D0467313

Dr Mortimer and the Aldgate Mystery

Williams, Gerard.
Dr. Mortimer and the
Aldgate mystery /
2001.
33305016511846
LA   10/18/01

DR. MORTIMER AND THE ALDGATE MYSTERY

Gerard Williams

Thomas Dunne Books
St. Martin's Minotaur
New York

SANTA CLARA COUNTY LIBRARY

▪ 3 3305 01651 1846

THOMAS DUNNE BOOKS.
An imprint of St. Martin's Press.

DR. MORTIMER AND THE ALDGATE MYSTERY. Copyright © 2000 by Gary Newman.
All rights reserved. Printed in the United States of America. No part of this
book may be used or reproduced in any manner whatsoever without written
permission except in the case of brief quotations embodied in critical articles or
reviews. For information, address St. Martin's Press, 175 Fifth Avenue, New
York, N.Y. 10010.

www.minotaurbooks.com

ISBN 0-312-26920-X

First published in Great Britain by Constable & Company Limited

First U.S. Edition: August 2001

10 9 8 7 6 5 4 3 2 1

1

I am that James Mortimer who in the year 1889 had the good fortune to bring the facts in the case of the Hound of the Baskervilles to the attention of the illustrious Sherlock Holmes.

Today is the twenty-fourth of July 1939, which marks the tenth anniversary of the death of John Watson, MD, whom I had the honour to call friend. I think it singularly timely, therefore, that I should now set down for my successors an account of the second – and most challenging – case that has ever come my way.

As this narrative unfolds, the reader will understand the reasons which have prompted me to direct that this, and other accounts of my life and cases, be held in a secure place until a period of not less than sixty years has elapsed.

Time presses, and not even the salubrious air of Torquay and the devoted care of my dearest wife can delay much longer that event which must inevitably close a long and strenuous life.

I open my story, then, with the first great grief of my life: the death of my first wife, Ruth, from diphtheria, in March 1890, not long after my arrival back from the sea-cruise on which I accompanied Sir Henry Baskerville after his ordeal under the claws and fangs of the Grimpen Hound.

Those who have known the final parting will scarcely need any description of the first pangs of bereavement. Suffice it to say that the hospitality and tactful companionship of Sir Henry in the first difficult days of stunned loss did much to put me back on an even keel.

I felt immediately on Ruth's death that I could no longer go on with life in Grimpen, and this sentiment persisted in the weeks that followed, so that at last I entrusted the sale of my practice to my solicitor. Along with the proceeds from this, I had the handsome bequest of a thousand pounds left to me by the late Sir Charles Baskerville, to say nothing of my late wife's consols, which yielded a steady hundred a year.

I found myself then very much on the sunny side of the

financial street and, at one point, I even toyed with the notion of devoting the rest of my days to my old passion of archaeology. It seemed to me, for instance, that the kist-burials of the North Durham coast had been unaccountably neglected.

It was Watson who pointed the way for me. After my affairs at Grimpen had been wound up, I was invited to stay with him and his wife Mary – herself, alas, soon to be taken from us – in their charming house in Kensington, where Watson then had a practice. We were sitting at dinner on a golden May evening when I raised the matter, only to see Watson's square face set in mock rage.

'What?' my friend exclaimed. 'Retire at thirty! Preposterous! Activity is what you need, Mortimer: London!'

'Another practice?' I murmured doubtfully. 'I scarcely think I'm up to it, Watson. Ruth's death has completely taken the wind out of my sails.'

The grey eyes softened.

'You've been through the mill, I know, Mortimer and, well, some losses aren't for mending this side of Jordan . . .'

Mary shot me a tender glance: thank God we cannot see into the future!

'But you must know,' Watson went on in a low, earnest voice, 'that in the end, it's our work that's our salvation. You're a medical man, and Lord knows there's plenty of call for your services, especially here in London. No need to try for a practice, either. Something in the way of a little foray, just to prime the pump, so to speak.'

'Er, have you anything in mind?' I asked. I had the distinct suspicion that something had been arranged.

'You are a lost man, James!' Mary remarked with a chuckle. 'Once John gets his teeth into something, he never lets go!'

We all laughed, then Watson spoke again.

'Well,' he said gruffly, 'something of the kind. Thing is, a friend of mine, Ferraby – we were at Barts together – urgently needs a locum for his practice in Eaton Square. His father has just died at Angmering, and his mother's quite gone to pieces, and if that weren't enough, it seems there's some irregularity in the accounts of the family business. Really, Mortimer, you'd be saving Ferraby's life. And think of the valuable introduction it would give you to London society!'

To cut a long story short, I allowed myself to be persuaded, and at ten o'clock the next morning, I was bustled into the drawing-room of Eustace Ferraby's elegantly appointed house in Eaton Square.

'Damn' providential your having turned up, Mortimer!' spluttered the beleaguered physician, after introductions had been made. He was a tall, pale man, beginning to run to fat, with a long, egg-shaped head, and a perpetual look of indignation in his eyes.

'Absolutely vital that I should get down to Sussex!' he exclaimed. 'Got a wire not half an hour ago: wretched chief clerk of my father's scooted. I shall be up to my neck in auditors, police, whole bally boiling! Oh, I forgot. Anything I can get you?'

'Not at this time, Ferraby: I was thinking in terms of an immediate start.'

'Oh, capital!' the doctor exclaimed, his long, hairless face lighting up. He leaped up from his chair and smoothed his immaculate frock-coat. 'No time like the present, hey? Better come along to the dispensary. Oh! You'd better meet Dolly; she'll surely be down to breakfast by now.'

I was whisked out into the hall, then over to the dining room, where Mrs Ferraby, a billowing, expensively dressed lady with a brilliant smile, was breakfasting in style, with two maids in attendance. I was from Devon? Charming. I knew Sir Henry Baskerville? Delightful. Did I hunt? She seemed not quite so charmed this time by my reply: amateur archaeology evidently cut no social ice in Eatonian circles. Still, the smile lost none of its candlepower. A gracious nod of dismissal. So looking forward to getting to know me better. Ferraby carried on the conversation as he led me down into the inner recesses of the building.

'You shall be living in, of course. I've sent Watson a note asking him to send along your things.'

Ferraby quickly introduced me to my duties: indeed, quick was the word, for my first patient was due at eleven. Transport was to present no difficulty, since I was to have the use of Ferraby's carriage and coachman for the duration. He and his family were to travel by cab to the station, en route to Angmering.

I recalled that Ruth and I had rented a cottage one summer in the village of Patching, not far from Angmering. I recalled the hot turf, and Ruth's solemn remark as we sat together on the crest of the Downs: 'It is all so beautiful, James. If only one could live forever . . .'

By a quarter to eleven, Mrs Ferraby and the two misses had already set off in a four-wheeler for the station, and the doctor was standing at the front door with me, giving me some last words of advice as, watch in hand, he awaited his cab.

'Shouldn't be away longer than a fortnight,' he said. 'Dolly can't abide Angmering: well, this time she'll bally-well have to lump it! Where is that confounded cab! Oh, yes, Mortimer: every confidence in your tact and all that, but, er, thought I'd better let you know that your last visit today – '

I consulted the ledger which I'd carried to the door.

'Miss Lavinia Nancarrow,' I read out loud. 'What a singular and charming name, Ferraby.'

'Ditto the young lady, Mortimer! Utterly, but needs careful handling; very careful handling.'

'Influenza?' I queried, with eyebrows slightly raised, this time referring to the entry 'Ipec. op'.

'In this case, but highly strung. Very highly strung.'

I winced inwardly. Some pampered baggage, no doubt. Still, I supposed Ferraby needed all the rich patients he could get to keep up his sumptuous style of life, and I would have to do my best not to ruffle Miss Nancarrow's feathers. Rich, though? The East End address hardly confirmed this impression. I mentioned this.

'Damn the fellow! I shall lose my train! What's that? The address? Ginger Lane, behind Aldgate Station. My dispenser will give you written instructions how to get there. Rum sound to it, hey? Boynton-Leigh – that's the young lady's guardian – comes of a distinguished line of India nabobs. Indigo trade originally, I believe, but they have a finger in every pie. Where is that cab? He has a young son, too: Lance.'

'And Mrs Boynton-Leigh?'

'He's a widower: some chaps have all the luck. Oh! I'm dreadfully sorry, Mortimer! I didn't mean ... Why, here I am, preaching to you about tact, and all – '

'It is of no consequence, Ferraby. You were saying about Ginger Lane, the Boynton-Leigh ménage?'

'Ahem, yes. Well, seems Boynton-Leigh – you will be careful with him, too, Mortimer: Evangelical and all that – inherited the whole street from an old uncle, who was my father's patient. It used to be known as Boynton's Rents, back in Seventeen Hundred and Frozen Stiff! In fact, it's a rather fine old William-and-Mary terrace. Boynton-Leigh chose to come and live in Number One when he and his household came over from India. Sought seclusion from the wicked world, or something of the sort. It's a rum arrangement all round, but ours not to reason why. He knew his uncle had been my father's patient and asked to be put on my books when he arrived here about eighteen months ago.'

'And the son?'

'Lance. He's sixteen. Bit of a hothouse flower: back on compassionate leave, or whatever they have, from Dartmouth, on account of Miss Nancarrow's illness. He was sent to Dartmouth to have a man made of him. Uphill task, I should say.'

Just then there was a rattle at the foot of the steps.

'And not before time!' Ferraby exclaimed. He grabbed his Gladstone bag in one hand, shook mine with the other, and, with a cry of 'Good luck, old man!' scuttled down the steps and into the hansom. As the cab jerked into rapid motion, Ferraby's top-hatted head emerged from the window.

'Don't on any account give anything besides medicine to Miss Nancarrow, Mortimer!'

How flagrantly I was to disregard this curious advice!

2

At about twenty-to-six on that smoky, mild evening, I stepped out from the grimy portico of Mark Lane Station and made my way up Fenchurch Street to Aldgate Station, then turned up into Middlesex Street, which was as 'behind' the latter station as I could think of.

I had dismissed Ferraby's coach outside Gloucester Road Station a few minutes after five, as I had not wished to arrive outrageously late for my last appointment in the far East End, and had taken the five-seven train. Typically, in my hurry I had left my purse – along with the written instructions Ferraby's excellent dispenser had given me – on the counter of the station ticket-office. I had, however, heeded the coachman's dire warnings about carrying large sums on one's person in the East End, to the extent of entrusting my pocket book to him before entering the station.

The remark of my housemaster at Clifton came to mind: 'Your incorrigible woolgathering may land you in Queer Street ere long, Mortimer, but I fancy you'll see more of life than most of us do!'

Be that as it might, I had no more than the change from the purchase of my train ticket – fourpence-halfpenny – in my pocket when I left Mark Lane Station, so that, short of pledging my watch or hiring a hansom for the rest of the evening, a cab was out of the question. As the comings and goings of the local omnibuses were incomprehensible to me, it would have to be Shanks' Pony, then, and pretty briskly at that.

I soon reached the intersection with Wentworth Street and the neighbourhood took on a distinctly exotic air. I know the Hebrew alphabet through my interest in archaeology, and my rudimentary German enabled me to decipher the Yiddish invitation on the bill opposite me to come and enjoy a 'song, a laugh and a tear' at the East London Palace in Fieldgate Street. As I crossed the busy road, I pulled out my watch – when would I learn caution – and saw that I had just six minutes to be at my appointment in time.

'Ginger – G-I-N-G-E-R – Lane,' I repeated slowly to a plump lady who was selling old clothes from a barrow.

A shrug and a wry smile, then, in guttural English: 'Sorry.'

Then a little foxy-faced man in a shiny-visored cap, who was peddling pastry-rings from a wire rod. The same incomprehension, until I found the sense to hand him a silver threepenny-bit from my tiny budget and take one of his pastries off the ring. If you want to know the time, buy a watch!

'Right at the bottom!' the man said with a grin and a backward jerk of the head.

I walked briskly – four minutes left – down what turned out to be Cobb Street till, near the end and on the left, I saw what looked more like a gap in the wall than a public thoroughfare. I looked up at the faded street sign: GINGER LANE.

It was so very quiet down there. Well-kept mews on the left and a terrace of substantial old houses on the right. The lane ended in a graveyard of the sort which will be familiar to those who have read *Bleak House*, and its gateway, which once must have allowed access to White's Row through the high, otherwise blank wall backing the cemetery, was bricked up.

The first three old houses appeared to be unoccupied – at least the windows were shuttered – and the neglected state of the outside fittings, including some fine, late seventeenth-century doorcases, backed this supposition. These three houses looked as if they had not received a coat of paint for generations.

The fourth house – Number One – whose side windows gave on to the graveyard, was clearly the only occupied one in the whole ensemble, for the windows were visible and smoke was drifting lazily from the chimney. The front door was dark green and the brass knocker, in the shape of a hand clutching an orange, brightly polished.

However, the object which immediately grasped my attention was leaning against the nearby graveyard railings: a bicycle of the latest make and model. I looked at my watch: a minute in hand. I cast my eye over the unkempt waste of the graveyard and my mind wandered irresistibly to the last cemetery I had been in, in a dark Dartmoor dell. A sudden glint from the far corner dazzled me for an instant, breaking my reverie. Surely it came from a piece of very thick glass, with considerable reflective powers.

The door of Number One opened abruptly, and a sudden commotion engulfed me as I was sent reeling by a violent blow to my shoulder. It was only by dint of my letting go of my medical bag and clinging on to the iron rail which lined the steps that I was able to keep upright.

A hand grasped my elbow firmly, and I looked up into sympathetic grey eyes, fringed by tow-coloured lashes and masked by gold pince-nez, of a short, sturdily built young woman. And what a young woman! Clad from little, feathered trilby to bloomered legs in Jaeger tweed, she was the very image of the free, modern woman. She handed me my bag with a solicitous smile, and I studied the high-coloured face, every line of which showed strength and regularity, but without in any way diminishing its essential femininity.

'I do so beg your pardon!' the Amazon said in a well-modulated voice.

'Don't mention it!' I said. 'I should have been looking ahead of me!'

'A pity a lot more people don't look ahead of them, sir!' she remarked, glancing back at the now-closed green door. Then, nodding at my black bag, she remarked: 'A colleague, I think?'

A lady bicyclist was *rara avis* enough, but a lady doctor!

'I am a physician, ma'am, yes.'

'Then perhaps we may work together.'

Before I could reply, she had thrust a card into my hand and, turning on a sturdily booted heel, mounted her bicycle and pedalled off, her back as straight as a guardsman's, in the direction of Cobb Street.

The distant boom of a church bell reminded me of my duties, and I pushed the visiting card into my waistcoat pocket. I seized the brazen hand and knocked, and the door opened just as the last chime of six was dying away.

The raw-featured man in an alpaca jacket bore the true mark of the boxer: the ears. He was not tall, but very solidly built. His thin mouth was turned down like an inverted U, and the expression in his eyes was implacable.

'Yerss?' he growled.

'Please tell your master the doctor has come to see Miss Nancarrow.'

'You ain't Dr Ferraby.'

Mastering my annoyance, I fumbled in my pocket and fished out yet another card, which I handed to the man.

'You will please give your employer this. I am expected at this hour.'

To my disgust, the door was shut in my face again, and I was left for a full minute to contemplate the churchyard where, on turning my head, I once more caught the glint of glass. An extraordinarily powerful reflection. The door opened again, and this time the human Cerberus stepped aside and nodded me an invitation to go in.

'Mr Boynton-Leigh will see you direckly, sir.'

I walked into a dark, spacious hall which was panelled in polished wood and floored with black-and-white marble tiles. The heavy outside door shut with a metallic boom and the servant led me to a fine old staircase. We climbed the stairs to emerge on to a broad landing, on whose walls were displayed half-a-dozen portraits of eighteenth-century notables, some in military red, and among which two group portraits showed Indian servants in idealised native dress. The male European subjects portrayed showed much the same square, narrow-eyed features, and seemed to be squinting at some strongly lit, distant prospect.

I was led down a thickly carpeted corridor on the right, and through a double door into a dark, richly furnished study, with book-lined walls and a number of Eastern curiosities, including antique weapons. There was also a rather spindly set of library steps, to which I would not have cared to entrust even my modest weight. Two long, narrow windows at the bottom of the room, their blinds drawn, framed a grand old dark-teak mandarin's desk, cut into a veritable lacework of carving, behind which a broad, sparely fleshed man in black broadcloth was standing with my card in his hand. His shining, domed head dipped as he consulted the card, then he looked at me without visible enthusiasm, before flapping out his arm like some crow's wing.

I felt a gentle pressure behind my knees, and could hardly help flopping back into the chair which had been put there so quietly by the pugilistic-looking servant. The bald, square man behind the desk bowed curtly at me and I nodded back rather awkwardly. He sat down.

'I had expected Dr Ferraby,' he sighed in a deep, weary voice. 'You are his assistant?'

'I am his locum tenens, sir.'

'Mmph! I trust you were not incommoded on the doorstep just now.'

'Ah! You refer no doubt to the remarkable young lady on the bicycle, sir.'

'Yes, indeed, though "remarkable" is a far milder epithet than the one which springs to mind! Consider the impudence of it, sir: she, a perfect stranger to me and mine, presuming upon the reputation of her late father – he served with some distinction in the Army in India – to get her foot in my door, in order to enquire upon the "conditions of my ward's confinement". To have to suffer bluestockings of that stripe peering in at one's windows! Intolerable interference!'

The bald dome dipped again and the nabob wiped his face with his hand, as if to brush away the recollection. His mention of his ward reminded me of the business in hand.

'I take it you are Mr Boynton-Leigh?' I asked.

'I beg your pardon, sir! I forget my manners! Yes, I am Archibald Boynton-Leigh. I trust Ferraby is well? Nothing untoward has befallen him? I am accustomed, you see, to his keeping me informed as to changes in his arrangements.'

'You will readily forgive that, sir,' I explained, 'when I tell you that Dr Ferraby's father died only the day before yesterday, and that the unfortunate event has necessitated his immediate departure for Angmering.'

'Then I am distressed to hear it, Dr . . .'

He peered down again at my card.

'Mortimer, sir.'

'Yes, just so: Dr Mortimer. Then I see I must acquaint you with my ward's condition.'

Here I scented that loathly animal, the lay physician, always worthy of suppression. I decided to begin as I meant to go on.

'I understand that Miss Nancarrow is a highly strung young lady who has influenza,' I said, and Mr Boynton-Leigh got up again from his chair, his face twitching.

'Her nervous constitution is balanced upon a knife-edge, doctor! All the more imperative that I should protect her from the uninvited attentions of female Paul Prys, who might push her over that edge. I had thought that we – your colleague Ferraby and myself – had been making some progress towards bringing her back to normal, then this vile influenza! Has Ferraby not at least acquainted you with the facts in Lavinia's case? The medicaments required, et cetera?'

I chose to ignore all this: I had my self-respect.

'I'm sure you'll agree, Mr Boynton-Leigh, that the surest road to my treating your ward is by my actually seeing her. Let us by all means talk afterwards about what is to be done.'

I rose and turned towards the door, and Boynton-Leigh hurried forward to open it.

'If you will follow me, doctor,' he said, with the coldness of tone with which he had first received me.

The nabob paused on the stairs just before the second and final landing. He turned and seemed to study me.

'I think I should warn you, Dr Mortimer, that Lavinia may from time to time ask you for little things – '

'Little things, sir? What kind of little things?'

'Oh, trifles, bagatelles. It is a sort of restless mania with her, I fear, and not to be encouraged . . .'

'Can it be that you suspect her of seeking some object with which she might harm herself?'

'No, no, nothing of the kind! It is simply that I think such a habit unsettling: Lavinia must, above all, be kept calm. In any case, I do not consider it unreasonable to insist that all objects you may wish to, er, offer my ward shall first be given into my hand. You will oblige me in this?'

This last sentence was uttered more in the tone of a command than a request, and my hackles definitely rose. I paused and looked squarely into the narrow, grey eyes.

'I assure you, sir,' I said coldly, 'that while I am under your roof, I shall respect all reasonable requests of yours. I hope too that you will not take it amiss if I further assure you that I am not in the habit of passing objects to my patients surreptitiously.'

Boynton-Leigh's expression lightened.

'I think we understand each other, Dr Mortimer!'

We turned right along the landing and, at the end of the corridor, stopped before a door with a high-backed armchair immediately to one side of it.

'This is Lavinia's room,' Boynton-Leigh said almost reverentially.

The bedroom blinds were drawn and all was dim within. The bed itself was situated between two high, narrow windows and, at each side of the bed and under the windows, two massive, bronze oriental candelabra stood sentinel. Gas-mantles on the walls above clearly indicated that the role of the stout, scarlet candles which topped the bronze sticks must be purely ornamental. There were vaguely discernible cabinets and other furniture in other parts of the room and rather high up on the walls to the right and the left were half-a-dozen dark, heavy-framed pictures. In an armchair to one side of the bed sat a homely looking old body in a voluminous calico dress and widow's cap. She made as if to get up as we entered, but my host gently gestured her to remain seated. Her eyes followed us anxiously.

The boyish figure who was leaning – nay, lying – across the bed as he grasped the long, pale hand of the invalid and whispered so urgently in her ear, was, however, shown no such consideration. Boynton-Leigh strode over to him and, bending down, hissed and spat some words into his ear, among which I fancied I could make out, 'pack', 'Dartmouth' and 'morning train'.

The lad in the Eton collar and tight, black suit shot to his feet without a word and made for the door and, as he passed, gave me such a look of pained resentment that I had to turn my face away. There was something girlish in his blond good looks and I wondered for a moment how such a youth might fare amid the coltish rough-and-tumble of the great naval public school.

At last, I had my patient to myself. I looked at her and went on looking. As for externals: olive skin, with a slight underlying blush that even illness had not entirely effaced; fine, sharply defined features, tending to the aquiline; and glorious, questing dark-brown eyes. The most striking feature, however, was the silver streak which sundered the crisp waves of jet-black hair covering the heightened pillows. Those were the individual traits of her appearance: taken together, they made up, quite simply, the most beautiful girl I had ever seen or have seen since.

I smiled in as reassuring a fashion as I could muster, and gently took the slim wrist. A mixture of alarm and confusion came into the dark eyes.

16

'Has Dr Ferraby gone away?' she whispered huskily and anxiously in my ear as I bent over her.

'His father has just died, Miss Nancarrow, and he cannot be here today. I am Dr Mortimer: I am standing in for him for the time being.'

'I feel such a cheat, doctor! Really, I am quite well now. I can get up . . .'

She grasped my hand for support and tried to raise her slim body higher, but sank back breathlessly against the pillows. She seemed all eyes.

'My dear,' her guardian broke in, his voice gentle but full of authority, 'you must let us – I mean Dr Mortimer – decide whether you are well enough to get up. You see how absurd it is. You are quite exhausted.'

'Mr Boynton-Leigh is quite right, Miss Nancarrow,' I said. 'The worst of your fever is evidently past, but there is nothing quite like influenza for pulling one down. We must concentrate all our efforts now on building you up, then, when your strength and spirits are equal to it – '

'Just so!' Boynton-Leigh interrupted. 'We will decide then.'

Just then I glanced at the little bottles on a side table, behind which the old nurse in the calico dress had now taken up position. Suspense could be read in her pug-dog features, and she eyed me as if I were about to take some sort of cue. I turned to my host and, to my surprise, he was glaring disapprovingly, not at the medicine table, but at my hand, which I realised was still holding Miss Nancarrow's. She gave it the slightest of squeezes before I gently disengaged it from her grip. There was an imploring look in her eyes which made me feel uneasy. I felt a pang of pity, then, when I could make out the inscriptions on two of the bottles in the dim light, a gathering surge of indignation.

'Well,' I said, holding up the bottles, 'I think we may dispense with these now, Miss Nancarrow, since you are evidently well on the mend.'

Boynton-Leigh breathed in sharply and the old nurse looked at him with something like panic in her eyes. Nothing was said, however, as I put my bag down on the little table and, opening

17

it, put in the two bottles and took out my prescription pad and pencilcase. I scribbled a prescription for a tonic mixture and a patent beef-extract, which I left on the table. I then snapped my bag shut, stood back from the bed, and studied my beautiful charge.

'I think that will be all for now,' I said. 'And may I suggest – just to keep off the fantods! – a little harmless diversion? Perhaps you enjoy reading, Miss Nancarrow?'

'Oh, yes, doctor! I'd so love my *Morte d'Arthur* and – '

'I shall attend to any, er, diversions my ward may need, Dr Mortimer,' the nabob interrupted again. 'I think you may safely leave that in my hands!'

I nodded curtly, then turned to give my patient a leave-taking smile. However, instead of turning immediately to follow Boynton-Leigh back to the door, I walked briskly up to the window.

'I think a little evening sunlight would do no harm,' I said and, before any of the company could respond, grasped the tapes which worked the blind. In doing so, I blundered against the stout, red candle in the candelabrum of the pair which flanked that particular window. The tall bronze stick tottered slightly, but the candle itself did not budge, a curious effect which I ascribed to its extraordinary fixity in the socket.

I righted the candelabrum then pulled on the blinds. The sun flooded the old room with gentle light, but somehow the light only served to deepen the ominous gloom of the chamber. The window was encased in a grill of stout, iron bars.

3

I left the sickroom in sombre silence, and my host followed me on to the landing, where I placed my bag on a side table. I opened the bag and took out the two anomalous medicine bottles.

'I do not believe that my colleague would have prescribed these particular drugs, Mr Boynton-Leigh,' I said, holding up one of the bottles.

'Nor he did, Dr Mortimer, nor he did. They are a relic of our Indian days: laudanum is sovereign against the dreadful headaches and sleeplessness that attend tropical fevers. Sovereign!'

I held up the second bottle, and now the nabob looked definitely uneasy; guilty, almost.

'And bromide of potassium, Mr Boynton-Leigh: pray what is that sovereign against, in Miss Nancarrow's case?'

'Ah! The ladies, you understand, doctor, they are prone to vapours, conniption fits. Bromide works wonders in restoring them to a state of rest, of calm.'

Or of doped submission, I thought. This particular drug had fuelled many a lecture-room snigger in my student days. Among other applications, it had been recommended for 'townswomen who were going out of their minds', and 'frightful imaginings'.

I turned my attention again to the laudanum bottle.

'My colleague Dr Ferraby prescribed powders – in measured doses – of ipecacuanha and opium for your ward's influenza,' I remarked.

'Pah!' the bald man snorted. 'Dover's Powders! That remedy came out of the Ark, Dr Mortimer. Any old fishwife might recommend it.'

I kept my temper and framed my next question in calm, measured tones.

'Mr Boynton-Leigh, have you any idea why the good, if antediluvian, Dr Dover should have chosen to mix ipecacuanha with opium in his remedy?'

'Hmph! None, sir. I know nothing of patent remedies.'

'Because, sir, ipecacuanha taken in excess of a certain dose will cause violent vomiting, so that when the two drugs are taken together in the correct proportions, it becomes impossible for the patient to taken an overdose of the deadlier opium. Laudanum on its own carries no such safeguard and, if the quantity is misjudged, the sleep that certainly ensues may be of the permanent variety.'

'I do not take kindly to this sort of catechism, Dr Mortimer!' the nabob barked. 'I have merely applied tried and tested remedies to my ward's illness. Tried, sir! And tested!'

'You will allow me, all the same, to dispose of these drugs?' I countered in the same suave tones.

'Oh, by all means! You are the doctor, after all!'

I saw that I had driven home my message, and placed the offending bottles back in my bag, which I snapped shut. I followed my stocky host downstairs, where the grim manservant was waiting at the door with my hat, stick and gloves.

'I shall look in again,' I proposed, 'in three days at, say, eleven in the morning, if that is convenient.'

Boynton-Leigh grunted and bowed in apparent consent.

'Ord here informs me, doctor, that for some reason you arrived here on foot. May I ask if you have made arrangements for your departure?'

I explained about the contretemps at the ticket counter at Gloucester Road Station.

'Then Ord shall drive you to Mark Lane. I bid you good evening.'

The nabob made his final bow and, turning on his heel, went back upstairs, leaving me to the baleful mercies of Ord, who bade me wait until he had got out the carriage. I stepped out on to the front step and thanked God for the sunshine, as I thought of the girl I had just left. How wrong it seemed to me to withhold the sunlight from a young and splendid animal! What more precious gift could God have given us than the sun? 'The Lord giveth, and the Lord taketh away ...' He had taken my wife away. She would never see the sun again.

'Carriage is ready!' Ord announced, breaking my reverie.

Back in Eaton Square, I ate a splendid, if solitary, dinner, then as the night was mild, and the sky like dusky, pink silk, I decided to take a turn in Kensington Gardens. To tell the truth, I was looking forward without relish to the sixty-first night I had spent without Ruth beside me.

I had done a double circuit of the Gardens, enjoying the desultory talk – so reassuringly ordinary – of the sauntering couples, when I became conscious of a recurring figure, always three or four paces behind me. I stopped at the Round Pond, and he promptly flopped down on to a bench and rattled open a newspaper, somewhat absurdly in the fading light. I continued on my way for ten yards or so, then paused in my steps to consult my watch. Sure enough, not far behind, my follower found something to admire in the blank greensward on his left.

In these situations, the direct method is often the best, so I swung round and confronted the fellow.

'I feel we must be acquainted,' I said.

Certainly no intimidating figure, the man looked on the contrary more like a startled rabbit, with an updrawn upper lip and rather ridiculous little moustache. His pale, prominent eyes evaded mine, and he wriggled in his tight, dark suit, as if unsure whether to tackle me or bolt. I drew back a pace and hitched up my stick in my hand, but he had evidently decided on the diplomatic course, as he briefly tipped his neat little dark-grey bowler and addressed me. The words tumbled out in a cultivated torrent and I was half-expecting that at any moment he would whip out a watch and begin to protest he was late for the tea party.

'I beg your pardon, sir,' he said, 'but I have to confess – for the best of reasons, I assure you – that, well – '

'You've been following me!'

'A low trick, I know, Dr Mortimer, but needs must – '

'How do you know my name?' I demanded, not amused.

'Er, on your bag, when you put it down to talk to the old-clothes woman in Wentworth Street this afternoon.'

'You mean you followed me all the way from the East End? How did you know I'd be going there, anyway? And how do you come to know me at all?'

'I saw you with Dr Ferraby this morning. On his doorstep in Eaton Square. I marked you – '

'The devil you did! Do you mean to say, then, that you've been following me all day, on all my calls?'

'Yes, but please let me explain myself. Oh! Perhaps you would care to join me in some refreshment?'

I considered anew the slight, neatly dressed figure who, if there was anything in his story, could not really have eaten all day. He was unmistakably a gentleman, and yet so singular, so out of his element. Yet there was something that predisposed me in his favour – a kind of pathos – and I made a decision.

'Thank you,' I said, 'but I have just dined. I suggest you join me for a chop and a pint of porter. I know a decent place not far from here.'

'Really, sir, that is good of you!'

'Please come along, then, Mr . . .'

'Tooke: Percival Tooke. Here is my card.'

It told me that Mr Tooke – if that was his real name – was a chartered surveyor, whose business address was No. 11, Crutched Friars.

We talked as we walked along.

'I seem to have brought you considerably west of your usual stamping ground, Mr Tooke.'

'More of a shared perch than a stamping ground, Dr Mortimer! A mere postal delivery-box for impecunious, would-be professional men! I have yet to establish myself in my profession here in London. Happily, I am able to scrape a living coaching military men up for examinations in mathematics. My actual lodgings are more, shall we say, prosaic.'

In that case, I thought, it had better be two chops.

'It is the old story, Mr Tooke,' I said. 'The mere act of putting up a brass plate seldom ensures an immediate rush of clients! You say you are establishing here; have you been long in London?'

'No, indeed, just eighteen months. I was in India before that: the Engineers, after Wellington and Woolwich. My people have always been Army.'

'India, Mr Tooke?' I said, pausing slightly in my steps.

The little man paused too and stared searchingly, almost hungrily, into my eyes. It was as if he was looking for a sign.

'Yes, Dr Mortimer: India. That is where my illness – this thing that is eating me up – began. So many of us receive our death-blow in that accursed land. I fear it will kill me in the end!'

'I am truly sorry to hear it, Mr Tooke!' I said, genuinely alarmed by the sudden change in the surveyor's mien. 'May I ask, then, what is your complaint?'

The odd little figure drew himself up to his full height and the pain in his eyes was plain to see.

'Dr Mortimer, I am out of my mind with love for Lavinia Nancarrow!'

4

After Tooke had done full justice to his meal we sat back in our tavern pews with tankards of porter in front of us.

'India, then,' I resumed.

'Yes,' Tooke said, the haunted look again coming into his eyes, 'India. I'd been seconded from the Engineers to the Trigonometric Survey, and had been doing some work in the Himalaya.'

'When would this have been?'

'Just before the Christmas of eighty-eight: about eighteen months ago. I had quite a bit of accrued leave, and had been driving myself rather hard up in the mountains, so I decided to rest up for a few weeks in Simla. It was the cold weather farther down on the Plain, of course – or as cold as it ever gets down there – so things were pretty quiet up in the hills, but that was just what I wanted: peace and quiet away from the eternal, filthy heat of the South.

'Christmas is always a fairly wretched time if you're single and in a foreign country, and I knew that India would always be that to me, however long I might stay there. Anyway, there I was, in a hotel in off-season Simla, at a loose end, and with Christmas coming on. Boynton-Leigh filled the gap.'

'Try as I may,' I remarked, 'I cannot see that gentleman in the role of a boon companion!'

'Precisely! You cannot have any conception of what Boynton-Leigh was like before, well, I'll be coming to that. Lavinia and Lance were with him, but I could only see Lavinia. It was all pretty obvious, I suppose. If you've ever tried any of Kipling's stories, you'll have some idea of the tattle and gossip that goes on up there: ritual adultery – nearly all talk – and all that. I filled the bill as the young officer on leave and on the lookout for fun and games. Even then, Boynton-Leigh was a bit of an old hen as far as Lavinia went, so you can imagine how wary he was towards me. There were other would-be dashing young subalterns, of course, but he soon sent them off with their tails between their legs! He learnt pretty soon, though, that as far as I was concerned, it was admiration with a capital A. That, and all the sentiments that a half-decent man can ascribe to what our friend Kipling refers to as a 'piece of rag and a hank of hair'. And what hair! Raven's wing, streaked with pure silver!

'They were really kind to me over the Christmas then, when they had to go back to Calcutta, I simply trotted along after them. I still had three weeks' leave left, but I think I'd have cheerfully deserted if it had meant another minute in the vicinity of Lavinia Nancarrow.'

'And Miss Nancarrow?' I asked tentatively, for I thought I could guess what his answer would be.

The little man gazed ruefully into his tankard.

'Oh, she was nice to me, as you are to a faithful little Scotch terrier. Any woman responds to admiration. That was about all, though – I can see that now – but then, in the first delirium, I was ready to clutch at any straw. With a week left of my leave, I invented a crisis, a parting of the ways: all on one side, of course. I even – this will give you some sort of idea of how mad I was! – sought a formal interview with Boynton-Leigh about my prospects.'

'No good?'

'Oh, he was very decent. He'd always value my friendship, and if ever he could find any opening for me, but as things stood . . . No tin, you see. Works like a charm.'

Tooke laughed bitterly and took a long draught at his tankard.

'So it all just petered out?' I asked.

'No! On the contrary, it blew up like a nine point-two inch shell! Boynton-Leigh suddenly turned on me like a mastiff who's been stroked the wrong way.'

I slammed my tankard down so loudly that the waiter dashed over, so I ordered two more pints of porter.

'How do you mean, "turned on you"?'

'A couple of days after our interview, I went along to their house to try to turn things round – again, mere desperation, of course – only to be ordered off the premises by the burra sahib himself.'

'What was that for, then?'

'He said that Lavinia must never marry – anyone – and that I

24

must never try to see her again. If I did, the servants would chuck me into the street. And that was that!'

'What do you think was the cause of his change of attitude?'

'I simply don't know. It was if he'd become another person. Anyway, I wasn't to be given the opportunity to find out the whys and the wherefores for, three days later, on the very eve of the expiry of my leave, I paid a final visit to his house, in spite of everything, only to find the place closed up, in the care of a native caretaker. He told me the whole family had simply packed their bags and taken ship for England!'

'Good Lord!' I exclaimed. 'Sounds like some sort of brainstorm!'

'That's what I thought. Well, on the following morning, I got a wire with notification of my next posting: Dum-Dum. It's a sort of anteroom to hell, where those who don't succumb to the heat or fever perish from sheer boredom. That settled it: I just sent in my papers and took the next boat home. I think that first slash of sleet on my face as I disembarked six weeks later at Tilbury was the most exquisite sensation I've ever enjoyed.'

'Tell me, Mr Tooke, how did Boynton-Leigh and his ménage live in Calcutta?'

'Off the fat of the land. As you may know, he comes of generations of bigwigs – burra sahibs – out there. They originally went out as soldiers, then settled there to trade. Made their pile in the indigo boom, but Boynton-Leigh's also in jute, shipping, sugar, a finger in every pie. A warm man and a shrewd one. He has the Midas gift of being able to forecast what's going to pay in the future. Wish I had some of it!'

'Bit of a pew-renter, too, I understand.'

'Oh, yes! He had some sort of experience in his youth which apparently made him see the light, I gather. It evidently didn't blind him to the art of making money, though. He was a sidesman or warden or whatever in St John's Church in Calcutta. That'll have been how he got to know Agar – '

'Agar?'

'Ah! I take it you haven't had the pleasure of meeting Jack Agar yet. I'm surprised he wasn't in attendance in Ginger Lane this evening. He's by way of being my hated rival, don't you know!'

The little man gloomed into the bottom of his pot again before taking up the thread of his narrative.

'Or one of my rivals. Damn it, Dr Mortimer, I don't see how any man can look at her and not be ... Well, anyway, Agar. Artist: pretty good one, too, if turning out a decent likeness is anything to go by. I'll allow him that.'

'What was an English artist doing in Calcutta?'

'Zoffany: big man in the last century, produced spectacular set-piece paintings, some of them group portraits. He spent some years in Calcutta during the late seventeen hundreds, doing grand paintings for the nabobs. Agar was on a sort of roving commission for an American collector, seeking out and buying up long-lost Zoffanys in the artist's old stamping grounds all over the world. Apparently bumped into Boynton-Leigh while studying Zoffany's *Last Supper* in St John's Church in Calcutta. Having two eyes in his head – very much so! – and blood in his veins, he immediately got to work on Lavinia!'

'To Boynton-Leigh's great dissatisfaction, no doubt.'

'Oh, no. At least, not at first. No: Agar's a downy bird. Drawing lessons, for both the young persons – '

'Ah! Master Lance serving as chaperone, hey?'

'Correct. Agar was soon quite one of the family. Began to wax cocky, in fact.'

I noticed Tooke's knuckles whiten round the handle of his tankard, as if in reaction to some memory of a slight. He drained off the contents of his pot, then fumbled in his pockets in a studied way, so I offered him my open cigarette case, from which he selected a cigarette, which he lit with a vesta from his own box, and drew a draught of smoke.

'Civil of you,' Tooke remarked, as he toyed with the case for a moment, catching the reflected glare of the gas-jet above on its polished surface, before handing it back to me. 'Fine case you've got there, remarkably fine. Well, as I was saying: Agar. Yes, he'd order the servants about to the manner born. Even twitted Boynton-Leigh – in a subtle way, of course – about his Bible-thumping. Mr Agar: so witty, such a card!'

And what a contrast to you! I thought to myself. How Tooke must have hated his self-confident rival!

'How do you think he got away with it?' I asked.

'Well, he was one of those fellers who can carry things off, if you see what I mean. He had a sort of lounging insolence about him. Nothing seemed to ruffle his feathers. I-know-something-you-don't, sort of thing.'

I quite knew what he meant.

'Until?'

'The brainstorm,' Tooke exclaimed.

'You mean just before Boynton-Leigh suddenly decamped from Calcutta?'

'Yes! In fact, I've often wondered since just how much Agar had to do with that. If I thought he'd done anything to harm Lavinia – '

'You alluded to the possibility of my meeting him?'

'Mmm. He's apparently *persona grata* again in Ginger Lane.'

'You've seen him there?'

'Well, I've seen him go in, which is easy enough during the day, I suppose.'

'Oh, how is it easy to go in during the day, then?'

'You haven't noticed the front-door knocker?'

'A brass one, like a hand grasping an orange.'

'It's a pomegranate, as a matter of fact. No, if you yank it up and to one side, it lifts the latch, and you can just push open the door and go in.'

I recalled seeing such a knocker on the front door of Lamb House in Rye on a visit there with Ruth five bright summers before.

'A rather free and easy arrangement for such an otherwise well-guarded house,' I remarked.

'Oh, there are always servants about during the day, and of course it's securely bolted from the inside last thing at night. Really, the only way one could get in and past the ground floor undetected would be if no one was in at all, which is never.'

'I see. You haven't been in yourself?'

'Not for the want of trying! Boynton-Leigh's human mastiff Ord has standing orders to drive me from their doorstep if ever I show up there!'

I wondered what influence the rakish-sounding Mr Agar could have over Boynton-Leigh which even the expanse of four oceans could not diminish.

27

'What about the old nurse?' I asked. The pug-dog features with the constantly worried eyes remained sharp in my memory.

'That's Demmy: she rejoices in the name of Demelza Penruddock. Widow of a company sergeant killed in the Mutiny, as far as I could gather. She seemed all at sea in Calcutta, though: clearly not used to Bengal. Damn' steambath of a climate.'

'Was she with the family when you met them in Simla?'

'Oh, yes. Wherever Lavinia is, there will go Demmy. Her charge will be twenty-one in July, and Demmy still refers to her as her "baby"!'

It seemed so very bizarre and unhealthy: a young woman near her majority being treated like a nurseling! I was quickly becoming fascinated by Lavinia Nancarrow's sheer apartness. I beckoned the waiter and paid the reckoning.

'Well, Mr Tooke,' I said, as we were rising to our feet, 'what do you want from me?'

'Just to know that all is well with Lavinia, Dr Mortimer. Seeing Ferraby so regularly in attendance in Ginger Lane has made me desperately worried.'

I must say, he seemed to me to be a bit quick off the mark in assuming that it was Miss Lavinia who was ill in the household, but love is blind to all save its object.

'Oh,' Tooke went on, 'do not expect me to ask you to break any professional confidences. I know better than that.'

'I am glad to hear it, Mr Tooke!'

Our conversation spilt out into the mild night.

The little man was eager again as he drew himself up before me. I could smell the porter on his breath.

'To know that you have been with her is almost like actually meeting her!'

'I can certainly tell you that Miss Nancarrow is well on the mend from her recent influenza: I don't think the Royal College of Surgeons will burn me at Smithfield for revealing that.'

'What? Influenza? And she is recovered! That at least is music to my ears, Dr Mortimer! I wonder if you can know what it means to care desperately for someone and know that they are beyond your reach.'

Yes, I did know.

'Dr Mortimer,' Tooke went on, with downcast eyes, 'you have been so kind already, I hardly know how to ask – '

'Anything within reason, Mr Tooke, and which does not in any way compromise the professional proprieties.'

'It is just this: when next you see Lavinia, could you possibly give her a message from me?'

'I am bound to say that it is most likely her guardian will be present throughout the consultation, Mr Tooke, and I must tell you here and now that I have no intention of acting as a go-between!'

'And let me assure you, Dr Mortimer, that I would never dream of suggesting that you pass on any message to Lavinia which I would wish to conceal from her guardian or from anyone else who might be present.'

'Very well, then, on that understanding. What is the message?'

'That I was asking after her.'

I looked at the little man incredulously. Had he dogged my steps all day just for this?

I stopped and looked him in the eyes.

'But is that all, Mr Tooke?'

'You will do it?'

'Of course, but it seems so small a thing!'

Tooke's eyes narrowed as he held my glance for a couple of seconds, as if he was weighing me up, and for an instant it seemed as if something akin to mockery stole into them before he briskly squeezed the rim of his bowler and started down the street in quite the opposite direction from the nearest cabstand. His voice faded as he went.

'Again my sincere thanks, Dr Mortimer. You can't know how much you've helped me. Goodnight!'

5

The next couple of days were consumed with calls in the more exclusive residential districts of London. It was the height of the

Season, and many of my cases were simply the results of over-indulgence of one sort of another. It did not take me very long to have my unwillingness to set up practice among the tuberose-scented drawing-rooms of the West End fully confirmed. To add to the oppression of my surroundings, the weather had turned hot and sultry, and I longed for the wind off the sea and the scent of the moors and downs. And, underneath it all, the Ache. What a mockery the sunshine seems to a desolate heart! Winter has its fires and inglenooks, before which one may take refuge within oneself and dream one's dreams, conjure up one's dear memories, but in the glare and jangle of summer thoroughfares: no refuge!

Activity: that was the thing! I had set aside the whole morning for my second appointment in Ginger Lane, but first the Charing Cross Road, and Krolick's, one of the bookshops of my student days.

Old Krolick recognised me, and there was the inevitable bright enquiry after Ruth, followed by the equally inevitable embarrassed condolences. I made my request quickly in order to loosen the tightness in my throat.

'The *Morte d'Arthur*, Mr Mortimer. Mmm, that'll be Lord Tennyson's version, I take it?'

'I really don't know, Mr Krolick. Er, what other versions are there?'

The bookseller peered over his small spectacles in a speculative sort of way.

'Malory. We have him in the, um, scholarly edition.'

'I take it, then, that Lord Tennyson's is the popular one? Well, I had better take a copy of that.'

Krolick spread out his hands.

'Sold out, I'm afraid, but I can order it for you.'

'No, I mean to offer it as a gift this morning, and I have no time to browse in the other shops for it. It had better be the other one, then – '

'The Malory.'

'Yes, that will have to do. I fancy it may come as a pleasant surprise to the recipient!'

The shopman opened his mouth briefly, as if about to say

something, then shut it with a smack, as if battening down the hatches on a momentary doubt.

'Certainly, sir! Shall we re-open the old account?'

I had not thought of that. How long would I be in London? I felt like a student again.

'Er, cash for the time being, Mr Krolick, until I have had time to look around me.'

A professional smile and nod from the shopman, and I was soon outside amid the cordial din of 'Soldiers of the Queen' from a barrel-organ with a neatly wrapped copy of Sir Thomas Malory's *Morte d'Arthur* under my arm.

At the house in Ginger Lane, Ord admitted me without any ado and I was shown, clutching my package, straight into Miss Nancarrow's room. I was gratified to note that Boynton-Leigh had the confidence to leave me alone with my patient this time, always allowing for the presence of the faithful Demmy, who rose from her armchair at my entrance. As before, she wore the expression of an old bulldog who wasn't sure whether he was about to receive a kick or a titbit.

'Please remain seated,' I said, then, wishing to return my host's confidence, I turned to Ord, 'Your master is at home?'

'Yerss.'

'You will please give him this, with my compliments. Tell him I trust it will be suitable as a gift to aid Miss Nancarrow's convalescence.'

The manservant took the package without looking twice at it and ambled down the corridor.

The blinds were up this time and my patient was sitting upright in bed. She looked ravishing. Her eyes had the same hungry, searching expression as when I had first seen her.

'No need to ask if you are better, Miss Nancarrow,' I said. 'I can see the improvement already! I fancy this morning's consultation will be something of a formality and that you will be up and about in no time.'

Demmy stiffened in her chair, her expression now one of unmistakable fear. To my dismay, I saw that tears were coursing down Lavinia's cheeks.

'Oh, come!' I said as gently as I could. 'It cannot be as bad as

31

all that! It is a little nervous reaction, no doubt: some degree of depression always follows a bad bout of influenza. Let me examine you now.'

Demmy was at hand immediately to ease off the upper part of my patient's negligee and shift, and I sat lightly on the bed and began to sound her lungs. She was lithe and wiry, these characteristics no doubt having been accentuated by her illness: her milliner would have a thin living in the matter of corsets. The curve of her back was exquisite, and I confess that the harsh fragrance of her hair, mingled with that of her warm body, filled my nostrils somewhat disturbingly.

'No sign of congestion in the lungs,' I pronounced, but what I thought was: How beautiful is woman!

'Oh,' Lavinia said, 'I am quite well, doctor. I feel up to anything, but it is no use!'

This statement was followed by a flood of tears and, to my consternation, my lovely patient writhed round in the bed and flung herself on to my chest. She clung to me like grim death and sobbed in that way that evinces as much alarm as pity. The long, surprisingly strong fingers clutched and gripped at my arms and chest.

'It is no use, no use, no use! I shall never be free! It would be better if I were dead!'

I gently disengaged the clutching hands and, with the nurse's help, got my patient settled back in bed.

'Let us hear no more of that!' I said firmly. 'It will be a very long time indeed before you are dead, and in the meantime we must try to see that you are strong enough in body and nerves to have a full and happy life.'

The dark eyes burned into mine, and she clutched my hands with both of hers. Her grip was as strong as it was hot and dry.

'If only, Dr Mortimer. But no, it is too late – '

'Why is it too late? Too late for what?'

'Baba says I shall never be well enough to be free, to live as I choose, but I feel so strong! Baba says it's my nerves, and – '

'But who is this "Baba"?'

'That's Miss Lavinia's guardian, sir,' Demmy explained. 'Mr Boynton-Leigh. When she was little it was her way of saying his Christian name: Archibald.'

Baba! That living tombstone in black broadcloth! I remembered what Tooke had said about the change in Boynton-Leigh just before he had left India. A sea change, evidently. But as to immediate purposes, I knew the signs of incipient hysteria, whatever the cause. I must change the subject immediately.

'Oh, I almost forgot to tell you, Miss Nancarrow: Mr Tooke was asking after you.'

My patient calmed down with gratifying suddenness.

'Ah, yes. Poor Percy. Please tell him I'm getting better.'

Poor Percy indeed, if this was all the return he was to have for all his constancy!

'Dr Mortimer,' Miss Nancarrow said in her hoarse, eager voice, 'please tell me what London is like!'

'Why, surely you have been in London long enough to have formed your own impressions!'

The nurse stood up again and grew agitated.

'Beg pardon, sir, but I can see she's going to get all muddled again. Now, don't take on, my baby! Of course you're going to see London when you get well. Now we must help the doctor to help us get well, mustn't we – '

'Mrs Penruddock,' I said, frankly angry, 'do you mean to say that Miss Nancarrow has not been out of doors since she came to London?'

Demmy's silence and downcast eyes were answer enough. By God! If this was what being a society physician was like, I'd sooner live on bread and cheese for the rest of my life! How these old rooms, with their grotesque antiques, were stifling me, let alone my poor young patient, who was virtually imprisoned in them! Mr Archibald Boynton-Leigh had much to answer for. I took my patient's pulse – too fast for my liking, but strong and steady – then got up and faced her.

'Miss Nancarrow,' I said, 'I am satisfied that you are well enough to be up and about, and now propose to prescribe the next stage in your treatment.'

She sat up bolt upright in the bed and her lambent eyes glowed.

'What is that, Dr Mortimer?'

I snapped my bag shut.

'Life, Miss Nancarrow: life!'

33

6

I confronted Boynton-Leigh in his study.

'I find that Miss Nancarrow has completely recovered from the influenza, and I think that my future treatment of her will be limited to observing her convalescence. However, in that respect I have some very definite suggestions to make – '

'That will not be necessary, Dr Mortimer. I appreciate your professional zeal, and sincerely thank you for the interest you have taken in Lavinia's case, but you will please leave her convalescence in my hands and those of her nurse, Penruddock.'

'No, Mr Boynton-Leigh!'

The nabob rose from his chair.

'I beg your pardon!'

'No, sir,' I repeated, 'that will not do!'

'Do you dictate to me, sir?'

'In medical matters, yes. While I act as your medical adviser – '

'May I remind you, Dr Mortimer, that you are merely standing in for Dr Ferraby, and that there are other medical advisers to be had!'

'And may I warn you, Mr Boynton-Leigh, that you will find it extremely difficult to find another reputable physician who will, shall we say, wink at your untutored and unauthorised use on your ward of powerful and dangerous soporific drugs!'

Boynton-Leigh dashed up to me, his face working.

'I have absolute discretion over Lavinia's activities until she reaches the age of majority. Absolute!'

I lowered my voice to a calm and agreeable one, and strolled past the angry man to the window.

'Is it not a lovely morning, Mr Boynton-Leigh, though a little warm and close – '

'What! Do you trifle with me, sir!'

'Do you never feel the urge to take the air, sir?'

'Ha! Now I see what you are driving at: Lavinia is to take her morning promenade now, is she? Perhaps pay calls, put on "at

34

homes" and so forth! Nay, open a salon. Why not? What a pleasant picture! And for how long do you think she will be received in society when once she has staged one of her hysterical scenes? I could not help hearing some echo of the little exhibition she has just made of herself with you just now, but that is nothing. Dr Mortimer, nothing! Do you think I do not know her, I who have cherished her since she was in her cradle, who have watched and struggled to understand her ways, who have kept and guarded her from all manner of evil, especially since she has blossomed into what she is. Yet you seem to imply that I wish to keep her from her place in life, in her generation. I would be pained, angered even, were it not so absurd!'

Boynton-Leigh strode over to me and seized my right hand and elbow in an odd, clumsy gesture, like a child who is trying to secure the attention of an unheeding adult. His eyes were full of confusion and hurt.

'Dr Mortimer, if anyone could convince me that they had the means to advance Lavinia an inch towards health and wholeness, I would willingly give them all I have in exchange for it!'

'Sir,' I said quietly, gently plucking his hands from my arm, 'you are overwrought. You will allow me to assist you to your chair – '

'Yes, yes, you are right. Forgive me, doctor, but whatever touches on Lavinia's welfare – '

'Yes, I see that, and it only makes it more imperative that you accede to my wishes in the matter of her recovery.'

Boynton-Leigh seemed to have shrunk in his chair and the skin of his face was moist and leaden. A hunted look came into his eyes and he sat in silence for a while, then wiped his face with his open hand, as if to try to brush away his anxiety.

'And furthermore, sir,' I went on, 'I shall prescribe a tonic for you before I leave here.'

The nabob waved his hand faintly.

'No, sir,' I said. 'I insist!'

'You clearly mean well, Dr Mortimer, but I think I have made my position clear.'

The doubt seemed to clear from his eyes, then he stooped over the drawer of his desk, which he opened, and drew out a book, which he handed over to me. The Malory.

'I am glad that you gave this into my keeping, Dr Mortimer.'

Boynton-Leigh glared at me in a sombre fashion, but said nothing.

I fingered the book and looked at the merchant in dismay.

'You do not care for the book, sir?'

'Care for it, sir? It is a filthy and depraved work, imbued with the morals of the pigsty! Written by a medieval brute, a lewd brigand proscribed by even his own faction!'

'The shopman did not have Lord Tennyson's version, sir, but I thought – '

'Make no mistake, doctor, I yield to no man in declaring Lord Tennyson to be our noblest intellect. His so frequent enjoyment of the company of our Gracious Majesty at Osborne would be sufficient patent of that. In happier circumstances, I should not hesitate in recommending his works to my ward, but even his fine, clean works are romantic and unsettling to a degree which has driven me to the reluctant necessity of removing them from Lavinia's possession. But Malory! Pah! Sooner hand her prussic acid!'

'You have then read Malory's book, sir?'

'Pray read out the first sentence of the third paragraph of the editor's introduction, Dr Mortimer,' he bade, evading my question. 'The part which deals with Malory's life and lamentable career.'

I found the place and began to read out loud from Dr Stutthofer's Introduction to *The Most Piteous Tale of the Morte Arthur Saunz Guerdon.*

'As to the actual events of Sir Thomas Malory's life, we know little, save that in the intervals between battles during the Wars of the Roses, he had been no stranger to the prisons of whatever Majesty was on the throne at the time, on account of such peacetime pastimes as rape and highway robbery.'

'Enough?' Boynton-Leigh interrupted me as, embarrassed, I closed the book and slipped it into my bag.

'Perhaps not indeed,' I stammered. 'I had not thought – '

'I suggest your kitchen maid may find a use for that volume, doctor, when next she lights the stove in the morning!'

Boynton-Leigh cradled his head in his hands and sighed

wearily. 'If you will excuse me, Dr Mortimer, we shall part for now: I must be alone with my God.'

'Till next week, then, sir,' I replied, and scribbled out a prescription and put it on the desk, then left the merchant with his conscience.

7

Not being so pressed for time on this occasion, I had brought along Ferraby's coach, and it was in the comfort of that vehicle that I pondered the stormy interview I had just had. The situation in Ginger Lane was potentially explosive, and Boynton-Leigh clearly near the end of his tether: whatever the source of his torment, it must be connected with his beautiful ward. And what a home for a sensitive young girl! Both my professional and personal concerns were engaged here. As a man and as a physician, I could not – would not – see a bright young life crushed out by an irrational imprisonment founded, so far as I could see, on nothing more than the religious mania of an overwrought businessman. Over and above this, developing with equal step, was a deepening curiosity about the relationships of the inmates – fitting word! – of Number One, Ginger Lane, and a nascent passion to get to the bottom of the mystery. That taste for detection which had first been enkindled in me by the events of the Baskerville Case was reawakening with redoubled force.

I winced as I recalled my gaffe over the Malory book and, as the carriage jolted lazily over the wooden sets of the road, I drew the volume from my bag and riffled through the pages. The English was of the fifteenth century, and scarcely comprehensible without constant reference to a glossary which, as is so often the infuriating case, had been placed at the end of the book. However, behind the 'ye wots' and 'ywisses', showing up against the barbarous syntax like sword-flashes amid the smoke of battle, were crude but forceful descriptions of brawls, battles, abductions, lecheries and treacheries. All very far indeed from the chaste idylls of Lord Tennyson, with his teas on the lawn at Osborne with our dear Majesty! At all events, scarcely fit reading for a highly strung young lady. But was it as simple as that? Why had Boynton-Leigh dodged my question when I had asked him if he had actually read it? What lay buried in the actual text that must not be brought to mind, nay, must not even speak its name? Perhaps I was making a mountain out of a molehill, but the book might repay further study, when once one had got the hang of the rough-hewn lingo.

And with what indifference Miss Nancarrow had received poor Tooke's enquiry after her health! I must be diplomatic with him about this, when next I met him, for I was sure he would seek me out again. Perhaps he was on my trail even now.

I looked at my watch as we clip-clopped down Middlesex Street, en route to the City, where I intended to eat in a tavern I knew off Cornhill. Twenty minutes to noon. A smoke would not come amiss. I had had to lay aside my tin of Virginia and rolling papers along with the rustic clothes of Dartmoor days, and my day's supply of cigarettes now lay in my rather grand, new silver case, which went better with my frock coat and silk hat, and which Tooke had admired so much in the Kensington tavern. Where on earth was it, though? I found my vesta case in my trousers pocket, then remembered that there were three or four loose cigarettes in my waistcoat pocket. It was while rummaging for one of these that my fingers encountered a forgotten visiting card and, as I took it out and looked at it, my memory rushed back to my first visit to Ginger Lane, and the extraordinary young lady bicyclist in tweeds who had literally bumped into me on the steps of Number One.

'Dr Violet Branscombe,' the card read, followed by the abbreviations of a French medical degree. Extraordinary! The address was given as 154, Whitechapel Road. I was intrigued and, being in the neighbourhood and with time in hand, I decided to look up Dr Branscombe before making for the City. If nothing else, it would provide relief from the stuffy drawing rooms of the West End. I gave the coachman his orders, and we swung round by Fashion Street into Brick Lane, which soon led us into the Whitechapel Road and all the squalid, roaring cheerio of the deep East End.

Number 154 was in a court off the main thoroughfare, where my coachman was hard put to it to thread a way through the midday traffic. Barefoot children were playing on the greasy cobbles of the court and slatternly, shawled women, some in men's caps and boots, stood gossiping at the openings of inky passages. Our vehicle drew instant attention, expressed through ribald comments, and I began – as I have done at so many junctures of my life – somewhat to regret my impulse.

A sign was affixed above the common entrance to Number 154: CLEAN BEDS FOR SINGLE MEN – FOURPENCE. I touched my hat to one of the shawled women a door up the court, and asked for Dr Branscombe.

'Straight up, squire! First floor landin'.'

'Yus!' some humourist joined in from across the court: 'Up them stairs!'

It was thus amid a general roar of derision that I left the coachman to disengage the unofficial urchin passengers who had already affixed themselves to the back of the carriage. Halfway up the creaking stairs I had to press myself against the wall to let pass two stoutish, painted young women in bedraggled picture hats.

'Reg'lar bloomin' lamppost,' I heard one say as she glanced insolently into my eyes.

'Wouldn't take much ter get yer legs rahnd 'im!' quipped her blowsy companion, which sparked off more ribald laughter.

I hurried up the stairs and at last stood on a dingy landing, covered – more or less – in scrubbed brown linoleum much the worse for wear. An open door confronted me, with the white cardboard sign above it, in simple black stencil: THE PEOPLE'S SURGERY AND DISPENSARY. There was a pervasive, institutional stench of carbolic acid.

Immediately inside was a bare waiting room of sorts, with broken-down kitchen chairs along two walls. The floor was of bare deal boards, scrubbed white as chalk. Only two chairs – those nearest the door in the wall which faced me – were occupied by a type of woman far removed from the plump

Delilahs I had met on the stairs. They were thin and their ruined clothes were drawn about them with a sort of pathetic modesty. Their eyes were sunken and fugitive under their tightly laced bonnets and they immediately began to make way for me. I smiled and signalled gently for them to remain seated, while I took the third chair in the row and looked about me.

It was rather like being on board ship, with all the scrubbed wood and, directly on my sitting down, a little girl of about fourteen, in a dress with mutton-chop sleeves and an apron, emerged from the door clutching an expertly wrapped medicine bottle to her chest. She wore a purposeful expression on her pale, candid face. A rather hoarse, cultivated woman's voice, which I recognised from my encounter on the steps of the house in Ginger Lane, caused the bustling little girl to stop in the doorway.

'Straight home to your dinner now, Queenie, as soon as you've delivered that,' the voice urged. 'And don't forget: I shall be testing you on sums tomorrow morning, so I'll want you here half an hour early!'

'All right, Dr Branscombe,' Queenie replied as she made for the door. 'See yer tomorrer!'

The bell rang for the next patient and while I waited, I mused on poor women and what they must endure, and thanked God for places like this. The London Hospital might just be down the road, but there were no doubt troubles that might not be unburdened, confidences that might not be entrusted in the harsh gaslight of a public out-patients' department. What a contrast, too, to Ferraby's grand establishment in Eaton Square! I had not previously given much thought to such matters: my routine work had been sufficient unto the day. After that, archaeology and my dear Ruth had filled my thoughts. Perhaps grief sharpens the understanding.

After another five minutes, the bell tolled for me and I went in, to be confronted by five-feet four of sturdy English woman-hood, straight as a guardsman, standing at the side of an American roll-top desk. This time, the tweed bloomer ensemble had given way to a most becoming skirt and blouse. The tow hair was up in a bun and the eyes danced a welcome behind the pince-nez. The hand was strong and shapely, the pressure on mine firm and dry. A fresh odour like apples emanated from the girl.

'I seem to have caught you at a slack time,' was my prosaic remark.

'We do not have many of those, here, Dr Mortimer,' she replied, 'but the British workman's dinner must be on the table promptly, so my patients tend not to dawdle here. They are my last of the morning. Please sit down.'

I obeyed, and my interlocutor sat down again at her desk.

'Your patients then are exclusively women?'

'Only since men choose not to come here – yet – as patients but, yes, women are my principal care.'

'I have studied your card, Dr Branscombe, and with such qualifications – I see you were at the Sorbonne – it struck me, if I may observe – '

'That I might find a far more lucrative crib elsewhere?'

'Well, the thought had occurred to me – '

'Even if I am "only" a woman, hey?'

'Really, ma'am, I had no intention of suggesting – '

'No, Dr Mortimer, of course you didn't! Please forgive me. I fear I have become something of a tease in the matter. As to your question, I simply choose to exercise my profession where the need is greatest, and where I may be of the most use: that is all.'

I would ponder those words deeply in the days that followed.

'Do I take it that the young person in the apron is by way of being your dispenser, Dr Branscombe?'

'Queenie? Not yet, Dr Mortimer, but she is an invaluable helper and is coming along a treat in her lessons. She is as bright as a button, and I have great hopes of her, but her family circumstances are unfavourable. Her father is bedridden after a stroke, and her mother is, well, seldom at home.'

I recalled how outrageously we medical students had treated the subject of women doctors – even rarer then – during my Charing Cross Hospital days. I determined there and then that I should give her no other occasion to tease in self-defence.

'When we, er, bumped into each other in Ginger Lane, Dr Branscombe' – again the throaty laugh – 'you seemed to suggest that I might be of some assistance to you. I am at your service.'

'I am grateful that you should have come so far to oblige me: I appreciate that this little court is far from the pleasant purlieus of the West End!'

'The company there is rarely as pleasant as the surroundings, Dr Branscombe; and in any case, I feel far more at home in the country.'

'Ah! May I ask which part of the country, Dr Mortimer?'

'The West Country: I was born in Exmouth and educated at Clifton. My first practice was on Dartmoor.'

'I too hail from the West Country – Cheltenham – though I was, in fact, born in India.'

The combination seemed to ring a bell with me.

'May I ask if you are any relation to Lieutenant-Colonel Hereward Branscombe, of the Chitral Scouts, who made the heroic stand at Maiwand?'

The tow-haired girl blushed.

'My late father, Dr Mortimer.'

'Then that explains your presence here, your work. Service is clearly in your blood, Dr Branscombe. But now, what can I do for you?'

'Let me lay certain facts before you, quite without comment, and then you may be in a position to say what you will do for me.'

I nodded, but Dr Branscombe had hardly drawn breath when there was an unholy clumping on the stairs, and the door burst open to reveal a tallish, fat man in dungaree slops and a deboshed cricket cap a size or two too small for him. His face – and notably the heroic nose – was of that plethoric scarlet which betokens fondness for the bottle.

'Where is she?' the fellow roared. 'Where is the f****** bitch?'

I jumped to my feet, clutching my stick.

'That is no way to talk to a lady, my friend!' I said.

The man ignored me entirely as evidently beneath his notice, and made as if to approach Dr Branscombe's desk, whereupon I stood in his way and, grasping my stick by the ferule, brought the heavy silver head crashing into my other palm. The man eyed me up and down and sneered, but went no further.

''Ark at 'im, Gilbert the bloomin' filbert! Where you on, then, tosh: the 'Ackney Empire?'

He redirected his gaze at my colleague.

'I wants my missus, Dr Bloody Branscombe, if you are a doctor, that is. I've a right ter know where me f****** missus is!'

My fists tightened round my stick.

'Your wife is in a place where you cannot inflict any more injury upon her, Mr Bettridge,' Dr Branscombe said calmly.

'The 'orspital? Which one? It ain't the London: I've just come from there. Yus! Gave 'em a piece o' me mind, an' all!'

'You are in drink again, Mr Bettridge,' my colleague said in an even tone. 'I suggest you go home and rest before we talk again.'

'Oh, do yer now? Well, let me tell yer one thing that ain't two: if my missus ain't back 'ome in one hour from now, I'm going ter come back 'ere and f****** swing for yer, so 'elp me if I don't! One hour, see!'

The man turned to me.

'And as for you, Gilbert, yer gig-lamps 'as saved yer this time, but don't let me see yer around 'ere again, or I might just lose me self-control!'

The fellow gave a last look at the company, then threw his head back, then forward, as he spat across the room. The loathsome moisture bespattered the papers on Dr Branscombe's desk, but she remained perfectly calm, her hands lightly clasped with fingers interlaced on the blotting pad in front of her.

As for myself, my hands were shaking with rage, and I do not know what I should have done if the drunken ruffian had not chosen that moment to stagger back down the stairs. Judging by the clatter and angry roars, mingled with the laughter of the gossips in the court, I judged that he had fallen down the last half-dozen or so steps. I leant over the desk, and Dr Branscombe's calm, humorous gaze met mine.

'My dear Dr Branscombe,' I said solicitously. 'What an appalling incident! You must allow me to order my coachman to send for a constable. In the meantime, I shall of course remain here until – '

It was Dr Branscombe's turn to get up.

'Please do sit down, Dr Mortimer. And leave the police where they are needed.'

I sat down grudgingly and faced her again.

'But if the fellow comes back, especially in that drunken state – '

'Oh, Bettridge will come back, Dr Mortimer, but only after he has further fortified himself, and then he will be in his maudlin stage. Then it will be tears and grovelling: he will be polishing the desk with his neckerchief that he has just soiled here. It is a familiar pattern. In fact, I am not sure that I do not prefer his aggressive mood.'

'But his poor wife – '

Dr Branscombe sighed.

'Safe for the time being. We must be grateful for that. She has had eleven children to him, seven of them still living; that is, in the sense that they are still walking and breathing. She is thirty-seven but dwells in the body of an ailing sixty year-old. I assure you that her plight is far from uncommon.'

'I wonder that you can bear such acquaintance.'

The grey eyes lost their friendly openness and the lenses of the pince-nez glinted.

'There are far worse men than Bettridge, Dr Mortimer. He may be one of the damned, but there are devils who rule over the damned, those who profit from distress, exploit innocence. From them there can and must be no consideration, no mercy . . .'

The blonde physician seemed to gather her thoughts, then twitched up the little watch which was affixed to her blouse.

'Lord!' she exclaimed. 'It is twelve-forty already and I am to take luncheon at Seymour Place at one-thirty: the New Hospital for Women, you know – '

'Yes,' I added. 'Frances Morgan and Elizabeth Garrett were the first women to operate there, were they not?'

'Indeed they were. Elizabeth Garrett's struggle has been the chief inspiration of our cause, Dr Mortimer. But no more of that: I am afraid I must impose on your kindness further.'

I got up and began to assist her with her outdoor clothes.

'My carriage shall take you to the station, Dr Branscombe, and from there you may take the Inner Circle Line to Baker Street and the nearest cabstand. You shall keep your luncheon appointment.'

'You are most kind, Dr Mortimer. Would it then be convenient for me to call on you when my duties next allow so that I may continue with the matter I broached before we were interrupted?'

'I should be delighted, but perhaps it might be more convenient for you – given the difficulties of transport – if I were to make the call.'

Dr Branscombe's eyes brightened.

'Perhaps you would care to take supper with me this evening, Dr Mortimer, at my Club.'

'That will be top hole, Dr Branscombe!'

'Shall we say seven-thirty, then? Number Eleven, Coptic Street.'

As we made our way downstairs to the carriage, I reflected on what remarkable Britons India can breed.

8

I do not know quite what I expected to find at a ladies' residential club, but the Coptic Street establishment, nestling, as it were, under the aegis of the British Museum, was as sober and well-run as any of its masculine equivalents of my experience. Only the opulence of an institution of longer foundation was lacking, and with it – shall I admit it? – the self-indulgence of the male preserve.

No complacent red faces to be seen in the club- and dining-rooms, no cigar fumes or loud, assertive voices. I tried to catch the tone of the place as my hostess, charming in a white summer dress, signed me in in the quiet lobby, then led me straight into the dining-room. I soon hit it: an Oxford or Cambridge college. I had no experience of Somerville or Girton but I imagined such places to have a feel to them like that of the Junior Minerva. I mentioned this to Dr Branscombe as we took our seats at a quiet table against a window. I could see that she had chosen a place where we were least likely to be overheard.

'You have hit it off pretty well!' she replied. 'Not surprising, in view of the fact that many of our members are in fact graduates – or would be, if they were allowed to sport the degrees they have earned – of those very institutions.'

Odd – and shameful – to recall that in those days women graduates of English universities were not awarded degrees.

'The proximity of the Museum must be a great advantage to those of your fellow members who are engaged in intellectual work,' I said.

'The Reading Room is quite indispensable to those of our members who do research into political and social questions. Our voice is being heard increasingly in journalism, Dr Mortimer! A day will come when women are represented on the staff of every paper, every publishing house in the land!'

I smiled at this but admired her spirit unreservedly. The soup arrived, an excellent cold vichyssoise and, after we had done some justice to it, a change in the topic of conversation.

'I have had my eye on Number One, Ginger Lane for some time,' my hostess said.

'You are acquainted, then, with the inmates?'

'Not personally, though my name's Indian connection gained me admittance to the house on the one and only occasion when I actually got inside and, of course, no one with any acquaintance with the Subcontinent can be ignorant of the name of Boynton-Leigh. I knew of the existence of a young woman who was said to have been seen behind barred windows there, and even if I had had no other reason to investigate the place, that would have sufficed. But it was in quite another connection that I was orginally interested in the house.'

'To do with your work, Dr Branscombe?'

'Precisely! You may recall a remark I made at the surgery in Whitechapel, after we were interrupted by Bettridge, about the existence of men much worse than he?'

'Yes, indeed: about exploiters of innocence.'

The expression of my *vis-à-vis* hardened, just as it had done that forenoon in Whitechapel.

'Yes, Dr Mortimer: exploiters of the innocent, of both sexes – '

'But surely you cannot mean Boynton-Leigh!'

'No, I do not mean him. I do not refer to the local ruffians – less than men – who live off girls. You will encounter them in any low public house, any wastrels' cafe within a two-mile radius of our surgery. I refer to the – shall we say – wholesalers in the trade. Purveyors – like high-class grocers – to the nobility and the gentry.'

My hostess's rather square jaw set grimly, and she leant forward slightly, no doubt to give emphasis to her words.

'I have had occasion to treat girls, Dr Mortimer, who have passed through the hands of the wealthy, those who can afford to indulge any whim within, or indeed out of all reason, the well-born, the – save the mark – cultured, even, and what I have seen has sickened and angered me. The apes and baboons of the jungle are gentlemen compared to those fiends! But they are base, flabby, weak. Without their agents, pandars – call them what you will – they could scarcely indulge their twisted passions. Well, then, Dr Mortimer, I now have incontrovertible proof that one such middleman is at work in this locality. I am on his trail, I am gathering evidence – '

'In a case of such flagrant nature, you will need only one reliable witness, and – '

We paused as the soup plates were collected then, after looking round the room with a vague smile, Dr Branscombe returned to her narrative.

'You clearly do not know the East End, Dr Mortimer! It is the unwritten law there that thou shalt not bear witness against thy neighbour. And if that law is unwritten, it is most rigorously enforced.'

'Intimidation?'

'Both moral and physical. It is a strong man – or woman – indeed who will break ranks, whatever the indignation aroused by a particular deed. Besides, there are those who have a strong interest in this case in seeing that my bird is not brought down. He cannot ply his vile trade without the compliance of the local bullies, who will exact a handsome tribute from him for the use of their pitch.'

I was half-prompted to warn her against the dangers of the course she had chosen, but I glanced again at the firm set of her jaw, and reflected that it would take more than a parcel of shiftless slum-denizens to deter the daughter of Hereward Branscombe, the Hero of Maiwand!

'And who is this scoundrel, Dr Branscombe?'

'Hmph! What was once a gentleman, and a man of some education, but rotten, rotten to his blackened teeth! Some would find him handsome in a worn-out way, and he draws on an old account of studied charm. For those with half an eye, however, the account has long been overdrawn and should be closed, forthwith. For the rest, he poses as an artist and a dealer of sorts, with a studio in an old former silkweaver's house in Fournier Street. I suspect, however, that his real dealings are done in the Warsaw Café in Whitechapel. It is a rookery where one may hear half the languages of Europe and brush shoulders with some of the worst rogues who have ever made the Russian empire too hot to hold them.'

'And when did this paragon first appear on the scene?'

'About a year ago, some four or five months after the Boynton-Leigh establishment came to Ginger Lane.'

'And the connection?'

'None that I have been able to make as yet, save that he is one of the very few callers apart from daily servants and tradesmen who is ever allowed past the front door of Number One. That is what I am most anxious to learn: what can this creature have to do with such a staid and secluded household? But I have not told you the man's name, Dr Mortimer: it is – '

'Jack Agar!' I announced, with a touch of melodrama. I would be a liar if I denied feeling any pleasure at the surprise in Dr Branscombe's eyes as I produced this card. I now felt no qualms or professional reservations about telling her all I knew about Agar – he was not, after all, my patient – though my information was second-hand and entirely in the Percival Tooke version. By now we had long since done full justice to our cold beef and salad, and had lingered as long as one decently could over our ices, so we rose and shifted the conversation to the cool and quiet clubroom, where the company was thin and the talk subdued.

'How clear the air is in here,' I hinted.

'There is no bar to smoking,' my hostess said with a laugh. 'So you may rest easy. And you would not perhaps find the air quite so fresh if Hettie Ovingham were back from her last expedition to the Karakoram: her cheroots are the curse of the clubroom. But our steward Miss Mainsforth has drawn a bead on her and I fear she is heading for a fall.'

I reached in my inside pocket with a sigh of relief but no cool, polished surface met my touch and I remembered with an inward curse that I had missed my new cigarette case that morning. I should have to abstain till I got home.

We returned to our more serious topic.

'I cannot approach the police about Agar,' Dr Branscombe explained, 'because of the difficulty of obtaining witnesses against him and his accomplices. Even if I could persuade anyone to come forward, my being seen to work hand-in-hand with the police force would fatally compromise my position with the local people.'

'The People's Dispensary would then be seen as a sort of listening post for the police,' I suggested.

'Exactly! That is to be avoided at all costs. I decided, then, to approach the matter from the Indian side. My father's name still opens many doors there, Dr Mortimer, and I can tell you in confidence that a couple of months ago I was able to convince a very high-ranking official of my acquaintance in the India Office that, as a matter of public interest, my enquiries might justify the use of a few signals of the official telegraph.'

I pause here to explain that at this time twelve years were yet to elapse before the British Empire was linked by the 'All-Red Line' of public electric telegraphy in 1902.

'And your enquiries are already afoot.'

My interlocutor smiled and nodded.

'Yes, I have engaged the services of a reputable private detective agency in Calcutta, run by a Mr Kearney, formerly of New York, an old Pinkerton's employee.'

'You did not then approach the official police authorities in Calcutta?'

'I was advised by my connection in the India Office, again in confidence – '

I nodded.

' – that I might find the police there, shall we say, unreceptive to enquiries of such a sensational nature concerning an old, established Calcutta family of such distinction. Even more so in the absence of cast-iron proof. The face of the British Raj must be saved at all costs!'

'I see. And when do you expect to receive a report from this Mr Kearney? I assume he will not be allowed to use the official wire from the Indian end?'

'Scarcely, Dr Mortimer! My initial message was a considerable privilege, a tribute to my late father's reputation, and I cannot expect it to be repeated. No, a bulky report – perhaps with photographs and other objects – will have to take its chances with the mail packets. But as I have told you, it has been a couple of months now, and I may expect something in the coming weeks, I hope, depending on Mr Kearney's progress. I do not know if Agar's activities in the East End have any necessary connection with your patient, but after what you have told me, I hardly think it can be coincidence. I fear that from now on, Dr Mortimer, you will have to view her as potential prey!'

It was a chilling thought, especially when put in such stark terms.

'I hope, then,' I said, 'that the information I have been able to give you has been of some use in your quest to bring this man to book. Yours has certainly put me on the alert with respect to my patient's welfare.'

'Your information has been invaluable, Dr Mortimer. I feel I can now proceed with even greater confidence towards nipping Agar in the bud.'

My colleague gave me an appraising look.

'And Dr Mortimer – '

'Yes, Dr Branscombe?'

'May I ask if you are well-established in practice here?'

'Why, no, I am at present serving as locum to help out a friend of a friend in the West End. I fancy my stint there will soon be finished. Moreover, I do not mind confessing that such a position is scarcely congenial to me.'

'I thought as much. Well, I wish you to know that, whatever you decide as to your future activities, there will always be a berth for you at the People's Dispensary: we have much to do in the East End.'

The offer took me aback, but I recalled the remark which Dr Branscombe had made at our last meeting and which had given me much food for thought: 'I simply choose to exercise my profession where the need is greatest, and where I may be of the most use.' Yes, there was something of a clarion-call to that. I should give the offer most serious thought.

'I shall give your offer the most earnest consideration, Dr Branscombe,' I replied. 'I should consider it an honour to work with you.'

She blushed in her charming way and, my carriage having just then arrived, my hostess showed me to the door. She spoke to me on parting on the steps of the club, amid the dappled light of the plane trees which lined the street.

'I think it will be in our mutual interest, Dr Mortimer, to exchange information as to developments in the matter we have just discussed: yours in the promotion of your patient's welfare, and mine in that of my girls in the East End.'

'First of all, Dr Branscombe, allow me to say that in any case I should need no pretext for seeking to make better acquaintance with you – ' another blush, and a nod ' – and that I greatly admire the work you are doing in the East End. Of course we shall keep in touch, and please do not hesitate to call upon me any time you feel you might need a helping hand.'

We shook hands warmly before I mounted the carriage.

'Very well then, Dr Mortimer, I shall not hesitate. For the time being, then, goodnight, and au revoir!'

Back in Eaton Square, I mulled over what Dr Branscombe had told me, and my head was soon so abuzz with speculations as to what might be the connection between Agar – given that his tutorial function had apparently come to an end in India – and the Boynton-Leigh household, that an early night was out of the question. And could he possibly be the villain of the piece that Dr Branscombe had portrayed him as being? Much as I liked and respected the lady, it occurred to me that Agar's evident bohemianism might have caused her to draw the wrong conclusions. It might well be that he kept queer – and even low – company, but surely it was the way of the artist to mingle with all sorts and conditions of men and women? Again, when I remembered the vehemence with which Dr Branscombe spoke

51

of Agar, the adage about the 'woman scorned' came immediately to mind . . .

There was nothing for it: I must make the acquaintance of Mr Agar; or at least, since I now knew the name of one of his haunts – the Warsaw Café – I could savour for myself the atmosphere in which he apparently chose to immerse himself. Instead of turning in, then, I changed into my oldest country suit and well-worn boots, left my watch-and-chain on my dressing table and, pulling the rim of my oldest and most disreputable bowler over my eyes, slunk out again into the night. The game was afoot!

9

I found the Warsaw Café in Osborn Street, not far from Aldgate East Station and just beyond the southernmost confines of the former Huguenot weavers' quarter. Though the clientele of the Warsaw was cosmopolitan, it scarcely presented the appearance of the thieves' kitchen which Dr Branscombe had depicted earlier on in the evening. There were decent white cloths on the tables, a waiter in attendance, and – after the Continental fashion – newspapers for those who wanted them. I came in and made quickly for one of the few unoccupied tables, at which I installed myself. All around me was the chatter of Eastern Europe, liberally intermixed with assertive cockney. No chatter, however, emanated from the half-dozen two-man tables where deep games of chess were in progress. Here a seeming ruffian in the sorriest rags could be seen solemnly confronting a bespectacled savant who would not have looked out of place in the academic cloisters of Heidelberg or Jena. I was particularly struck by a fine-looking, broad-shouldered man in light, loose-fitting clothes who might have been a poet or an artist and who was in deep play with a man with pale wolf's eyes clad in a Russian blouse and visored cap. There was something vaguely familiar about the man in the cap, but I could not quite place him. No one paid me the slightest attention – or so I thought – until, at length, a waiter was at my side.

'What can I bring you, sir?' he asked in a sort of whisper, his cheek twitching nervously as a neighbouring client shouted impatiently over to him for service.

I ordered tea and lemon and, as the waiter scurried off, a little yellow-skinned man, sporting a drooping moustache and with his hair greased down into a calf-lick, came up, tipped his curly-brimmed bowler and gave me an oily smile.

'You voot like to play, sir? My partner has not come tonight, and it is definite I must heff my game.'

'Why, yes!' I said, forgetting in my surprise to disguise my accent. 'I may be a bit rusty, mind, but yes, I'll give you a game!'

The quaint little man who, I noticed, carried much gold about him in the form of watch-chain, rings, cufflinks and so on, positively beamed and, bawling across the room at the harassed waiter for a board and chessmen, sat down in the seat which faced mine.

'Chess, sir,' he said, as the waiter plonked down a tall glass with my tea and a slice of lemon and began to set out the chessboard, 'is a republic. And vy?'

'Please tell me,' I said, taken by the man's oddity.

'Because anyvorn who can play, may vin. No matter who he is, sir. No matter how he spiks, no matter if he has no money in his pocket. Is dat not a republic?'

'It seems a pretty good working definition of one.'

The little man nodded solemnly, waved his hand gently at my tea, of which I took a sip, then, gripping the edge of the table, slightly bowed his head, as if in dedication. He positively glared at me.

'And now, sir, ve play!'

And play we did, for a good hour. I did my best to put up a decent show, but kept enough of my attention free to watch the comings and goings in the café. Towards midnight, as the chess games broke up, an altogether flashier clientele started to trickle in, types who, I dared say, would normally have gone in for games rather rougher than chess. They congregated round a couple of tables in a far corner, talking in low and vehement tones. A pair of them – young sparks in bookies' suits and rakish, pearl-grey bowlers – started to scan the rest of the clients in what I took to be an appraising sort of fashion. I was on the alert.

My game at last ended, with me as manifest loser, and my opponent got up and bowed grandly, while waving to the waiter.

'It has been a pleasure, sir!' he declared, and insisted on paying my count. He gave another bow and stalked away, and I began to think I might be happier elsewhere. I took a last look round at the dwindling company and my eyes met those of the two sparks in the checked suits. As I was turning for the door, I noticed one of them turn to his mate and nod slightly. I quickened my steps and, once outside, decided to evade any possible pursuit by ducking down into nearby Angel Alley, all the while keeping my eyes on the entry to the café. I watched for quite five minutes, but no one emerged from the street door, so I darted out from my cover, having decided to make quickly for the nearest cabstand in Whitechapel High Street. I had hardly got past the opening to Gunthorpe Street, when I heard a low whistle behind me, and someone suddenly emerged from the street-opening in front and drove his fist into my abdomen with a force that left me sprawling and gasping on the ground.

The next thing I knew, feet were clattering up from the direction of the whistle and I felt a terrible kick in my side. I am thankful I had the presence of mind to throw up an arm to protect my head for, almost simultaneously with the kick, my forearm took the full force of a blow from what seemed like a cudgel or life-preserver. I made a desperate attempt to roll over, only to receive another kick, this time on the hip.

Just then I heard the unmistakable sound of a revolver shot and my assailants seemed to melt away like snow before sunshine. I felt strong hands raising me up, and a light, cultivated voice asking me if I was all right. My Good Samaritan propped me against a low windowsill, where I struggled to regain my wind while he whistled up a passing cab. With my rescuer's help, I clambered into the cab and, after he had given directions to the cabbie, he climbed in beside me. The cab jerked into motion, and in the dim light afforded by the street-lamps, I made out the features of the artistic-looking gentleman whom I had noticed playing chess with the man in the visored cap in the

Warsaw Café. He leant forward and brought his face close to mine.

'Are you in much pain, sir?' he asked. 'Your ribs must have had quite a basting!'

I fingered my side gingerly and decided that, while it was hurting like the devil, there did not seem to be any broken bones. By morning it would be all the colours of the rainbow! My arm was similarly sore, but quite sound.

'Nothing broken, sir, thank you,' I said. 'You were in the Warsaw Café not five minutes ago, were you not?'

'As I am most nights: I have not the gift of sound sleep, so providence has endowed me with a passion for chess. At a guess, sir, I should say you had come quite a long way for your game.'

'Indeed! And the game was far rougher than I had bargained for! But my dear sir, I am most infinitely obliged to you for your timely help. Please let me know your name.'

The rangy chessplayer cocked up the brim of his wideawake hat with his long, delicate forefinger.

'My name is Agar, sir, Jack Agar. At your service!'

10

Agar insisted on taking me back to his studio in Fournier Street, where he sat me in a cane chair and gave me a brandy-and-seltzer. The place was no more than a single vast room on the top floor of the house, with a broad north window and a skylight let into the roof.

'The old silkweavers were artists, too,' the long, lounging man said from his low cane chair, which was backed by an easel covered by a cloth.

'Yes,' I agreed. 'I can imagine they would need good light, too. I have seen similar windows in the old weavers' cottages in Yorkshire.'

The room was a jumble of paintings, paint, sketches, statues and albums, exactly what I imagined an artist's studio to be. I sipped my brandy and examined my discovery. So this was the Great Beast of Dr Branscombe's good crusade! I had to own, I had found nothing beastly in the way – however theatrical – he had rescued me from those ruffians in the opening of Gunthorpe Street. There was nothing bestial, either, in the frank, manly features, with the Cambridge blue eyes under thick, black lashes. His gaze was steady and frank.

'You have not asked me my name, Mr Agar,' I remarked.

'It has often been my experience that the best way of finding out something is by not asking,' he riposted.

'Ah!' I said. 'I see you are a disciple of Mr Wilde.'

I fancied that my remark had momentarily startled him, but he merely smiled gently with the corners of his lips.

'Wilde is something of a forerunner,' Agar said. 'In many things.'

'My name is Mortimer, sir, James Mortimer, and I am a physician by trade,' I said, handing him my card.

'If I may abandon my Wildean course of not asking,' Agar went on, 'I should like to know what a member of the Royal College of Surgeons should be doing in the Warsaw Café until near midnight. Admittedly, one can get a decent game of chess there, but there are other such places in London where the company is rather more select . . .'

'But I may be down on my luck, Mr Agar. Surely there is nothing of Harley Street in my present attire?'

'If you were really down on your luck, that fine ring you are wearing – sapphire, is it not? – would have been the first thing you would have popped.'

I cursed myself inwardly: it had never occurred to me to take the ring off before going out. Ruth had given it to me when we had first become engaged.

'You think, then, that the ring may have been the reason why those ruffians waylaid me?'

'A fence would give them a couple of sovereigns for it, easily. More if they stood out for a good bargain.'

'But they could scarcely have spotted it from the opposite end of the café,' I objected. 'Unless of course there was a fence sitting conveniently nearby.'

'What did you make of the old card who invited himself to a game of chess with you, Dr Mortimer?'

'Oh, the "chess is a republic" man. Very droll. A regular, no doubt.'

'Very regular, and you may know that in the best theoretical republics, goods are held in common.'

I sat up, now bolt upright, and put down my glass on the Egyptian table at my side.

'You mean, he tipped them the wink?' I exclaimed.

Agar laughed, covering his mouth with his hand as he did so. He then brought his lips together and tapped them with his forefinger, as if to enjoin silence.

'Good Lord!' I said. 'Then it really is a thieves' kitchen! She was absolutely ri – '

Agar simply stared at me coldly.

I felt as if I could bite off my tongue.

'What I mean is . . .' I began, but the artist only smiled.

'Please don't trouble to explain. I think I can piece it together myself. A West End physician in mufti comes slumming in the Warsaw Café to see if it is as black as "she" has painted it. While playing chess, he spends quite half his time scanning the company. Now I confess that my vanity is colossal, but I take it I am the object of your quest, and as for the "she", I think we need to look no further than the redoubtable Dr Branscombe. Your expression confirms it. The lady is indefatigable, Dr Mortimer. Indefatigable!'

I hardly knew which way to turn.

'Still, sir,' I stammered, 'I am indebted to you for your prompt intervention just now. Do you, er, always carry a revolver?'

To my astonishment, Agar whipped out the revolver, held it about a yard away from him, the barrel aimed at his own chest and, his thumb on the trigger, fired. He then sat back in his chair and laughed, his hand again across his mouth.

'Ah, blanks!' I said. 'But the ruffians, will they not be looking out for you in future?'

'Not they! For one thing, the Warsaw is not on their pitch. They looked like Houndsditch men, no doubt well in drink and looking for trouble. Well, they got it tonight, and I fancy we'll not be seeing much more of them yet awhile. Our chess-playing republican friend will no doubt also be looking elsewhere for a game!'

'But what made you follow me?'

'God knows I'm no moralist, Dr Mortimer, but I could see what you were in for, and I don't care to see a gentleman set upon by ruffians. And besides, they upset my game! And while we're on the subject of morality, I daresay your colleague Dr Branscombe has told you all about my manifold iniquities.'

My hackles rose a bit over his attitude to my colleague, whom he was discussing as if she were some sort of vaporous hysteric. I felt I must redress the balance.

'I fear Dr Branscombe has formed some very specific suspicions concerning you, Mr Agar, which she insists are founded on ample evidence.'

'Ah, let me see, now. I have it! Agar the pandar, Agar the corrupter of innocence! Agar, the Shame of our Cities! Well, perhaps I have occasionally acted as, shall we say, philosopher, guide and friend to a few young chaps of our own sort – Varsity men, down on the spree, don't you know – down here to taste the nameless sins of the East End. A smoker here, a gaff or a spieler there, and – now and then – a terrified brush with a streetwalker. But innocence! Believe me, the only innocence I've seen in danger has been that of those young fools. Most of them wouldn't know which end of a woman to start with! No, Dr Mortimer, the reality of Wicked Jack Agar is rather more prosaic: I'm an artist whose pictures no one wants to buy, and I have a studio here in Spitalfields because I can't afford to fork out Chelsea rents. I scrape a living by tutoring poor devils in an art I can't practise profitably myself and, when there aren't enough of them, I'm reduced to piloting ships of well-heeled fools round the night-spots of the East End. All rather humdrum, I fear. She's been here, you know – '

'Dr Branscombe, you mean?'

'Yes, to beard me in my lair. I've had two ultimatums so far: mend my wicked ways, or else. Really, she's a damn' fine woman! Bags of spirit, backbone. Breeding, you see: caste. But wrong about me: hopelessly wrong. Simply a case of her allegedly reformed magdalens telling her what they think she wants to hear. They do, if you feed them, you see, like animals. Chuck 'em a biscuit, and up they go on their hind legs! Fact of nature.'

Agar had by now lit a strong cheroot and was gazing up at the ceiling with a dreamy sort of smile on his face. I could see through the gap introduced by the cheroot that his teeth – or at least, the ones I could see – were quite spectacularly rotten, like black pearls in appearance. I wondered about the smile, connecting it somehow with the remark about Dr Branscombe being a 'damn' fine woman. Perhaps he and she... And again the adage: 'Hell hath no fury like a woman scorned' reverberated round my mind. But surely not.

'But enough of this!' Agar snapped, suddenly leaping out of his chair and beckoning me up with his cheroot in a theatrical gesture. 'You are my prisoner here, Dr James Mortimer, foreign visitor in the Republic of Chess, and in spite of the lateness of the hour, it is my fell intent to inflict my paintings upon you! Come, sir.'

I could not help laughing at this sally, and I rose rather stiffly, on account of my maturing bruises, while Agar rushed over to the walls to put up the gas-jets. They were fine paintings, too, evidently done with a truly professional confidence of stroke. The draughtsmanship was impeccable, the tone right, but then a doubt started to creep into my mind. They were nearly all copies of the works of former masters, notably Gainsborough and Reynolds, and when we came to Agar's own work – his contemporary portraits from life – my doubt hardened into certainty. My heart sank a little and went out to the dandyfied man who talked so wittily and bravely for, in spite of their technical proficiency, his paintings showed not the slightest spark of originality which, for any artist, must surely be the all-in-all. My eyes met his and, as if he saw that I knew his tragedy, he averted his gaze and swung round to the back of the cloth-shrouded easel.

'I think this may interest you, Dr Mortimer!' Agar announced, and tugged away the cloth from the picture. There on the canvas, dressed in the costume of the eighteenth century, was Lavinia Nancarrow.

11

'It is remarkable!' I stammered, for, alone among all the other canvases Agar had shown me, this one had the breath of life. Could it have been that the artist could only find himself with the inspiration of Lavinia Nancarrow before him?

Uncharted waters, indeed. The more I delved into this mystery, the more I was engrossed in it. I stepped forward a pace, the better to view the painting. The eyes in particular – at once anxious and hungry – conveyed the very essence of my beautiful patient, but the canvas was dark and positively dirty-looking. Even with the gas-jets up full, I should need to approach even more closely, but no sooner had I made my move than Agar, with a deft movement like that of a toreador plying a cape, whipped the cloth back over the canvas.

'It is not ready yet, Dr Mortimer. I hope she is well.'

'I have been led to believe, Mr Agar, that you were in a better position than most to keep up-to-date on Miss Nancarrow's progress.'

'It is some while since I was in Ginger Lane. You will understand that one's visits there are always at the mercy of the egregious Archibald and his caprices.'

I was determined not to be pumped further, and decided to bait my hook so that I might land Agar this time.

'Miss Nancarrow is making a good recovery from her influenza,' I said cautiously, 'given the somewhat sombre domestic arrangements down there. The view from her window, I find, is particularly gloomy.'

'Yes,' Agar said through a blue cloud of cheroot-smoke. 'The constant sight of the backside of Bell Lane can scarcely be very conducive to robust health and spirits.'

So! I had smoked Agar out! He could not then have ever set foot in Lavinia Nancarrow's room, for the windows of her chamber faced out from the end of the house on to the disused cemetery, from which no aspect of Bell Lane was visible. He must have assumed by analogy that her windows would have looked out on to Bell Lane, like those of the rest of the windows along the back of the house. He should not find me so easy to gull in future. I did not carry the topic further.

'She is perfectly beautiful, Dr Mortimer, and I don't mean the squishy-squashy chocolate-box stuff! Caste again! In the Spanish sense, I mean: a type developed to perfection in all its characteristic traits. Not much prized in this brummagem age, I'll grant you, but we all recognise it when we see it. We mark, we wonder, and we are silent. All except us chumps of artists, of course, who must immediately attempt to chase it with our brushes, only to sink into the Slough of Despond when it inevitably eludes us. But our Archibald won't have it, Dr Mortimer. Why was he born so pigheaded, why was he born at all!'

'I am led to believe that his obstinacy in that respect has its origin in India, Mr Agar – '

'But how well-informed you are, doctor!' Agar said skittishly, squashing out the butt of his cheroot in a filthy saucer. 'Don't tell me Archibald has been pouring out his heart to you. Yes, I was given my marching orders in Calcutta without a word of explanation, except that I was a thoroughly importunate and objectionable fellow.'

'And yet you are allowed to call on the family in Ginger Lane. May I ask if you and Mr Boynton-Leigh have patched things up?'

Agar darted me a shrewd look.

'If you call being glared at by him while I exchange remarks with Lavinia about the weather for five minutes "patching things up", then I suppose there must have been a reconciliation of sorts. But then again, there is no accounting for Archibald's whims, Dr Mortimer. If I go along there tomorrow, he may well kick me downstairs! One really need look no farther than Lavinia for the key to his behaviour: he wants to keep her all to himself. Like a jealous old stag in the rutting season. How's old Lance, by the way? I've hardly seen him since he was packed off to Dartmouth.'

'I have only seen him once, and he did not speak.'

61

'Charming little fellow, in his way,' Agar sneered, 'but I suspect there's only one naval tradition he's likely to take to, and that's scarcely mentionable in polite society.'

I now began to feel the full effects of my mishap and, thanking Agar again for his help, I made my excuses and followed him downstairs in search of a cab. As I walked down the street with him, it struck me that, whatever else he might be, Jack Agar was thundering good company. We found a free cab at last and he helped me up into it. Before it drove off, a question sprang to my lips.

'Mr Agar,' I said. 'Do you know where Lavinia Nancarrow comes from?'

'One or two people would give their right arm to know that, Dr Mortimer.'

The cab drove off.

12

Early next morning I climbed stiffly into Ferraby's carriage and drove to Coptic Street, where I dropped in on Dr Branscombe at the Junior Minerva. I joined her for a cup of coffee in the dining-room, where she was eating breakfast.

'You should have consulted me before setting off on such a madcap errand, Dr Mortimer,' she remarked after she had listened eagerly to my account of my doings of the previous evening and had commiserated with me over the drubbing I had had. 'It is of the first importance that you know your way round the East End, especially before venturing into its darker recesses late at night. However, what you have learnt from Agar is of the greatest interest. Now that he appears never to have set foot in Miss Nancarrow's room to visit her sickbed, there would seem to be a real possibility that his principal business in Ginger Lane is with Mr Boynton-Leigh.'

'He was dissembling, then, on the subject of Boynton-Leigh's hostility towards him?'

'Not necessarily, but the true relation between them is yet to be established. I fancy money will not be far away from it, in spite of Agar's artistic pretensions.'

I did not mention to Dr Branscombe Agar's assessment of her orientation in pursuing the matter. We went over my experience in the Warsaw Café again and something dropped into my memory.

'The man in the visored cap!' I exclaimed. 'The little man with the wolf's eyes who was playing chess with Agar! I remember now where I first saw him: he was the man who was selling the pastries in Wentworth Street, the man I asked for directions to Ginger Lane.'

'He may well have reported your movements to Agar, as part of a general watch kept on the approaches to Ginger Lane. And last night's business of the attack on you and his seemingly dashing rescue may have been a put-up job; a mere ploy, serving both to warn you away from the Warsaw, and then to pump you for what you knew.'

'And not a mention of Zoffany!' I remarked.

'No, but there is still much we do not know. From now on we must be perpetually on guard, and, above all, we must agree to take no action in this matter without prior mutual consultation.'

Though somewhat taken aback by Dr Branscombe's forwardness, I now realised just how much the thrill of the chase had overtaken other considerations in my attitude to this affair. From this juncture I date the fixing of my penchant for private detection that has formed the leitmotiv of my life since then. I returned to the matter in hand.

'I do agree to that, Dr Branscombe.'

'United we stand, Dr Mortimer!'

Having come to an understanding with my new-found ally, I rejoined my carriage and set off for the West End and the prosaic round of my morning's consultations. The days wore on as the Season waxed, and June began to lose its bloom. I had received no word of fresh developments from Whitechapel, and the report Violet Branscombe was so avidly awaiting from the private detective in Calcutta was, so far as her silence went, still on the high seas. Nor, to my surprise, had the lovelorn surveyor, Percy Tooke, darkened my doorstep since our confidential chop in the tavern off Kensington Gardens. Perhaps he had at last found a post worthy of his abilities and had put his hopeless love behind him. More immediately irritating was the continuing silence from Angmering, and I was beginning to lose hope of handing back the baton of endless calls and petty humiliations at the hands of pampered clients to Ferraby at any early opportunity. On the very eve, then, of my third appointment in Ginger Lane, on my arrival back at Eaton Square from my rounds, I found Lance Boynton-Leigh waiting in my consulting room.

I entered quietly and the thick pile of carpet must have so deadened my footfalls that he was unaware of my entry. He was standing gazing out of the window on to the busy, early-evening traffic. He made a graceful figure, but there was something in his expression that I thought no one of his age should experience: broken resignation.

'Why, Lance!' I said. 'What can I do for you?'

'Got sacked from Dartmouth, sir!' he said with a jauntiness belied by the look in his eyes. 'Hopeless case, don't you know.'

'Sacked?' I said in a puzzled tone, and waved him into the visitor's chair and took mine behind the table.

'Well, crocked-up, sir. Anyhow, it looks as if I'm beached as far as that institution's concerned. I've a letter for you, sir, from the M.O.'

He handed a sealed envelope across the table, which I opened with Ferraby's fancy little poniard. A single stiff sheet inscribed in a rapid, medical hand. I read, and my heart sank, but I did my best not to show it.

'Mmph!' I muttered with what I hoped was a conspiratorial grin. 'I smell a good, long spot of leave here. How do you feel now, Lance?'

'Oh, pretty well, sir. Something to do with my balance; falling over chaps in the dark. Had a bit of a lark with the M.O., sir. D'you know what he made me do?'

'No, Lance, what was that?'

'Blindfolded me and asked me to make my way back from memory – on all fours – to the door of his surgery. Priceless, hey, sir?'

The Medical Officer at Dartmouth strongly suspected a brain tumour and, in the letter, suggested I consult Crowninshield or Cary-Evans.

'What does your father say about this?' I asked as I scribbled a note to Sir Edgar Crowninshield, whose lectures I had in fact attended as a student. I knew from the Dartmouth physician's letter that he had already written to Boynton-Leigh, but I was curious as to the nabob's reaction.

'Mmm. Dunno, sir. Fact is, I haven't been home yet to see him. Came straight here.'

I folded the note I had just written, sealed it into an envelope, on which I had written Sir Edgar's name, then handed it to my patient.

'I should like you to take this to the Charing Cross Hospital as soon as you like tomorrow after you've reported back home. Sir Edgar is by way of being our leading expert on, er, falling over chaps. I shall in any case be calling on Miss Lavinia tomorrow, when I shall no doubt have the opportunity to talk to your father. Now I really think you should be cutting along home. Have you the money for the train?'

'Oh, that's all right, sir! Decent of you to ask, but I'm rolling in tin at the moment. Perfectly all right.'

As Lance showed no sign of rising from his chair, but merely sat staring at me with wide, blue eyes, I put down my pen and folded my hands on the table.

'Out with it!' I said simply.

It was like summer rain after thunder. His little rosebud mouth twitched, and then he laid on his face on the tooled leather of the tabletop as his body shook with sobs. At first he made only straining, coughing noises, then he threw his head back and found speech.

'I'm at the end of my rope, Dr Mortimer! I really can't stand it any longer! Sometimes I think it's all an awful nightmare, and I'll wake up again in my room in Calcutta, and things will be the same as they were before, before . . .'

I paused, but no further revelation was forthcoming.

'I can well understand that Dartmouth can't have been much good for someone of your temperament, Lance, but well, it doesn't look as if you'll have to put up with it for much longer. If you like, I shall speak to your father about it.'

'Oh, it's not so much Dartmouth – though that's bad enough, with the stupid rules and traditions and the ragging: I don't ever want to see another lanyard! – it's, well, Pa, and everything. You must have sensed it, Dr Mortimer.'

I let this remark pass.

'I'm sure your father means well, and wants what's best for you, Lance.'

'I wish I could believe that, sir! I wish I could see some sense in the way he's been behaving since, since, well, Calcutta . . .'

I got up and walked over to the armoire, where I opened the door of the cabinet and mixed a brandy-and-seltzer, which I gave to my patient before I resumed my seat. He gulped a mouthful and coughed violently, then sat quietly and forlornly, his rather girlish face reddened and swollen with crying. How cruel and heedless nature's gifts can be!

When I thought the emotional storm had subsided, I returned to my questioning.

'Tell me, Lance, what happened in Calcutta?'

The boy was silent for a while and fixed his gaze on the tabletop.

'Oh, big row, sir. One among many. Hardly worth talking about, really . . .'

I sensed the return of caution in Lance's words. Perhaps he felt he'd already blurted out too much.

'Please tell me, Lance. It may help.'

The lad hesitated, shot me a fugitive glance, then went on.

'Oh, I suppose it arose out of a redeeming, sir – '

'A redeeming, Lance?'

'Yes, it's one of Pa's ways: if you do anything wrong, he says you redeem yourself just by owning up promptly. If you wait till you're put on the carpet, you lose face altogether. He never actually whacks you or anything, just looks as if you were something the cat had brought in and, well, stares. Sometimes he looks angry, sometimes as if he's just disappointed. Then you almost think he's going to blub! It's pretty awful, really, sir, because he can keep it up for ages. When I was little I'd even own up to things I'd never actually done – just made them up – so he'd be decent to me. I soon chucked that wheeze, as it meant he'd only add lying to my sheet. It, it, builds up inside you, like steam-pressure. Well, after the last big row – just before we left India – he started to treat me like a criminal, then he put Vinnie into purdah like a Mohammedan woman, and we had to come here. "Home", he calls it! Ever since, he's been – I don't know how to say it – tightening things. He's even taken away Vinnie's books.'

'Books, Lance? What books did your father take away from, er, Vinnie?'

'Oh, her King Arthur stuff: Sir Lancelot and Guinevere and all that rot. She used to be quite potty about it! Now we're only allowed to read schoolbooks – maths, and geography and so on – but even then Pa has to choose them.'

'What about the Bible?'

'Oh, that! Pa reads bits of it out to us every day, but he keeps it.'

What then was this topic that must not be read about, even in the Bible?

'And on this last occasion in Calcutta, Lance, what was it you were supposed to have done, do you think? The sin that you had failed to, er, redeem yourself from?'

Again the blue eyes evaded mine.

'Oh, dunno, sir. Can't really remember; there were so many rows . . .'

I could sense that Lance's defences were now up on that topic, so I changed the subject.

'How do you get on with Miss Nancarrow, Lance?'

'Oh, we rub along pretty well together. Now.'

'Why the "now"?'

'Well, Mama died when I was eleven – that was pretty beastly – and just after, Pa was really decent to me, decenter than he'd ever been before.'

'Why not before?'

'Oh, I suppose he was disappointed in me, because I hadn't the "makings of a modern major-general", or something like that. He once even took me into the mofussil with him, to watch some pig-sticking. Ugh, all that blood and squealing! I howled the place down. It was as if he wanted me to be somebody else all the time. Mama always took my side, too. Dear Mama. They had lots of rows about me: "Adelaide, you are making a perfect Molly of that boy!" Mama liked a joke, and if she saw you couldn't take one, watch out! Pa never sees a joke: they really weren't each others' sort. But he was really kind in the first few weeks after Mama died. Then along came Vinnie.'

'Hadn't you known anything about her before she arrived?'

'Not a thing. One morning about six weeks after Mama's death, Pa came into the nursery with Demmy and Vinnie – and her calling him "Baba"!' I didn't know what to make of it.'

I, on the contrary, had no difficulty in imagining Boynton-Leigh's previous unwillingness to spring a winsome little ward on his contentious wife. From Lance's description of his parents' relationship, I could think of nothing more likely to have provided the final straw to the camel's back of their incompatibility.

The lad went on.

'I remember I fairly gaped at that stripe thing in her hair! Anyhow, he said Vinnie had lost not only her mother, but her father, too, who'd been a bosom pal of his when he'd been young, though it was the first I'd heard of it.'

'And who had brought her up till then?'

'Well, later on she told me she'd only ever really known Demmy, who'd brought her up from a baby in Simla – she went to a sort of dame school there, run by a Frenchwoman – but that Pa used to come and see them fairly often ever since she could remember. She'd never known her parents at all. Well, Pa told me she was to come and live with us from then on, and I was to be nice to her always.'

'And were you?'

'Oh, not half, sir! Although she was the same age as I am now, on that very first meeting I jumped up and grabbed her by the hair and pulled her down on to the ground! I'd have given her a good pummelling, too, if Pa and Demmy hadn't separated us. After that, Pa wasn't so nice to me: it was all Lavinia this, Lavinia that. She's quite a decent old beast, though, when you get to know her, even if she is a bit hysterical at times. Too much of her own way. Vinnie'll do, though. We've been through a lot together.'

'I understand it is customary for Anglo-Indian children to be sent home to England to be educated. That did not occur in your case?'

'Ah! That caused one of Mama and Pa's biggest rows. Went on for months! Pa wanted to pack me off here to a prep school when I was eight, but she wouldn't have it: threatened to leave Pa and take me with her. He gave in for once, then, as I got older, I suppose he saw that I wasn't cut out for that sort of stuff.'

'Did you go to school in India, then?'

'Lor' no, sir! Isn't done. You might come out of it with a cheechee accent, for one thing. All right for country-bred wallahs – loco-engineers' and shopkeepers' sons – and half-castes, but not for the sons of burra sahibs. No, Vinnie and I had tutors. One was a clergyman, then Jack – '

'Was this, er, Jack the last of your tutors, Lance?'

'Sright, sir. Oh, by the way, he's called Agar.'

I feigned enlightenment.

'Ah Agar. I see. Was he your tutor for long?'

'No, no, sir, just for a few weeks round Christmas a year-and-a-half ago. As I said, he was the last of our tutors, in fact.'

'Do you think his occupying the post for such a brief time had any connection with your father's decision to leave India, Lance? His attitude to Miss Lavinia, for instance – '

Lance actually laughed, a high, giggly shriek.

'Lor'! You can't mean Jack, sir, going soft on Vinnie? Heavens, no, sir! All they ever talked about was art, and in any case, she never really took much of a shine to him as a chap. Sulky beast! He taught her to paint pretty well, though, but that was about all the use she had for him. Art, art, art. He was forever fossicking around the family paintings, looking for Zoffanys. Had a bee in his bonnet about Zoffanys. You've heard of Zoffany, sir?'

I nodded.

'And did you, er, take a shine to this Mr Agar, Lance?'

'Oh, rather! He was a real sport, as well as a ripping artist. Pity you haven't met him, sir.'

13

Before I saw my regular patient in Ginger Lane next morning, I discussed Lance with Mr Boynton-Leigh in his study, and in particular the Dartmouth Medical Officer's report.

'What does it mean, Dr Mortimer?'

'Difficulties with balance can indicate a number of conditions, Mr Boynton-Leigh,' I said diplomatically, 'not all of them equally serious, from a simple infection of the inner ear to, well, graver ailments.'

'And in my son's case? Please speak plainly.'

'I can hardly pronounce upon that, sir, since I have not examined him, but his Medical Officer recommends that he see – as a simple precaution – Sir Edgar Crowninshield – '

'Who is a specialist in what, Dr Mortimer?'

'In affections of the brain.'

The nabob threw himself back in his chair and closed his eyes, and remained quite still for a moment.

'I see,' he said at length, in a voice like the rustling of dead leaves. 'A tumour.'

'It is far from certain, and until the results of Sir Edgar's examination are known – '

'Very well, Dr Mortimer: it is in God's hands. His will be done. Allow me to ask you: are you a parent?'

It had been Ruth's dearest wish, now never to be fulfilled.

'No, sir, I am not.'

'I say it without blasphemous intention, but it is crucifixion, and the deeper one loves, the deeper, the more cruelly the nails are driven in . . .'

I could make no reply to that, but simply told Mr Boynton-Leigh that I was ready to see his ward. He nodded and made as if to get up, whereupon I begged him to remain seated and started to make for the sickroom. The nabob got up all the same.

'No, Dr Mortimer, not that way. She is in the garden with Penruddock.'

'I am gratified to hear it, sir!' I said delightedly. 'Fresh air can do nothing but good for her.'

I wondered at Boynton-Leigh's apparent change of tack. Or was it tactics?

Ord was deputed to show me down into the overgrown back garden, which was fenced off from the churchyard by high, iron spiked railings. I was gratified to behold Lavinia, radiant in a white summer dress, seated, brush in hand, at an easel, apparently absorbed in a study of the adjoining churchyard. Demmy sat knitting at her side in a basket chair.

'Gravestones are scarcely the kind of tablets I should prescribe!' I said with a laugh, and Lavinia, swinging round to face the door, gave a shout of 'Dr Mortimer!' She placed her brush on the ledge of the easel, got up and ran over the cleared patch of newly grown grass to my side. She seized both my hands in hers in her impulsive way, and I heard a little cough behind us.

'All is in order, Mrs Penruddock,' I said. 'Please carry on with your knitting.'

My patient's dark eyes sought mine hungrily.

'Oh, thank you, dear Dr Mortimer!' she said. 'Thank you for getting Baba to let me come out into the garden: it is all so beautiful!'

The grip – a formidable one for a young lady – became even tighter, and a momentary cloud passed over her eyes.

'Dr Ferraby isn't coming back, is he?' she asked in a hoarse whisper. 'I mean, not too soon.'

I laughed.

'Not just yet: he is still occupied in Sussex.'

She smiled again, a tigerish smile, and dragged me to the cane chair that Ord had left for me.

'I'm glad,' she said confidentially, then: 'Please do not misunderstand me, Dr Mortimer: I have nothing against Dr Ferraby, but, well, he doesn't listen. And always so jokey, all the time.'

'And I'm not jokey, hey?' I said with mock severity.

'Not in that way, but that is one of the reasons why I like you so.'

Demmy seemed to be troubled with a particularly persistent cough that lovely morning, a cough which seemed to clear up abruptly as soon as I changed the subject.

'Your recovery is now evidently complete,' I said, 'and I am delighted!'

Miss Nancarrow poured me out a glass of barley water from a carafe on a little cane sidetable.

'Do you know what Baba has promised, Doctor?'

'No, what?'

'That we are to travel soon.'

'That is splendid!' I exclaimed, though I felt a little chill of foreboding at my heart.

'Yes, it is to be in part to celebrate my twenty-first birthday in three weeks' time.'

'An ocean cruise perhaps?'

'Baba hasn't said yet: he says it is to be a surprise. But it will be wonderful to travel again.'

'If you had the choice, Miss Nancarrow – '

'Please: Lavinia.'

Demmy didn't cough this time.

'Well, then, Lavinia, if you had the choice, where would you travel to?'

My patient put down her glass and pondered for a moment.

'I would have said India, Dr Mortimer, but it occurs to me that while we can go back to a place, we cannot go back to a time, and then I am not so sure.'

'Yes, you are absolutely right. You must have been happy in India.'

'India is all I know. My life was so different there. So different. Simla, the Himalaya – '

'And Calcutta? That must have been more different still.'

Her expression clouded over.

'Later, yes. But wherever we go, it will be so good to get away from England. Oh, but that sounds so disloyal! I am, after all, British.'

'Not at all. Having been born and brought up in India, it is quite natural that you should see England as a foreign country. But no doubt with the passage of time – '

'India shall always be my home, Dr Mortimer! It is always in my dreams: the hot sunshine, the bright colours, the smells. You would be surprised, for instance, how different smoke smells there, from fragrant woods, incense, spicy cooking, dung-fires.

Here everything seems, well, so small and mean. The smell of wet, heavy clothes, boiled cabbage and coal-smoke. But I have seen so little of it since I came here.'

'Well, then, we must learn to cook with curries and spices, so that you may feel at home, and – who knows? – if you stay a little longer, sarees and silken pantaloons may yet brighten the streets of London!'

We both laughed at my flight of fancy, and Lavinia took up her brush again. I admired the way the greens merged together in her treatment of the churchyard, creating a strange, underwater effect. It was all redolent of the canvases of Monet and the French Impressionists.

'There is certainly nothing mean or drab in the way you are painting that churchyard,' I remarked.

She seemed to redouble her concentration on her work, and it was some little while before she responded to my comment.

'Oh, I had a good teacher in India, before we came here. He was a good painter.'

'And did Lance share your flair for painting, Lavinia? Did your gifted teacher succeed in bringing out some talent in him?'

A wariness seemed to creep into Lavinia's reply.

'Lance couldn't sketch or paint for toffee, doctor!'

'Oh, then he can hardly have enjoyed your joint lessons!'

There was a longish pause as Lavinia applied a pale green to the canvas to do justice to some leaves with the sun behind them.

'On the contrary, doctor, Lance and Mr Agar – ' so it was 'Mr Agar' to Lavinia, not 'Jack' ' – Lance and Mr Agar got on like a house on fire!'

'You liked Mr Agar?' I persisted.

There was another pregnant pause, during which Lavinia plied her brush steadily.

'I have told you, doctor, he was a good teacher.'

Evidently, Agar had not made so favourable an impression as a man on Lavinia as he had on Lance. I recalled Lance's shriek of derision at the mere suggestion that there might be some sort of warm regard between Agar and Lavinia.

'I daresay he will look you all up again, when he comes back to England.'

'I don't think that is likely, Dr Mortimer.'

I could swear from her expression and demeanour that not only had she not seen Agar since his return to London but that she was unaware that he was even in the country again. So much for the artist's rigmarole to me in his studio about his having passed the time of day with Lavinia under Boynton-Leigh's basilisk stare here in Ginger Lane.

'Well,' I went on, 'Mr Agar has evidently taught you well. I notice that there are a number of interesting portraits in this house, clearly of your guardian's forebears.'

'Oh, yes, we brought nearly all of them back from India.'

'Nearly all? I trust none was lost in transit?'

'No, indeed, I meant all the ones we had in India, along with the ones we found already in the house here.'

'Ah, lost masterpieces, perhaps! You intrigue me!'

Lavinia chuckled and took up her brush again.

'Oh, hardly, Dr Mortimer! They were found wrapped in brown paper and covered in dust in the attics: just journeyman's work, mostly old ancestors of Baba's. The poorer ones. There's so much old varnish, lamp-black and tobacco-smoke on them, along with the grime of a century or so, that it's hard to make out just who or what the subjects are. There are some of them hanging in my room.'

'Yes, I've noticed them. One day it might be interesting to have them cleaned.'

Lavinia became thoughtful and returned to the topic of Lance.

'Dr Mortimer, is Lance really ill?'

'But has he not spoken to you?'

She shook her head sadly.

'Baba is always there.'

'But surely Lance has written to you from Dartmouth? It is absurd that you should be kept incommunicado! I shall speak to your guardian!'

Lavinia's eyes widened, and she flung down her brush and grasped my hand.

'For pity's sake, Dr Mortimer, I beg of you – I implore you – please do not even suggest to Baba that Lance and I should enter into correspondence! He would, he would . . .'

Show me the door, perhaps, I speculated, as he had shown it

to Tooke and Agar in Calcutta, then flee with his ménage to some other secluded bolt-hole somewhere else? So there must be a letter or letters in the case.

'Then of course I shan't do anything of the kind,' I said gently, patting the thin, gripping hands. 'Please dismiss it from your mind and get on with your charming painting.'

'Promise?'

'I swear it.'

The hands slipped out of mine, and she took up her brush and began painting again uncertainly.

'And try not to worry about Lance,' I went on. 'It is just that he needs certain tests. He is in safe hands: Sir Edgar Crownin-shield is one of the finest medical men in London.'

'Poor Lance! He is always getting into scrapes. It was the same in India. I don't know how many times he has taken the blame for me.'

'He must have resented you very much when you appeared out of the blue so soon after his mother's death.'

Lavinia darted a shrewd glance at me but went on painting.

'Why, Dr Mortimer, I see you know all about us!'

She laughed her husky laugh.

'His resentment soon wore off,' she went on, 'and in fact it wasn't long before he was running to me when . . .'

She paused slightly, and I might have finished her sentence for her: '. . . whenever his father was bullying and browbeating him.'

'Whenever he was in hot water,' were her actual words.

'I am glad Lance will have your sympathy and support while he is at home.'

'He shall always have that. Always. I own I feel protective towards Lance in a way I am at a loss to explain, Dr Mortimer.'

'Well then,' I said, putting down my glass, 'I can see that my professional presence will no longer be required here. Let me say again how delighted I am to see how much your condition has improved, in all respects.'

She put down her brush and seized my hand. Tears stood in her eyes.

'And don't think, Dr Mortimer, that I don't know whom I have to thank for that improvement!'

I gave her hot, dry hand a slight squeeze, then released it as I stood up to go.

'Dr Ferraby will before long be resuming his role as your medical advisor,' I said, 'and I hope it will be a very long time indeed before you need his professional ministrations again. It is goodbye, then.'

'Oh,' she said, 'say rather "au revoir"!'

'With all my heart. When Ferraby returns, and you are no longer my patient, perhaps I shall look in on you here as plain James Mortimer.'

At that moment, Demmy rang vigorously on a handbell, and I anticipated the early reappearance of Ord.

Lavinia's luminous dark eyes caught mine intently.

'Do not think badly of me, James,' she whispered.

Before I could express the puzzlement these words evinced in me, Ord was at my side, and the sun went in. I gave Lavinia a final nod and smile, and Ord escorted me up to his master's study again. As the results of poor Lance's tests had not yet arrived, this would be my last professional confabulation with Boynton-Leigh, as far as Lavinia went, anyway. The nabob bade me sit down.

'Well, doctor?' he said.

'Miss Nancarrow I consider entirely restored from her influenza and consequent nervous depression, and is evidently much looking forward to her planned foreign travels. May I congratulate you on that, sir. A tip-top idea!'

Boynton-Leigh nodded solemnly.

'Yes, Dr Mortimer, we shall seek a purer air than that which blows here. We shall see what that will do for my ward, and for my unfortunate boy.'

'You should not despair of Lance's condition, sir; after all, it may only be – '

A magisterial gesture and a grave look silenced me.

'It is in God's hands, doctor. His hands!'

I took my courage in both hands.

'You will forgive my curiosity, sir, but I cannot help wondering about your ward, Miss Nancarrow . . .'

The nabob shot me a searching glance.

'Yes, Dr Mortimer, what cannot you help wondering about her?'

'How you first came to, er, care for her.'

Boynton-Leigh rose and walked over to the window, where he stood looking out over the graveyard.

'Lavinia is the orphan of a dear friend of mine, Dr Mortimer, dead these twenty years.'

'From Indian days?' I ventured.

'From Indian days,' he murmured, almost to himself, and an awkward silence fell between us. The interview was plainly at an end.

'That is rather fine, sir,' I stammered, as I rose to my feet.

'Dr Mortimer,' was his parting shot. 'There is nothing I would not do for her!'

14

The summer leaves of the plane-trees grew dusty as June gave way to brazen July, and I plodded on my rounds, calling whenever I could on Violet Branscombe at the Junior Minerva Club. Still no news from India. I do not think Noah awaited the dove with more avid interest than we waited for the arrival of the Bombay steam packet! There were stirrings in the under-world, though, it seemed, and she expected to be in a position to give me more detailed news anon. Her vigilance regarding Jack Agar was unrelenting.

In fact, the ladies' club in Coptic Street was fast becoming a sort of home-from-home for me, and I looked forward with much pleasure to my breakfast briefings over coffee and our tête-à-tête suppers there. So assiduous, indeed, was my attendance that on one occasion I heard above the murmur of the dining-room a reference to myself as 'Branscombe's young man'.

I had not yet found time to pay my promised private call at Ginger Lane, but I was by no means easy in my mind as to Boynton-Leigh's apparent change of heart in the matter of Lavinia's 'purdah', as Lance had termed it. One or two alfresco afternoons in the garden under the supervision of Ord and Demmy did not spell liberation any more than one swallow made a summer, and I should believe in the announced trip abroad when it happened. As for Lance's own plight, the lad had engaged my sympathy, and I was interested to know the results of his medical tests. An early visit to Ginger Lane, then, was on the cards.

Then there was myself. What was I to do with my life? I have mentioned how my growing absorption in the enigma of Number One, Ginger Lane – the Aldgate Mystery – had fuelled an incipient passion in me for detection whose origins derived from my part in the Baskerville Case. At the time I am describing, however, it had never really occurred to me that this might become anything more than an absorbing hobby. What to do then in the meantime? Again and again I returned to Violet's words about her having chosen to work where the need was greatest, and where she might be of the most use.

It came like an order of release when, a week after my last interview with Boynton-Leigh, Ferraby returned, full of ado, from Angmering, and I was able to hand back to him the baton of the Eaton Square practice.

'No complaints from our worthy patients, I hope?' he had asked on our last meeting, which was at a tête-à-tête dinner at his house, Mrs Ferraby and the young misses having retired for a month to Broadstairs in order to recover from Angmering. 'Apart from their medical complaints, hey?'

I smiled dutifully at this, reflecting that if Watson liked Ferraby, there must be some good in him.

'Did you, er, manage to negotiate the shoals and reefs of Ginger Lane?' he went on, a sly look stealing across the long, pale face. 'No tantrums on Miss Lavinia's part?'

I explained the situation, including the news of Lance's having left Dartmouth, and the reason for his leaving there.

'Mmm . . .' Ferraby murmured with a slow, judicial nod. 'Crowninshield's about the top man in his field. Young Lance couldn't be in better hands.'

My colleague pushed the cigar-box over to me, and took a leisurely draw from his own Corona-Corona as he studied me.

'You've done damn' well, Mortimer, damn' well! Seems to me you're settling down to being quite a monster of tact.'

'God forbid!' I retorted with feeling, amid Ferraby's guffaws.

'Any idea what your next move's going to be? If not, I've been thinking: this practice is big enough now – more than big enough – to take a partner.'

Ferraby's words acted as a sort of catalyst to my lengthy ponderings about my future activities. To work where the need was greatest, and where one could be of most use . . . I thanked him for his offer, but told him I'd long been considering the offer of another post, one which I had now decided to accept.

'Oh?' he asked, rather crestfallen. 'Such as what, might one ask?'

When I gave him my reply, the long head of ash on the end of his cigar plopped on to his dazzling boiled shirtfront.

'As an unpaid dispenser at a social mission in the Whitechapel Road!'

15

Next morning, having decided to take up Dr Branscombe's offer of employment, I breakfasted early in the quiet rooms I had taken in a court off Fleet Street and presented myself at nine sharp at the People's Dispensary in Whitechapel. Little Queenie, as bright and brisk as ever, received me.

'Doctor ain't in yet, sir. She generally comes in about half-past nine for the ten o'clock surgery.'

'Well, Queenie,' I said conspiratorially, 'it's not really the surgery I'm after. Truth is, I'm looking for a job.'

'Cor!' the apprentice dispenser hissed, and the big, grey eyes popped in the peaky, freckled face. Indeed my statement might well have been borne out in her eyes by the rather tired, grey suit I was wearing, along with the businesslike bowler and spatless boots. For all the world, I might have been a shipping clerk. This time, I was determined to blend with my surroundings as closely as possible.

'I'm sure she won't mind if I put you in the surgery, sir, if you care to wait.'

'I'd rather wait in the dispensary, Queenie. This is where I'm hoping to find a crib!'

Queenie's expression brightened.

'All right, sir! It's this way. P'raps yer'd like a cuppa tea?'

'Please make it two, Queenie: I'm hoping we're going to be workmates!'

The dispensary was reached through an unobtrusive side-door off the consulting-room-cum-office, rather grandly referred to as 'the surgery', and had probably been a dressing-room in more spacious days. The equipment was spartan, though at first sight adequate, and spotlessly clean. I sat down on a high stool at the mixing bench and looked around me, and in no time at all Queenie had brought me a large mug of strong tea. I insisted that she join me.

'There ain't only but one chair, sir, but I can sit on this . . .'

She dragged a soapbox, which served as a port for mops and brooms, from the far end of the narrow room and, up-ending the box, sat down beside me. She carefully soothed her white apron over her meagre knees, smiled nervously at me, and clasped her mug of hot tea in her red, thin hands.

'You like working for Dr Branscombe, Queenie?'

'Oh, yes, sir! It ain't all work, though: last patient's at twelve, and I'm usually finished me deliveries by half-one. I 'as a bite to eat around then – a nice saveloy-an'-dip or somefink of that – then the doctor goes through me lessons wiv me, that is, if she ain't goin' inter town. I do me writin' and sums, and later on, if I do well enough in them, the doctor says we'll be doin' chemistry, so's I can be a proper dispenser.'

'I'm sure you'll knock spots off chemistry,' I said. 'And I'm not sure you won't be the first lady dispenser!'

She grinned and hugged her tea-mug.

'Doctor'll get us through, sir.'

'You think a lot of Dr Branscombe, hey, Queenie?'

'We all love the doctor, sir,' she said in a matter-of-fact voice. 'D'you really want to work here, sir? It'd be ever such a 'elp for the doctor. Sometimes she 'as to work right into the night, makin' up bottles. It's somefink crool in the winter!

Won't let me 'elp 'er, neither: says I'm to wait till I'm a proper dispenser.'

'I should very much like to help the doctor, Queenie, and I daresay I'll be able to give you a few tips on chemistry by the way!'

Just then firm footsteps could be heard on the stairs, and Queenie slammed down her mug, got up from her soapbox and made for the door.

'That'll be 'er now, sir!'

Dr Branscombe bustled in, greetings were exchanged, and I was bidden into the patient's chair. I made my acceptance without preamble.

'That will be capital!' she said. 'I shall be most grateful to have your services. However, be warned: this is not a romantic situation. There will be times when your patience is sorely tried: you have already had a little taste of that . . .'

I remembered my encounter with beery Bill Bettridge and nodded ruefully.

'I feel I wish to serve, as you do, where the need is greatest. I really believe, Dr Branscombe, that I can make a contribution here.'

The doctor clasped her sturdy white hands under her chin and gave me a sympathetic nod.

'That is the spirit, doctor! As long as you bear in mind that we do not have careers here. We have work. In fairness to you, I think I shall put you on three months' probation, and if by then you feel – or I feel – that your introduction to the more challenging side of medical practice need go no further, well, we shall call it a day and part friends. Will that be satisfactory?'

'Eminently!' I said, and I rose in concert with my new colleague and we shook hands.

Dr Branscombe briefed me as she ushered me back into the dispensary.

'Since we have a busy morning ahead, I suggest you begin your duties immediately. Queenie can deliver the prescriptions as soon as you have made them up. Really, Dr Mortimer, you are releasing much time to me for my other duties here. Oh, and when you have finished at midday, I should like to introduce you to someone.'

81

'Ah!' I said, thoroughly interested. 'Is it to do with Ginger Lane?'

By then a subdued shuffle and murmur could be heard from the outer room: the first patients had arrived.

'Later, please, Dr Mortimer. Meanwhile, to work!'

And work I did, tirelessly assisted by Queenie, right through till near noon. It was like student days again, getting experience in a busy dispensary. Then Dr Branscombe called me into the consulting room, sent Queenie off on her last round of deliveries, and asked me to come in and shut the inner door behind us.

The last patient was as obvious a Delilah as a brazen painted face and cheap finery could suggest. She swung herself round in the patient's chair and eyed me insolently, while twirling a soiled, furled parasol like a spinning top on the floor.

I went and sat lightly on the edge of the windowsill.

'Dolly,' Dr Branscombe said, 'I'd like you to tell this gentleman exactly what you've told me. I give you my word that this will remain strictly between the three of us.'

'That's good enough for me, doctor. I wouldn't do it for no one else. As long as 'e understands.'

The woman nodded at me as if I were a hatstand.

'I am a doctor, too,' I said to her, 'and I know how to keep a confidence.'

'Right you are, then: I should've known, but I see yer in yer shootin' togs! If you'll do for Dr B, you'll do for me. This is my story, then, an' if Deechy knew what I was up to . . .'

Her 'fancy man', no doubt, I thought.

'No word of this shall pass beyond these walls!' Dr Branscombe assured her.

''Ere goes, then. I, er, sometimes 'as occasion to stroll by the churchyard up Ginger Lane.'

I threw myself forward tensely.

'The other evenin' I 'appens to glance up through the railin's of the garden of Number One . . .'

From flat on her back, I surmised, and not alone . . .

'There was an absolutely beautiful gel, in a white dress, just flittin' back and forwards. There was still light enough ter see by, and she had long, black 'air, but yer'd know 'er anywhere 'cos she had a broad white streak in it, like on an 'orse!

'For a second I thought it was a bloomin' ghost! What wiv me bein' in a churchyard an' all! Gave me a fair turn, I can tell yer! Anyway, next thing I 'eard was an old woman's voice, callin' the gel in – "my baby", she called her, though she'd have been twenty if she was a day – and the gel just looked around her, as if she was in a dream, and went away back into the 'ouse.'

The Lady of the Parasol turned to Dr Branscombe.

'Does 'e know about Agar?'

'Yes, Dolly. Just tell him everything you told me.'

'Well, when you asked me what I knew abaht Agar – rotten, stinkin' villain! – I told yer 'ow Deechy took me to 'is place in Fournier Street that night.'

'Yes, yes.'

'Ter see if there was, er, anyfink worth 'aving, if yer foller me. Well, 'e deserves everything 'e gets, after what 'e's done to, well, some as I could name. Anyway, Deechy 'ad 'im on that 'e was bringin' me along, so's 'e could, well, take a look at me. Dirty sod! Well, there was all these pictures, drawins' and so on. Takes a lot ter make me blush, but Gawdelpus! Deechy tried to laugh, but it rung 'oller. Well, 'e 'ad one paintin' – proper, reg'lar one, no funny business – of a dark gel in old-fashioned clothes, little shawl over 'er back, 'air up' and bead things rahnd it – foreign-lookin'. It was 'er – '

'The girl in the garden,' my colleague prompted.

I was all ears, recalling the portrait Agar had so hastily covered up on my visit.

''Sright!' Dolly went on. 'Right dahn ter the streak in 'er 'air under the beads. I 'ad a look at 'er name, too – '

'It was on the label?'

'Yerss, at the bottom of the picture. I 'ad a peep at it on the sly. It was "Fanny" as far as I could make out.'

'Are you sure it wasn't something like "Vinnie"?' I asked.

'Might 'ave been, but it was 'er all right – sure as little apples!'

Dolly stopped twirling her parasol, and looked at me with disabused eyes.

'If that gel means anything to you, mister, and if yer'd seen those other pictures, well, yer'll look after 'er in future. In my experience – and I've 'ad quite a bit of it – men who go in for drorins' and pictures of that sort can't do much with a woman, if yer catch my meanin . . .'

I nodded tensely, and she went on.

'They're dangerous men – real dangerous – and it comes aht in other ways. What I say is, they're better put dahn!'

We heard a low whistle from below the open window and Dolly jumped to her feet.

'Gawd! That's Deechy! Quick, doctor, my medicine!'

Dr Branscombe handed her a neatly wrapped bottle.

'Don't worry about the dose, Dolly,' she said with a smile. 'It's mostly liquorice!'

'Yer couldn't 'ave put somethin' stronger in it, could yer?' the street-girl said with a grimace. 'Well, must dash!'

Dolly billowed towards the door, wafting cheap scent, but she paused for a few seconds with her hand on the doorknob.

'Don't forget what I said,' she remarked to me. 'Men like that are dangerous!'

16

My colleague was full of exultation after our interview with Dolly: to her it simply meant that the tide of revulsion towards Agar even from members of the underworld was bringing ever nearer the prospect of his successful prosecution.

'She is only one of my girls, Dr Mortimer!' she declared, after we had been left alone in the surgery. 'And I have many more on his trail, not to speak of their men, or those worthy of the name. We shall have him by the heels!'

She spoke of the growing file she had on the artist at the Junior Minerva, under lock and key in the safe of the formidable secretary, Miss Mainsforth. The trouser-wearer had not been born who could get past her! Then there were meetings she had had with all sorts and conditions of men and women in the darkest recesses of the East End: speak it not in Stepney, whisper it not in Whitechapel. But all of this would take time, and the mills would grind precious slow – if they didn't come to a dead stop, dead being the word – in the meantime. And against this sombre background, Lavinia would be travelling soon, destination unknown.

My own first reaction to Dolly's somewhat sensational recital had been to wonder how Agar could be producing such an evidently striking likeness of Lavinia without the original to paint from. Perhaps he had a photograph. And 'Fanny'? The nearest analogy I had come up with at the time had been 'Vinnie': this would require further thought. Then again, as far as the case for Agar's irredeemable villainy went – Dolly's account notwithstanding – only actual proof would finally convince me.

Presently my colleague went on her afternoon visits, and I to a pensive luncheon in Cohen's restaurant in Fieldgate Street, not far from the old bell-foundry in Whitechapel Road. I was gratified to note that my presence there attracted no attention whatsoever. By the time I had finished my cheesecake, my mind had been made up. I would see what a surprise visit to Agar might reveal in the way of depraved art.

I paid the waiter and, once outside, hailed the first idling hansom I saw, and ordered the cabby to take me to Fournier Street. As so often when one revisits in daylight a place one has only ever seen at night, I was dismayed to find absolutely no point of familiarity in the street. I met with more than one blank, fearful or downright hostile stare before, just three doors from the great Hawksmoor church, I dropped a whole shilling on to a matchseller's box and, on enquiring about the artist's studio, was told: 'Four doors down, next to the Jew place.'

The 'Jew Place' was not hard to find, for grave, bearded men in shawls and tassels were filing into one of the old terraced houses in ones and twos. Evidently some tabernacle or improvised prayer-house, of the sort known, I believe, as a 'shteebl' in the vernacular.

The house on the right of the tabernacle was occupied on all floors by a furrier's establishment, so I approached the steps of the house on the left, the street door of which was open. All was quiet inside the lobby, which was flagged, and whose walls were panelled with oak. I climbed up to the third and last floor, and found the door of Agar's studio ajar. I knocked, and popped my head inside the large, airy room, with its long windows and broad skylights, through which cold light was pouring in.

'Ah, Dr Mortimer!' came Agar's voice from behind his easel. 'Slumming again.'

I walked in, and quickly cast my eyes round the room, but at first glance I could see none of the artistic depravities Dolly had alluded to. The artist appeared to be working from a painting which was propped up on another easel facing him.

'You see what I'm reduced to!' Agar announced in a voice of theatrical declamation. 'Copying the reproduction of an original! "In the style of . . ." Pah! Take my advice, Dr Mortimer – do just tip that rubbish off the chair and sit down – and stick to doctoring, if you want to keep your sanity! I trust your ribs are improving?'

'I am well, thank you,' I said. 'It's about Lavinia.'

'Ah, Lavinia!' Agar echoed, without putting down his brush. 'The "Bird in a Gilded Cage". And what about Lavinia, pray?'

'She will be twenty-one shortly.'

'In a couple of weeks' time,' the artist said. 'The twenty-second.'

For whatever reason, Agar evidently had that date firmly fixed in his memory.

'Indeed. Well, I was wondering if that date would have any, er, pecuniary significance to her or her guardian.'

'Ah, I see: the sinister guardian mews up his ward with some dark design on her inheritance. Meanwhile the fateful twenty-first birthday draws near, and the plot thickens. That it, hey?'

'That's putting it rather melodramatically, but something of the kind may be possible. I know that you knew them in India, and I wondered if you had any idea of how Lavinia stands in that regard.'

'Well, as far as I understand it, Lavinia doesn't "stand" any-where in that regard, Dr Mortimer. Quite apart from the fact that Boynton-Leigh is as rich as Croesus in his own right, as far as I know, Lavinia has not a penny to her name, except what our Archibald sees fit to allow her. She lives solely by his grace and favour in every way, and I assume her majority will not make her a penny richer. The only escape route I can see for her will be through marriage, and I'm sure her guardian will do his level best to delay or prevent that contingency.'

'Why do you paint, Agar?' I asked.

'Why do I paint? Why do you doctor, Mortimer?'

'I want to do something well and I want to be of use.'

'Well, then, I want to do something well, too – God knows I want to do it well! – but I don't know how useful I am in that respect. I'm content to leave that to posterity.'

'I notice all your work seems to be portraits.'

'Yes,' Agar replied, 'I paint people because they represent life on the wing, so to speak. The expression on the face – so exquisitely fleeting! – the eyes, the corners of the mouth. To capture these is to capture the Now, the eternal, Mortimer! How many of us have ever come near this? Rembrandt? Velazquez? It is an endless quest.'

'And endlessly doomed to disappointment,' I countered, 'for how can the fleeting be fixed on canvas?'

'The artist's dilemma in a nutshell, Mortimer, but all he knows is that he must try. *Hic labor, hoc opus est.*'

Indeed, I saw plenty of evidence of the labour, and the work around me as I looked round the studio. I took up my hat and rose. Again I had not found what I had been led to expect.

'I will not keep you from your Muse, Agar,' I said, and the artist bowed as I made for the door.

'We must talk again, Mortimer. You know where to find me now, and do watch your step.'

As I made my way down the common stairs, a small, hunched figure shuffled past me on his way up, a figure which emitted a particularly rank cigarette-smoke, not at all like the mild fragrance of the Virginia favoured by Anglo-Saxon smokers. But it was not so much the smoke which caused me to look back upstairs as the curious, shiny-visored cap which the smoker wore. It was familiar to me somehow, as I clearly was to the man, for his eyes met mine as he took the foreign cigarette-butt, complete with a white cardboard tube or mouthpiece, from his lips, and cast it away, before going into Agar's studio. The man's eyes were pale, like a wolf's, and he looked at me much, I imagine, as a wolf looks at its prey. From now on I would be watching my step with particular concentration.

17

I resumed my voluntary duties at the Whitechapel Dispensary the next morning, and later on, in the course of a sandwich luncheon in the surgery with my colleague, we discussed developments to date in the Aldgate Mystery. Although the information solicited from Calcutta was yet to arrive, I divined from her air of expectancy that she was holding a further card for later on. Meanwhile, I described my visit to Agar's studio on the previous afternoon.

'I was able to form two conjectures,' I began to sum up. 'First, that the pastry-seller in Wentworth Street, whom I saw playing chess with Agar in the Warsaw Café and whom I passed on the stairs to Agar's studio yesterday afternoon, is his hireling, his spy. Secondly, I am bound to say that, although I dropped in on Agar completely out of the blue, I saw no sign of the sort of drawings described here by your protégée Dolly yesterday morning, nor did I see the portrait of Lavinia Nancarrow she described as bearing the inscription of "Fanny".'

'No doubt he arranges special showings for connoisseurs.'

'That may be the case,' I said, 'nor do I doubt for a moment the thoroughness of your investigations into Agar's activities insofar as they affect your girls, but as to actual proof, of the sort that might stand up in a court of law – '

My colleague leant over the top of the table, and brought her face closer to mine, triumph in her eyes.

'Perhaps I have something better now: a real, live witness who is prepared to come forward and testify in just such a court of law!'

'But who?' I asked eagerly.

'A burglar who got in touch with me through one of my girls. He hates Agar with his entire soul!'

'But what is his name?'

'I do not know his real name yet, though I know his unfortunate woman as Rosie Bartlett. The burglar is known in White-chapel as Sammy the Shiner.'

'You have met him?'

'No, that is what I wish to put to you . . .'

'Pray go on.'

'Sammy has offered to discuss terms with a trustworthy emissary – someone unfamiliar to the underworld in East Ham – and that would rule me out immediately. In any case, the sight of a respectable woman entering the Hot Cross Bun would inevitably arouse curiosity, to say the least – '

'What on earth is the Hot Cross Bun?'

'It is a public house in East Ham.'

'So far east as to be almost in China!'

'Yes, and where Sammy the Shiner is about as well-known. To a Whitechapel denizen, East Ham is scarcely less foreign than China.'

'Very well, I shall be your emissary, then.'

'That is splendid of you! We advance in leaps and bounds.'

'And how shall I know this Sammy?'

Dr Branscombe laughed her throaty laugh.

'You really are the merest babe-in-arms when it comes to our Whitechapel ways. Don't you know what a "shiner" is? A "beauty"! He will be quite the ugliest man in the house!'

'How am I to approach this Adonis, then? What shall I say to him?'

'Nothing. You are to sit at the same table as he and, without looking at him, place this on the table.'

She rummaged briefly in the drawer, then handed me a little triangle of cardboard, which on examination turned out to be half the head and bare shoulder of Miss Lily Langtry, the 'Jersey Lily'.

'And Sammy will then slide his half of the cigarette-card to mine,' I said. 'Neat. What then?'

'You are to wait, and not look at him until he either speaks or, if the occasion is not favourable for some reason, he takes back his half of the card and leaves.'

'What do I do in that case?'

'After we have consulted together, return to the public house the next evening. He will be there every subsequent evening from nine to ten until our business is concluded. You are to wear inconspicuous clothes, and keep your wits about you at all times. For the first meeting, listen to all he says without committing yourself in any way and volunteer nothing.'

'I shall go tonight, then,' I said, intrigued by this possible opportunity of making progress in unravelling the mystery.

'Splendid!' Dr Branscombe exulted. 'We shall have him, Dr Mortimer. We shall have him at last!'

I found that everyone in East Ham knew the Hot Cross Bun, though its fame was certainly not founded on salubrious prospects or choice furnishings, the hostelry being a long, smoke-filled gallery with sawdust-strewn floors and lit by sputtering gas-jets.

I went to the bar and ordered a pint of Scotch ale, and was served by a man who, by his well-fed and confident air – not to speak of the waxed splendour of his moustaches and coy arrangement of the large, oiled curls which adorned his temples – appeared to be the guv'nor. He shot me a searching look as he handed me the foaming mug, then turned his attention to a more clamorous client, whose tied-at-the-knees trousers and earthy boots betokened the navvy, thirstiest of artisans.

Before I turned away from the bar with my drink, I saw the origin and derivation of the house's title on the opposite wall. There were countless scores of blackened circular objects arranged in lines, like so many large Pontefract cakes, but the last on the line was enough on this side of petrifaction to be discernible as a hot cross bun. Evidently one for each year of the public house's existence.

I set to work as discreetly as I could, as I searched out one of the few vacant kitchen-style chairs, which stood, two to a little table, along the back wall. Though none of the occupants of the engaged chairs could with any conscience have modelled for Praxiteles, there was one who stood out above all the company for sheer sublime ugliness, and the other chair at his table was unoccupied. It was not the arrangement or proportion of his features which were gross, but the sheer exaggeratedness of each: the narrow top to his skull, surmounted by the tiniest of bowlers; the tropical exuberance of his pepper-and-salt eye-brows; the craggy coarseness of the great potato nose; the sagging satchel-mouth. His considerable bulk was barely confined by a rusty, black broadcloth jacket.

It was, I confess, with some trepidation that I took the vacant seat next to him, but I put down my glass on the table without giving away any sign of recognition, and took a draught of ale before relaxing my clutched hand on the table-top, to leave my half of the cigarette-card. I detected no movement from my neighbour as I contemplated the rows of mortified buns on the wall in front, but his hoarse whisper soon reassured me.

'Look straight ahead and whisper!'

'Righto!' I hissed, trying to suppress my lip-movements as the ventriloquists do.

''Baht Agar – '

'Yes?'

'On account of some gels you-know-who's interested in, and one in partickler . . .'

I remembered Dr Branscombe's file, locked away in the safe under the secretary Miss Mainsforth's watchful eye in the Junior Minerva Club. I remembered also Rosie Bartlett, the Shiner's 'woman' mentioned by my colleague.

'Yes,' I hissed. 'Go on!'

'First thing is, I 'ad nuffink to do with that lay – not direckly – but I know enough abaht it to get 'im fifteen years on the Moor, straight up and dahn! And the pitchers – '

My heart gave a little jump.

'Pictures? You have evidence?' I shot at a hazard.

'I know where he keeps 'em! It was the bloody pitcher-lay what done me in. You-know-who'll have told yer abaht the Pond Villa job, I suppose . . .'

'Damn' shame!' I muttered noncommittally.

'Yus! A cryin' shame, cully! Old josser was supposed to be as deaf as a stone, an' all! "Easiest job in me career" ', 'e says. No slopin' rahnd the country, wiv 'ayseeds watchin' yer every step. 'Ighgate: nice and quiet. So was the dog, mate, quietest dog that ever wrapped its jaws rahnd yer leg! I wasn't quiet, though, mate. I tried clobberin' it wiv me tool-bag, but the amahnt o' punishment one o' them dogs'll take is somefink crool. Thick skulls, I suppose. Any road, next thing I know's a copper's 'ead poppin' over the garden wall. Good job I'd 'ad the sense to sling me bag o' tools over the wall as soon as I saw the dog wasn't goin' ter let go. "Keep perfectly still, now", says the copper, and before yer can say "Jack Robinson" I'm doin' a sixer! Loiterin' wiv intent. Best of it was, Agar was goin' ter look after the missus if anyfink went wrong. When I gits aht, no missus, 'n when I goes rahnd ter Spitalfields, she's on the game, doncherknaw! An 'ere's a little somefink for yer trouble.'

A silence fell which I felt I could have reached out and touched: poor Rosie.

'Took three of 'is lads ter get me on the bottom but I took one of 'em's 'ooter off, or the better part of it! 'E'll be able to whistle through it nah! Get a job on the 'alls! Ter cut a long story short, I got aht o' the 'orspital last week wiv only one kidney ter me name and one thought in me mind: ter do Agar in. Right, then. A 'undred in gold and two tickets ter Noo York and I'll stand witness against 'im, but understand this, mate, and make sure yer tell you-know-who: the bargain stands whether 'e goes dahn or not, especially if 'e don't! Those are me terms, and remember, I gets me whack whether 'e goes dahn or not!'

I heard Sammy's chair creak, then realised I was alone at the table, which fact my first sideways glance of the evening confirmed. My half of the card was still lying – on its own – on the spot where I'd put it down.

I finished my pint. Paintings, then. If the Shiner was to be believed, Agar was a fence as well as an agent and, taking into account Sammy's six months in jail, and at least a month in hospital by the sound of his injuries, Agar had attempted an art theft at Ponds Villa in Highgate between seven and eight months ago. Why a theft, though, if he was flush with money from his share of the proceeds of the East End vice traffic? Why not a sweeping appearance in Highgate in full dandyish garb, followed by a handsome offer to the rightful owner, wrapped in devastating charm? It must have been a very big job indeed – or one which demanded total secrecy – to risk burglary, albeit through Sammy's agency. This would repay investigation, but after consultation with my colleague.

I tossed and turned for a long time in the course of that close, humid night in my rooms, mulling over the events that had drawn me into their meshes since my arrival in London. Faces seemed to appear to me in the dark, as the cast of a play will appear in the limelight to receive the applause of the audience. As the phantasmagoria unfolded, a stage actually appeared in my mind's eye, complete with footlights and curtains.

The first of the actors to make his bow was Archibald Boynton-Leigh, the personification of tortured wrongheadedness, or so I saw it. Next, Lavinia as the Lady in the Tower, she of the glorious beauty and haunted, life-hungry eyes, so friendless and vulnerable. Then, seeming to cower behind her skirts, Lance, forced on to the stage to play a part for which he was so clearly unfitted. Demmy and Ord – minor characters – but what they could tell if they chose! By way of comic relief, there was the March Hare, in the form of Percy Tooke, who also doubled in the character of Constancy Unrewarded. Finally, in a puff of blue smoke, cheroot in hand, Jack Agar – the Demon King – took his sardonic bow.

Faces and pictures, pictures and faces. Pictures. My mental stage emptied, the curtain fell, then parted again, and as a figure appeared in the spotlight, there was thunderous applause. There, taking a gracious bow, resplendent in powdered wig, cutaway coat, small-clothes, knee-breeches and silver-buckled shoes, was the leading actor in the drama, twinklingly alive for all his eighty years in the grave: Johann Zoffany.

18

The next morning, Friday, my colleague joined me again at a luncheon conference in the surgery, and willingly endorsed the Shiner's offer, as reported to her by me.

'His terms shall be met,' she said positively, 'and his conditions observed. I shall convey my acceptance through my confidential channels.'

'It is a considerable sum of money, all the same,' I put in as discreetly as I could. 'Are you quite sure – '

'There are more than myself who have an interest in downing Agar, Dr Mortimer. There is already quite a war-chest in existence. The plan shall proceed.'

My own news – Sammy's revelation about the attempted art-theft at Highgate – was of less interest to my colleague, since it did not touch directly upon the welfare of her girls, but she was determined all the same to leave no stone unturned in getting to the bottom of Agar's nefarious activities.

'I should very much like to know,' she said, 'what picture was there that Agar felt was so eminently worth stealing. In my pursuit of him, all is grist to my mill.'

She reflected for a little while.

'I find I have no engagements on Sunday afternoon, Dr Mortimer: what do you say to an excursion to the healthful heights of Hampstead?'

I fell in more than willingly with this suggestion and we made our plans accordingly. That Sunday, we took luncheon at Gatti's, then entrained for Hampstead. Highgate still retained something of a rural air in those days, especially the secluded lane not far to the south of the grounds of Athlone House, where we eventually found Ponds Villa. It was a delightful little Regency box with a shrubby garden all round. There was no evidence of a guard dog. Our knock at the wisteria-bedecked front door was promptly answered by a maidservant. I presented our cards and enquired if the owner was at home. The girl showed us into an airy, white-painted drawing-room, and left for a minute. It had all been recently painted. The girl returned: yes, Mr Peckfuller was at home: would we care to step into the library?

Another airy room, whose furniture was all in keeping with the date of the building. A small, rotund man of about fifty-five rose from a *chaise-longue* and blinked at us through Pickwickian spectacles, before retreating to an armchair and waving us into the *chaise-longue*.

'So, Doctors Mortimer and Branscombe: pray be seated and tell me how I may be of service to you. But let me assure you straight away that you may be of no service at all to me!'

'I am glad to hear you are in such, er, rude health, sir,' I quipped.

The little man chortled.

'Ha, just so, just so! Rude health! You will take some refreshment, perhaps: barley-water for the heat? Lemonade?'

We declined politely, and I began to explain our business.

'We are interested in the work of the artist Zoffany, sir, and we were led to believe that an example of his work might be found here in Ponds Villa.'

'Then, doctor, you have come too late: I sold such a painting not three weeks ago.'

'Ah,' I said, 'that is a considerable disappointment – '

'We should so much have liked to see the painting!' Violet added.

'Would you perhaps be so good as to describe it to us, sir?' I went on. 'We should like to follow it up.'

'It was a conversation piece, doctor, a number of portraits in a family group.'

'I see,' I said. 'But how interesting!'

This was not what I had expected.

'Sir Jonas Fairmead and his family,' the little man specified, 'of Rainton Park. That is all I know of the picture, from the gilded plaque which was set in the foot of the frame; apart, that is, from Zoffany's signature. I see you are not familiar with the picture.'

A sly look came into Peckfuller's eyes as he put this question to us.

'Alas, no, sir,' my companion answered for both of us. 'Is it then a lost Zoffany?'

'You are no collectors, at any rate!' our host exclaimed. 'How few of them will admit that a work of their particular hero is unknown to them. It is listed in the appropriate places, I understand, but – until I sold it – with the rider: Ownership unknown.'

I studied the man while he spoke. He was of mature age, to be sure, but sprightly, and hardly the 'old josser' the Shiner had described, nor did there appear to be anything wrong with his hearing.

'I beg your pardon, sir,' I broke in, 'but I suspect that our informant confused you with a quite different occupant of this house.'

'Ah! When would this have been?'

'About seven or eight months ago.'

'That would explain it, then, doctor: that would have been my late Uncle Edmund Peckfuller. He died just before last Christmas. I can tell you that this house would have presented an altogether different appearance to you if you had come here when he was in residence. That is, if you had been able to penetrate the jungle in the garden and evade the jaws of Prince. And the state of the house! 'Rats' Castle', the local people called it. Many a time I tried to take it all in hand for him, but each time I was driven away with a flea in my ear. Even after the affair of the burglar . . .'

'A burglar, sir?' Violet Branscombe said. 'But how alarming!'

'Yes, ma'am, caught in the act by Prince in the garden last autumn. You never saw such an ugly brute: I was at the trial. Attracted here no doubt by the rumours about Uncle Edmund's treasures. You know the silly tales a solitary man gathers round him! They couldn't make the burglary charge stick, since they found nothing on him. Not that my uncle would have known for sure exactly what he had in the Aladdin's cave this place was in his time. Burglar seems to have got rid of his tools, too, before they nabbed him, so he only got six months for loitering. My uncle was a human magpie, ma'am: he collected for collecting's sake, and in the end he quite forgot just what he had collected.'

'He must nevertheless have amassed some things of real value,' I suggested.

'Indeed he did, and the Zoffany was one of them. Oh, the dealers certainly kept him warm. Trust those jackals to sniff out anything fine. As I recall, he told me about someone who came to call about the Zoffany just before the burglar affair: some agent. Yes, I remember now!'

Mr Peckfuller wheezed with laughter.

'Yes! – ' wheeze ' – yes, I remember Uncle Edmund called him a "simpering dandyprat"!'

'How did he get past the dog, sir?' Violet Branscombe asked.

'I believe he waited for the daily help, and went in with her. Fly customer! Anyhow, he was no match for Uncle Edmund, who refused adamantly to part with the painting, and he would have sent the fellow packing directly, only he offered five guineas for letting him photograph the painting. Five guineas!

96

Uncle must have thought his birthday had come. Well, the fellow got his photograph, but he certainly didn't get the Zoffany!'

'I don't suppose you recall the agent's name, sir,' I said. 'We might look him up some day.'

'That I don't, doctor, not offhand. But perhaps you might care to look up the fellow I sold the painting to: he seemed to know all there was to know about Zoffany. I may have his card still somewhere.'

'We should be most obliged to you, sir,' my companion said with a disarming smile.

'May be in my desk here. Excuse me while I look for it . . .'

We exchanged eager looks as the little man went over to his desk and rummaged in a drawer.

'Drat!' he squeaked. 'Such wretched little things, calling cards. They all look the same . . .'

'You were quite happy to part with the painting, then, Mr Peckfuller?' I asked as he rummaged.

'That's not it, no . . . What was that? The painting? Oh, yes, flashy great thing, with dead, smug faces like contented dairy-cows. Not an artist I care for, and would you have hesitated, doctor, if you'd been offered a cool thousand for a painting you hadn't house-room for!'

A cool thousand! I made a low whistle under my breath.

'Ah, you're in luck. Here it is!'

I took the card and read: MR FRANCIS CORCORAN, DEALER IN FINE ART who was to be found, it seemed, at Number Four, Wharf Lane, Twickenham.

'We are greatly obliged to you, Mr Peckfuller,' I said, getting up and handing him back the card. 'We shall certainly follow this up. Tell me, if you would: what did this Mr Corcoran look like?'

'Dark-haired young fellow in a black suit like an undertaker's. Soft, black hat. Cleanshaven, too. Not my idea of an art dealer. More like a curate, I should have said. Still, his cheque was good. Let me clear it with my banker beforehand: act of a sportsman!'

Disappointment was written all over Violet's face, but I had an idea.

97

'Tell me, Mr Peckfuller, did he have a personal mannerism?'

'Mmm . . . I'm not sure that I – '

'When he smiled, did he put his hand over his mouth, like this?'

I made the appropriate gesture and Mr Peckfuller's face lit up. 'Why, you must know him already, doctor.'

19

After our meeting with Mr Peckfuller, we took tea in a charming little place in Hampstead, where we discussed our new information.

'This painting is clearly of vital importance to Agar,' my companion said, 'if after going to the extraordinary length of commissioning its burglary – albeit unsuccessfully – he is afterwards prepared to part with the remarkable sum of a thousand pounds for it! Yet I can scarcely believe that, had the burglary been successful, he would have sold it on to his American principal, who could never have shown it once old Peckfuller had raised the hue-and-cry. Even less so when the news broke in art circles that a hitherto-lost Zoffany was in circulation.'

'And I feel sure,' I added, 'that of all the dealers who pestered old Peckfuller during the period before the burglary, Agar, with his Zoffany agency, must have been prominent. If only the old man had kept his visiting-cards! Agar seems to have been content to let the picture go on his first offer being refused, so why not the second time last autumn? What had happened in the interval to make his acquisition of it so urgent, to make him go to the lengths of engineering a burglary in order to get possession of it?'

Dr Branscombe returned to her theme.

'And why acquire it at all if it can never be sold, except through a fence, who would give him only a fraction of what he paid for it, or shown by anyone mad enough to buy it?'

Something occurred to me.

'Your question,' I said, 'indicates a clear alternative. Perhaps its value lay not in its possession, but in its suppression!'

'But whatever for? What conceivable kind of plot demands for its success the suppression of something which, as far as the world knows, doesn't exist?'

'That, dear colleague,' I said, summoning the waiter, 'is what we must determine.'

After I had dropped off Dr Branscombe at her club, there was an hour or so before dinner, which I decided to fill by calling on Ferraby, to enquire about the results of the tests on poor Lance Boynton-Leigh, as well as any other titbits I might glean as to developments in Ginger Lane. Truth to tell, I was far from easy in my mind concerning Archibald Boynton-Leigh's apparent change of mind in the matter of Lavinia's captivity. The spiked railings of the garden in Ginger Lane were scarcely wide enough confines to constitute liberty, however conditional. And what exact destination had the nabob in mind for the mooted trip abroad?

In view of my not having dressed, my declining Ferraby's invitation to stay to dinner was as perfunctory as his offer. He took me into the library and we sat in easy chairs, brandies-and-seltzers at our elbows.

''Fraid the tests were positive,' he said in answer to my first question. 'Tumour. Crowninshield declined to operate – '

'What!' I said, putting down my glass and sitting up rigidly in my chair. 'You mean you're just going to let things take their course?'

'No, of course not. Ah! But you wouldn't know down in, er, Limehouse, was it?'

'Whitechapel,' I said rather coldly.

'Descadilhas is to take the case.'

'You mean the Director of the Clinique des Ursins at Montpellier, the specialist in nervous disorders? Are you then familiar with his work, Ferraby?'

'Not I, old boy! All Bee-Ell's idea. Seems to have quite made up his mind on the matter.'

The warning bells started to ring in my mind.

'Boynton-Leigh wanted him?' I parrotted, sitting up even more rigidly in my chair.

'Yes, he must've been making enquiries. This Discadoo feller seems like the goods, though, if a touch controversial: they tell me at the club he's had stuff published in the *Lancet*. I should say he'll be more than up to the job. Any road, better than the alternative, as far as poor Lance is concerned, hey?'

Fernand Descadilhas was certainly 'up to the job', being as brilliant as a surgeon as he was controversial in his methods of treating nervous disorders in his isolated clinic in the hills behind Montpellier.

'It's all settled,' Ferraby went on. 'Both the patients are to leave for France in a week or two – '

I put down my glass again with a clatter.

'Both of the patients, Ferraby?'

'Mmm, Miss Lavinia as well. We thought it would be an ideal opportunity to get at the roots of her neurasthenia: the peace and quiet of the clinic over there, the splendid facilities – '

I positively leapt to my feet.

'I thank you for your hospitality, Ferraby,' I said stiffly, 'but I really must dash: I have an appointment to keep.'

After my dash across the city, Boynton-Leigh received me seated behind his teakwood desk. He held me in a calm, unwavering stare.

'I had anticipated this irruption, Dr Mortimer, and I am prepared for it.'

'I feel responsible for your ward, Mr Boynton-Leigh, she having been until so recently in my care.'

'As she is now in your erstwhile colleague, Ferraby's,' the nabob reminded me coldly. 'Lavinia's case is out of your hands now, Dr Mortimer.'

'But you led me – Lavinia – to believe she was to go on a cruise to celebrate her twenty-first birthday,' I protested. 'Is this then the cruise you promised her: an indefinite sojourn in a French *maison de santé*!'

The nabob leant back in his chair.

'An indefinite sojourn, Dr Mortimer? You make it sound like veritable incarceration! You seem to imply an element of coercion: force, even. I assure you it is to be nothing of the kind.'

A suspicion came into my mind.

'Is it by any chance a lunacy petition you have in mind, Mr

Boynton-Leigh?' I quizzed the merchant. 'Is that it, sir? So that your ward may be in your charge indefinitely, her coming majority notwithstanding? If so, sir, I give you notice that I shall contest it with all the force at my command!'

Boynton-Leigh almost smiled: I had never seen him so clearly sure of himself.

'Dr Mortimer, my dear young man! You really must try to curb your tendency to melodrama. But, wait. There is a sure way I may set your mind at rest, and by the bye, this takes me back to our very first encounter when, you may recall, you stated that the one sure way of ascertaining my ward's condition was by your actually seeing her. Just so!'

The nabob rose and tugged at a sash on the wall behind him then, resuming his chair, looked at me with an ironical little smile. His grim manservant soon appeared.

'Bring Miss Lavinia here, Ord,' Boynton-Leigh ordered.

Lavinia appeared in a rich crushed-velvet dress of some dark-crimson hue. She gave me a shy smile and nodded in a tentative way.

'Lavinia, my dear,' the nabob said silkily, 'I have just been telling Dr Mortimer about our travel-plans: how they are going to make you quite well again in the clinic in France. The dear doctor seems to think you may not have been, er, sufficiently consulted in the matter. Why, we cannot have him thinking that, now, can we! Pray reassure him.'

The glorious eyes – undrugged as any I have ever looked into – turned on me with an earnest expression in them.

'Of course I shall go wherever Baba wants me to go,' she said calmly. 'It must be for the best!'

20

Neither the train of revelation sparked off by Ferraby's report nor, above all, the enigma posed by Lavinia's utterly baffling reaction to her guardian's latest ploy to keep her in his grip conduced to untroubled sleep that Sunday night.

I was fairly sure that she had shown none of the signs – particularly about the eyes – of being under the influence of any soporific I knew of. Then how to account for her seeming acquiescence in the planned extension beyond her majority of her state of wretched subjection? I turned it over and over in my mind until the odd statement she had made to me at the close of our meeting in the summer garden came back to me: 'Do not think badly of me ...' Could this have any bearing on the matter? But think badly of her over what? Something she had done? That she was doing? Or was about to do? It was with this insoluble conjugation tick-tocking in my brain that, in the uncertain whiteness of the summer dawn, I slid into a light slumber.

I recounted the puzzling developments in Aldgate to my colleague in the dispensary next noonday.

'I too suspect a lunacy petition,' she said straight away. 'The French plans may be mere persiflage to keep meddlers off the scent.'

'But Lavinia's apparent compliance – ' I objected.

'We do not know what arguments or inducements he may have brought to bear on her. He may be simply biding his time until the legal period has elapsed.'

'What legal period?'

'Ah, forgive me! I see you are not familiar with the new Lunacy Act: it just came into force in May. It is of direct importance to my work in that it touches on the plight of solitary and vulnerable heiresses, and on that of women in asylums and workhouses. The legal period I refer to is the stipulation in the new Act that no less than fourteen days must elapse between the presentation of a petition – accompanied by two separate doctors' certificates – and its acceptance by an appropriate authority. How long is it since Miss Nancarrow revealed to you her guardian's plans for a foreign journey?'

I made a brief mental calculation.

'Mmm, let me see. It would have been Tuesday, the twenty-fourth of June. A fortnight tomorrow! My God! Do you mean he may already have submitted the petition, and is simply waiting for it to be accepted. But surely even Ferraby would not have – '

'Dr Ferraby may be in blissful ignorance of the whole thing,' my colleague said. 'After all, there are other doctors to be had, less scrupulous than he. I have a copy of the Act in my quarters in the Minerva. I would look it up for you now, but I must stay here for the afternoon, in case there may be news concerning our business with Sammy the Shiner.'

I said I would see into the matter myself, and left Dr Branscombe till evening surgery. All ideas of luncheon having been driven from my thoughts, I made straight for the premises of Messrs Eyre and Spottiswood in East Harding Street, conveniently close to my rooms further down Fleet Street. At the venerable publisher's establishment, which also served as an outlet for government publications, three shillings obtained me a brand new copy of the Lunacy Act, passed that spring, and I scurried back to my lodgings to study it.

I must say that the appearance throughout the voluminous document of such creatures as the Commissioners in Lunacy, and the airing of such medieval mysteries as 'traverse and supersedeas', fuelled my exasperation to the extent that at times I wondered if I might not have strayed into the pages of *Alice in Wonderland*! However, after several hours' close study of the Act, I thought I understood that Violet Branscombe had been quite correct in her summary. The only faint hope I might have had of intervention – Part One, 6 (3), in which it is stated that the supposed lunatic may, at the presentation of the petition, name someone to be present with him or her – had presumably long since faded with my failure to be in at the beginning of the process.

Of course, it was all mere surmise that Boynton-Leigh had taken any such measures in the first place, but if he had, it seemed there was nothing I could do to stop them in their inevitable course. I finally flung away the legal tome in disgust, and went out for a belated beefsteak pudding in the Cheshire Cheese to make up for my lost luncheon. By the time I had emerged, replete, into the never-ending jangle of Fleet Street, it was long past teatime: in fact, I had only an hour in hand before I must set off for evening surgery in Whitechapel. I decided to use that hour to drop a message for Tooke at Crutched Friars, who I felt ought to be told about what further danger might be hanging over Lavinia, though as I negotiated the winding alley-ways, I damned the man roundly for his mystery-mongering in the matter of his private address.

When I got to the dispensary, I learned from my colleague that there had been no developments during the afternoon in the business of the rendezvous with the East Ham Shiner. It was still early days though and dismissing the matter for the time being, I flung myself with relief into work I could understand. Rolling pills and mixing tonics was mental balm after my wrestlings with the Dickensian contortions of the Lunacy Act!

That evening Dr Branscombe had a dinner appointment in the West End with her colleagues from the New Women's Hospital in Seymour Place and, after I had escorted her to the station, I found myself at a loose end. I had by now grown pleasantly accustomed to our cosy suppers at the Junior Minerva, and to her physical proximity. In fact, my feelings towards her were rapidly converging on those of the conventional way of a man with a woman. There was so much in her that put the fey glamour of such as Lavinia Nancarrow in the shade.

I strolled along to Fieldgate Street, where I had a bite of supper at Cohen's. I was reluctant to leave the cheery murmur of the restaurant for my impersonal diggings in Fleet Street. Nevertheless, the moment came when the bill was paid and I was out on the pavement again. I sauntered unhurriedly in the direction of the opening into the Whitechapel Road when, just as I was passing the opening to Plumbers' Row, I thought I heard a voice – a rough, cockney voice, with a familiar ring to it – call my name. I glanced down the dingy Row, but all was quiet and deserted, and I shook my head slightly: I had been overdoing things, and it was definitely time I cut along to bed.

'Dahn 'ere, cully. It's me!'

I stopped again. I had not been imagining things after all. And that had been Sammy the Shiner's voice! Things must have moved quickly, then. I took three or four steps down the Row, and the burly figure of the Shiner, with the tiny bowler atop his diminutive skull, stepped out from the passage to a court. I wondered if he would require immediate payment, but the question quickly turned out to be immaterial when in the dim streetlight I realised that the face I was looking into was not Sammy's.

'What the – ' I began, but an awful crushing pressure on my windpipe cut short my expostulations. Someone behind me was evidently pressing an iron bar against my throat. I was momentarily aware that the man in front of me who had been impersonating Sammy was fumbling in my jacket pocket. The pressure on my neck became unbearable, and I instinctively stamped my heels behind me, managing in so doing to make contact with a booted toe. I heard an angry yelp behind me and the pressure suddenly increased. I began to see stars.

Just as I was on the point of losing consciousness, there came another squeal behind me and the pressure on my throat suddenly relaxed, and I fell away, retching and gasping, into the darkened court. I was vaguely aware of a scuffle behind me, but it was a good half-minute before I was up to tottering back into the illuminated darkness of the Row to look about me.

A slight, bowlered figure with his back to me was holding, with thumb and forefinger, the arm of the bulking man with the little head, who was squealing in pain. His small tormentor deftly stepped to one side and swung the arm round the man's back as if leading him in some sinister Highland reel, then pulled the arm right up till the bone snapped with a sickening click. The heavy man fell into a heap on the ground and the little man in the bowler rushed towards me. I squinted at him and gasped in astonishment.

'Tooke!' I exclaimed. 'You! But how – '

'No time for that!' the surveyor snapped, harsh command now usurping the meek and mild tones he usually affected. 'Let's get to a cab. Come on!'

He seized my arm and I staggered back behind him towards the opening into Fieldgate Street, in doing so almost falling over the body of the man who had tried to garrot me. His arm was protruding from under him at an impossible angle.

'What about these two – ' I gasped.

'Bugger 'em!' came the definitely un-Tookean reply as he dragged me along into the Whitechapel Road, where we were lucky enough to be able to stop a disengaged hansom coming

105

from the direction of Aldgate Station. Tooke pushed me into the cab, giving the cabbie instructions to take us to my lodgings, but to take his time about it, then got in beside me.

'I take back whatever complaints I have made in the past about your dogging my footsteps, Tooke,' I said. 'I owe you – '

'Nothing, old boy!' the little surveyor said with his familiar amiable mildness of tone. The steel had gone out of the grey eyes. 'I got your message about your having news for me about Lavinia. I couldn't let those two flats get in our way, now, could I?'

'But where did you learn that trick with their arms?'

'Oh that! Just a little wheeze I picked up up Pathankot way: pressure on those nerves unbearably painful, you know, unbearably.'

A cold look again flickered over the grey eyes, a look commingled with the same expression of mild contempt he had shot me at the close of our very first meeting in Kensington Gardens.

'Did they take anything?' he asked.

I quickly patted my pockets to feel the comforting lumps of pocket-book, watch and so forth.

'No, everything seems to be in place.'

'Mmph!' Tooke snorted. 'Perhaps I didn't give them time. Got your message about an hour-and-a-half ago. Reckoned you'd be putting down Dr Branscombe in Bloomsbury at the usual hour, but no sign of either of you there, so on previous form, I thought the odds would be on Cohen's Restaurant.'

'Didn't it occur to you to try my diggings in Fleet Street?'

'This is a confidential pidgin, old chap. Landladies notoriously chatty old bodies.'

'And didn't you think of coming into the restaurant after me?' The familiar rabbity little smile.

'Wanted to see where you'd lead me: old shikaree's instinct!'

'I really don't know you, Tooke. You're a rum cove!'

'Not nearly so rum as the customers you seem to have on your tail, Mortimer! You must have trodden on some pretty sensitive toes. I should cover your flanks carefully in future. What's your news?'

I told him about the latest twist in the Ginger Lane mystery, and Tooke reacted with incongruous self-control, in view of his

106

declared adoration of Lavinia Nancarrow. He looked pensive for an instant, then spoke calmly.

'And you say there's nothing we can do, Mortimer? They can just put her away with a stroke of the pen?'

'I'm afraid so, Tooke, and with the Law's blessing.'

'I see. It's a possibility we'll have to take into account.'

'If I may say so, Tooke, you seem to be taking it all tolerably coolly!'

The eyes went cold again, and the same faint contempt flickered across them.

'Always keep a clear head, Mortimer, and be prepared for anything. You don't seriously think I'd let them do anything to her, do you?'

I thought of the two ruffians the little man had just dealt with and, no, I did not think he would let them do anything to her. We arrived at the opening of the little court where my rooms were.

'If I were you, I should get indoors and see to that throat.' Tooke's voice came from the cab as it clopped away with him. 'Many thanks for the news, and keep me posted!'

After I'd attended to my sore and swollen neck, I prepared immediately to turn in for the night. The attack that had just been made on me, if not an outright attempt to murder me, must have been a warning, since nothing had been taken from me. A very serious warning, and obviously connected with my dealings with Sammy the Shiner: that impersonation of his voice in the court-entrance off Plumbers' Row had been extraordinarily good. I should now have to remain on the alert at all times, and keep – whenever possible – to the main thoroughfares.

I emptied out the contents of my pockets on to the dressing-table with particular care that night. Yes, everything present and correct, but wait a bit . . . Besides the diagonally cut half of the cigarette card which had formed my portion of the talisman in the Hot Cross Bun, there was another, of identical shape. I fitted them both together to form the unmistakable likeness of Lily Langtry, the 'Jersey Lily'. I stared at the card sombrely. I feared now that our projected meeting with Sammy the Shiner would have to be postponed indefinitely.

21

'The outlook for Sammy seems dim indeed!' Dr Branscombe remarked as she frowned down at the now-united halves of the Lily Langtry cigarette card which lay on the top of her consulting room desk after surgery on that Tuesday morning.

'My meeting with Sammy in the Hot Cross Bun on Saturday night must have been remarked on,' I said. 'Agar's writ must run as far as East Ham!'

'So it would seem, and the attack on you last night. I wish you would take more care, James – ' it was the first time she had called me by my Christian name, and I was delighted ' – was clearly a warning, with Sammy's segment of the card to emphasise the point, rather than a murderous attack.'

'I must confess the harmlessness of it was lost on me at the time,' I said ruefully, stroking my bruised throat.

'This is a grave setback,' my colleague remarked. 'Sammy would have made a devastating witness against Agar . . .'

Just then a clumping was heard on the stairs, and I got up and moved instinctively in front of Dr Branscombe's desk, my heaviest loaded stick in my hand. The door burst open and a panting, wild-eyed woman stood gasping on the threshold. She was short and stocky, and had only a torn blue cotton dress on with a greasy bodice. Her lank blond hair was wildly askew. What drew one's eye immediately, though, were the black-and-yellow bruises which criss-crossed her coarse-featured face like some design of aboriginal warpaint. The lid of her left eye was swollen and the corner of the eye itself was bloodshot. Violet was on her feet in an instant.

'Rosie!' she exclaimed, and I remembered her mentioning Sammy's woman who, the Shiner had alleged, had been driven into prostitution by Agar. 'Who has done this?'

'Gotta 'elp me, miss!' the woman gasped. ''E'll do for me this time. That's definite!'

'Do you mean – '

'Agar!' the woman hissed. ''Oo else?'

I felt anger rising in me and my hands clutched at the knobbly stick.

'And Agar did this to you?' I asked.

''E did, mister, an' it ain't nuffink to what 'e's done ter me before, so 'elp me, if I'm lived and spared, I'll swing for him! An' I don't care 'oo knows it!'

Violet, as usual, got down to brass tacks.

'Is someone after you now, Rosie?'

'Dunno, miss, didn't wait ter see. I've just left that flat in a dead faint, wiv me scissors in 'is 'and. I've run all the way from Fournier Street – '

'Agar!' I exclaimed. 'You've just stabbed Agar!'

My colleague shook her head.

'Later, James. They cannot be far behind. We must get her away from here!'

Violet seemed to ponder for a while, then her face brightened, and she sat down and started to scribble a note. She called in Queenie from the dispensary, and the girl gaped at the bedraggled, panting woman.

'Are you ready for your rounds, Queenie?' Dr Branscombe said.

'Yes, doctor, medicines is ready.'

'Good! I want you to go straight away to the cab-rank outside Aldgate Station – take your basket with you – and tell a cabbie to drive round along Old Montague Street – remember, by Old Montague Street – behind here.'

'Right you are, miss!'

'Tell him to wait at the opening of Winthrop Street as it joins Brady Street. Can you remember that?'

'Winthrop and Brady. Righto, miss.'

'Good girl! Away you go, then.'

Queenie went back into the dispensary to collect her basket, then re-emerged and bustled down the stairs.

'What have you in mind?' I asked my colleague, while Rosie flopped into the patient's chair and attempted to regain her wind.

'Like so many eighteenth-century buildings, this one has a common loft, without partitions. I want you to take Rosie along the loft till you find the last trapdoor but one. Below is an empty, boarded-up oil shop. It opens on to the end of Winthrop Street – '

'I'm with you!' I said. 'Whoever may be watching this building will be watching the two entrances on the Whitechapel Road in front or on Durward Street to the rear, the only apparent places of egress. Using the loft, we may be able to sneak out unobserved by way of Winthrop Street farther east, and into Brady Street.'

'We must make assurance doubly sure, though,' my colleague said as she finished writing her note, which she slipped into an envelope, which she in turn sealed and superscribed. She then got up and stood away from the desk and pulled a pin from her hair, which she shook into a straggly mop.

'If Dr Mortimer will go and fetch the packing case crowbar from the dispensary, Rosie, we shall exchange clothes.'

Minutes later, I was escorting a caped and hatted Rosie through the dust and cobwebs of the long common loft which extended back from the court deep into Winthrop Street. Our way was lit by what dim daylight could penetrate the filthy slits of skylights. At length we stepped over the joists that encased the last trapdoor but one and, scraping in the dust for the crack, I brought the crowbar into play. A few hearty jerks and the trapdoor was open. I threw down the crowbar ahead of me and swung down by my fingertips on to the third-floor landing beneath. I caught Rosie as she flopped down after me, and we made our way briskly down the flights of stairs to the back corridor and the Winthrop Street side-entrance, whose steel bar I raised from its hooks, then levered off the door-lock, which came away, screws and all. After I'd popped out my head in order to spy out the land – all clear – I led Rosie out and along to Brady Street where our cab was waiting. I felt the thrill of the chase mounting in me as I handed Rosie her envelope and a couple of half-crowns for the cabbie when she got to her destination, the address of a sort of halfway house for wronged women in Hackney. I gave the cabbie the address, along with a shilling to speed him on his way and, with Rosie's thanks ringing in my ears, I watched the cab jaunt briskly up Brady Street.

My immediate duty discharged, I withdrew into the dusty oil shop, pulled the lockless door shut, and slotted the bar back into the four hooks that secured it. I took the three flights of stairs three steps at a time, then dragged an abandoned washstand out of one of the third-floor rooms and, by standing on it, managed – after flinging the crowbar back up in front of me – to haul myself back up into the loft. In no time at all, I had rejoined my colleague in the consulting room.

Dr Branscombe made a very passable simulacrum of our recent visitor, with her disordered tow hair and greasy, tattered dress.

'Rosie will be in safe hands in Hackney,' she said. 'They will know what to do. I have sent out for a cab to pick us up at the Durward Street back entrance. Come! It should be there by now.'

We locked the outer door of the dispensary as we left and, taking the back corridor, emerged at the Durward Street entrance where our hansom was waiting. My comrade-in-arms covered her face with a handkerchief, and I encircled her shoulders with a shielding arm as we hurried into the cab. I ordered the cabbie to drive to the Junior Minerva Club as fast as he liked.

'Did Rosie tell you any more while I was in the pharmacy hunting out the crowbar?' I asked, as we clattered citywards along Old Montague Street.

'She told me Agar had her dragged to his studio in Fournier Street in the early hours of Sunday morning – '

'Just after my meeting with Sammy in the Hot Cross Bun!' I said.

'Yes. Agar told her he thought she'd a good idea where Sammy might be, and when she refused to tell him anything, he thrashed her senseless with a rattan cane.'

'The despicable swine!' I muttered, then, calming down, observed, 'They can't have caught Sammy straight away, then.'

'No, but I suspect they must have done away with him sometime between then and last night, when they passed you his half of the cigarette card. We can scarcely hope they got the card without Sammy, especially when, an hour or so ago, Rosie heard one of her captors say to another outside the room in which she was being held that he'd be back to help him "see to her" later on.'

'Then they'd no longer need to pump her regarding Sammy,' I said. 'And the scissors?'

'Ah! Realising there'd be only one man outside in the corridor for some time, Rosie banged on the locked door of the room in which she was being held and demanded that her, er, receptacle be changed. Well, after much ado, the man complied and, as his arm appeared again through the open door, she opened her scissors – which she habitually carries secreted on her person to deal with clients who get out of hand – and ran one of the blades through the captor's hand, pinning it to the door-jamb. The man fainted away and Rosie dashed out in the clothes she stood up in. The rest you know.'

'Will she testify against Agar?' I asked.

'The will is certainly there, but I fear she has shown her hand too early. She has apparently been making public threats against him while in drink. Agar will be fully aware of her potential danger to him as a witness, so will presumably stop at nothing in order to silence her. We must tread warily.'

Just then, as our cab was turning off Bloomsbury Way into Coptic Street, a closed, two-horse van suddenly overtook us and, slewing in front of us, blocked our route. We heard the cabbie remonstrate with someone outside, then in a twinkling, a coarse-looking, unshaven fellow in a cricket cap appeared at the window. I reached for my stick as he raised what looked like a life-preserver – as if he was about to smash the window – and flung myself across my companion, but his jaw suddenly fell and with it the life-preserver.

The man looked over his shoulder towards the van.

'Gorblimey!' he yelled. 'It ain't 'er!'

He disappeared from view and the van soon jinked away from in front of us, and swung speedily back into Bloomsbury Way. Not so rapidly, however, that we were unable momentarily to glimpse, in one of the little circular windows in the back door of the van, the face, white with rage, of Jack Agar.

22

The next few days marked a lull in the series of frenetic events that had been put into motion by my meeting with Sammy the

Shiner on the previous Saturday night. A lull, perhaps, but certainly not a respite, for we were constantly aware, both at the dispensary and even in the vicinity of our respective lodgings, that we were being watched. A cab which, for no apparent reason, would come to a halt at the side of the road opposite my rooms, neckerchiefed loafers appearing in the sobre purlieus of Coptic Street where none had been known to appear before, and with increasing frequency. Clearly, no effort was being made at concealment, or even discretion for, equally clearly, none was intended. It was a show of strength, a sign – like that of the interception of our cab in broad daylight on Tuesday afternoon – that Agar's arm could reach beyond the bounds of the East End.

If Agar's present intention had been to intercept communication between us and Rosie Bartlett in the hope of its leading back to her, then his efforts had been in vain. The refuge in Hackney to which the forlorn streetwalker had been directed by my colleague was an independent entity, whose executives were perfectly capable, if necessary, of acting in Rosie's best interests without further referral to us. In any case, Violet assured me, she would by now have been conveyed in absolute secrecy to a safe house which might be anywhere in the kingdom between Land's End and John O' Groats. I was to learn more and more that the Women's Movement had a very long arm. For the rest, though we spared an eye for our own safety, we simply ignored Agar's febrile strivings to evade eventual nemesis, and got on with our duties.

Indeed, there was little else we could do, for, as far as the Aldgate Affair went, there was little corn in Egypt yet. The requested material from the Pinkerton's agent in India was presumably still in the hold of its mail-boat on the high seas – I estimated now somewhere between Marseilles and Gibraltar – and no dove flew across the enigmatic waste between us and Ginger Lane. Tooke, who had now revealed himself to me as being considerably more than just a chocolate soldier, did not so much as show his head above the parapet. I could not help but reflect that – masterly inactivity and his impressive vow to me on the Night of the Garrotters: 'Do you really think I'd let them do anything to her . . .' apart – if faint heart never won fair lady, then his claim to the heart of Lavinia Nancarrow must be one of the least well-founded since love began! In short, it seemed as if I was no nearer the heart of the mystery than I had been when first I had come up against the barred windows of the bedroom in Ginger Lane on that early summer evening an eternity ago.

I had pursued my enquiries into the possible ramifications of the affair of the lost Zoffany in Highgate, and during the course of my researches at various West End galleries, one collector's name had cropped up more frequently than those of all the others: Politis. This worthy was reputedly doyen of the trade, and what he did not know about Zoffany was not knowledge. I sent him a tentative note and this, with its coy allusion to a lost Zoffany, earned my colleague and me an invitation to tea with him on the forthcoming Sunday afternoon. In the meantime, an event occurred which clearly signalled that things had come to a head in the affair of the Disappearing Potential Witness.

We had just finished Friday evening surgery when, from my place at the mixing-bench in the pharmacy, I heard a sudden clumping and shuffling of several pairs of heavy boots at the door of the consulting room. My nerves were strung up from the tension of the previous few days of ceaseless surveillance of us, and I needed no further prompting before I grabbed up my loaded shillelagh from the bench and dashed out into the consulting room.

Two plug-uglies in vulgar checked suits and pearl-grey bowlers were standing sentinel on either side of the door from the waiting-room, and Jack Agar, resplendent in a wide-brimmed white felt hat and lavender gloves, was lolling in the patient's chair. He was arching and relaxing a vicious-looking rattan cane walking stick in his gloved hands while Dr Branscombe, rigid as an Easter Island statue, confronted him across the table.

'Agar!' I shouted. 'This is an unwarrantable intrusion, especially in view of your outrageous conduct in Bloomsbury on Tuesday!'

The two ruffians at the door made a step forward as I gripped my stick, but Agar motioned them back to their posts with a whanging backstroke of his cane.

'Bloomsbury?' he drawled. 'Not a place I frequent: too much

high-thinking there, for one thing, and blue, I find, is such an impossible colour for stockings.'

'You will please state your business, Mr Agar,' Violet said evenly, though there was murder in her eyes.

'Certainly, ma'am. Woman by the name of Rosie Bartlett: I gather she's known to you?'

My colleague continued to stare impassively through him.

'Well,' Agar went on, 'this Rosie is by way of being, shall we say, a model of mine. No longer in the first flush of youth but a woman of character who has lived. That type is always interesting. But women are kittle cattle, hey, ma'am? And we artists are always misunderstood: it is the mark of all our tribe. Well, now, it seems this Rosie has a bee in her bonnet, some bizarre notion that I have, er, made away with a man-friend of hers. Fantastic, do I hear you say? Now Rosie, I'm afraid, drinks, and has said, well, certain ugly things about me in public. If it were only my poor reputation, I would snap my fingers at the whole thing, but Rosie has recently been entertaining delusions about going to law – '

'What is all this to us, Mr Agar?' Dr Branscombe cut in coldly.

'Just this, ma'am: Rosie is beginning to pose a serious nuisance to me, a nuisance which I am determined to obviate. Oh, you may ignore the rumours of the gutter: I intend her no physical harm.'

I had it on the tip of my tongue to berate him on account of the weals I had seen on the poor woman's face, but I reined myself in in time: we must let him know nothing.

'No,' Agar went on, all the while bowing and straightening the cane, 'I had in mind a pact of, shall we say, bipartite supervision, as follows: Rosie will remain under your, er, tutelage, while I and my agents will retain right of access at will, all expenses to be met by myself, while you may in turn appoint whatever supervisors you may think – '

'You seem to assume, Mr Agar,' Violet commented in serene tones, 'that we know the whereabouts of this unfortunate woman.'

'A reasonable assumption, I should have thought, ma'am,' Agar said suavely, glancing up at the ceiling.

'These old buildings have such intriguing possibilities – concealed rooms, sealed-up chimneys and the like – do they not, doctor?'

'I assure you,' my colleague replied, 'that neither I nor Dr Mortimer have the slightest idea where the woman you describe is at present – ' the arc of the cane bowed to a semi-circle ' – and that there are no concealed dwellers in these premises. If that is all, I will ask you to give us leave to lock up the dispensary for the night.'

The cane snapped in two with a report like a gunshot and an electric hush fell for a full ten seconds. At length, Agar regained control of himself and, unfolding his long legs in his indolent fashion, lounged to his feet.

'I see,' he said quietly. 'And that is your last word?'

My colleague had got up and was already tidying the things on her desk. I stepped over to her side and, with a flick of my stick, swept the remains of Agar's cane off the table and into the wastepaper basket below.

'It grows late, Mr Agar,' Violet said, without looking up from what she was doing.

The artist looked at her with narrowed eyes.

'Later perhaps than you think, Dr Branscombe. Goodnight to you both!'

23

If his stopping our cab in Bloomsbury that Tuesday had not finally convinced me of Agar's nefarious intent, the fraught confrontation with him of the Friday evening would have dissipated any remaining doubt. We were now under notice, and every time we stepped into the street we felt a frisson in the small of our backs. It came as a welcome relief, then, when we were able momentarily to forget the tension of this crisis in our affairs by taking up our invitation to tea that Sunday afternoon in Bloomsbury Square with Mr Politis, the uncrowned King of the Zoffany experts.

Inside the fine William-and-Mary house we found ourselves

in a quietly opulent room, its walls hung with tawny master-pieces: conversation pieces, theatrical paintings and worldly portraits, the common characteristic of the subjects of the latter being a profound self-satisfaction.

'Such a Vanity Fair, no?' remarked our host, a thin, sallow man with eager, prominent brown eyes and much unruly, black wavy hair, as he served us tea and muffins. We looked around at the glowing walls and smiled and nodded our agreement.

'Very, um, worldly,' Violet said noncommittally.

'The worldliest paintings in the world, dear madam!' Mr Politis said with animation. 'Now you must tell me about this lost Zoffany of yours. You interest me unbearably!'

We explained and he nodded enthusiastically.

'Yes, yes, the Fairmead conversation piece! It has been out of circulation for – oh – sixty or seventy years! But this Corcoran, I do not know him at all: perhaps you can tell me something about him.'

One thing we could have told him: that on our enquiring, we had found that no one answering the description given to us by Mr Peckfuller the previous Sunday lived at the address given on the alleged Mr Corcoran's visiting card.

'I suspect, Mr Politis,' I said, 'that Corcoran is not his real name, but Agar, and that he is, or was until recently, an agent acting on behalf of a wealthy American collector – '

'Frohwein!' the connoisseur exclaimed, his face wrinkling in disgust. 'It must be him: Kurt Frohwein. He is a Croesus. Made a fortune as a pork-packer in Chicago. I am not at all surprised that his agents should go under assumed names, considering his methods of acquisition. He is a fanatic and will stop at nothing to add a new Zoffany to his collection. I should not mind so much if he showed some discrimination, some real appreciation of the paintings he collects, but I am sure he collects them merely as one would collect share-certificates or bearer-bonds, as material assets, as trophies to show that he can get the better of the next man.'

'Could you tell us something about the picture, sir?' Violet said.

'The Fairmead? Yes, I know by reading that it is a conversation piece: Sir Jonas Fairmead is with his family under a spreading

117

oaktree on their estate in Northumberland. It is in 1780. There is Sir Jonas, his lady, two sons and three daughters, the Misses Leigh – '

'The Misses Leigh?' I said, alerted. 'Please tell us about them.'

'They were the daughters of Sir Jonas' widowed sister-in-law, Constantia Leigh, of St Buryan in Cornwall. Upon her death, Sir Jonas took the sisters into his family. They were celebrated beauties. Dark like gypsies, apparently – '

'How "apparently", Mr Politis?' Violet asked.

'Because apart from the lost Zoffany – and presumably on the photograph taken by this Mr Corcoran of yours – there seems to exist no representation of them: no drawings, sketches, prints, nothing. But we shall no doubt see them again as soon as Frohwein has added the picture to his collection in New York. He will send me the first invitation to view, as he always does. It is his – how do you say? – gloating. A pork-butcher! Pah!'

'I fancy Agar will be keeping this particular Zoffany to himself,' I remarked.

Politis' exquisite Chelsea teacup was arrested halfway up his gorgeous silk waistcoat.

'Ah, is it so? I say it myself, but no one will give him a better price than Frohwein: no one!'

The excitable collector put down his cup and looked first at Violet, then at me. His eyes positively stood out on stalks.

'I have an idea, Doctors Branscombe and Mortimer!'

We in turn put down our cups and leant forward in our chairs.

'You shall be my agents! Yes! If you can find this Corcoran, or Agar, or whoever has the Fairmead, I shall back you for two thousand pounds, and you shall have five per cent each or seven-and-a-half per cent if you can get it for me for fifteen hundred. What do you say?'

I smiled indifferently, but Violet muttered under her breath: 'For the dispensary, James. You never know.'

We rose and Politis followed suit.

'I accept for both of us, Mr Politis,' I said. 'It is a bargain!'

The collector shook both our hands with enthusiasm.

'Something tells me you will find this man, and the painting,' he said, 'and I, Politis, shall add it to my collection!'

Our host waved his hand around the canvas-clad walls, then wrinkled his nose in disgust.

'Better to hang it here than in a pork-shop, no?'

We thanked Mr Politis and left, and discussed the events of the afternoon in the cab on the way to the Junior Minerva.

'It looks as if Agar made three approaches, then,' I said to my companion. 'To Uncle Edmund Peckfuller in Highgate, once as accredited agent of this American Croesus, Frohwein, before he, Agar, left for India – '

'Presumably under his own name,' Violet added.

'Yes, all above board, but without any luck as to his object of buying the painting for the American. Secondly, back in England and under what name we've no means of knowing, to make another unsuccessful bid – '

'Yes,' Violet added, 'but after photographing the picture this time. That would have some value for Mr Frohwein, presumably, as the painting hadn't actually been seen by anyone since heaven-knows-when.'

'Yes, it might be worth something, provided it was on Frohwein's account, this second bid being supplemented, though, by an attempted burglary. Finally, the third, successful bid, about a month ago, with Uncle Edmund's nephew and heir, for the tidy sum of a thousand pounds, Agar masquerading as Corcoran, whom Twickenham knows not. He opens a bank account there in the persona of Corcoran, deposits a thousand in cash, and makes out a perfectly good cheque for that amount to Peckfuller the Younger. Agar then gets the picture and Francis Corcoran disappears forever. But what does Agar do with the painting? And who were the Misses Leigh?'

'Yes!' Violet exclaimed. 'That may give some clue as to the relationship between Agar and Boynton-Leigh. Something Agar is handling on his own account. I should very much like to see these Misses Leigh.'

I thought of the Greek collector's remark about the two young ladies in the picture: 'dark, like gypsies'. Lavinia was dark like a gypsy. I wondered what she might be thinking at that very moment, in the light of her parting remark to me on the previous Sunday. Unfathomable!

As the cab pulled up at the club entrance, the boots dashed out and thrust a note through the window.

'For yer immediate attention, Dr Branscombe!' he said eagerly. 'Delivered by the perlice!'

Violet was half-in and half-out of the cab as she read the note. Her face became ashen, and she turned to me.

'We must go to the dispensary immediately, James. Something has happened!'

24

There was a police constable on duty in the court, outside the door to the dispensary, but the blackened hole where once the window had been told the story, as did the charred items that lay in a heap on the ground. I recognised some of the drugs and equipment from the pharmacy among them. We hurried over to the constable, who touched his helmet and stepped forward to meet us. We introduced ourselves, and he addressed Violet.

'Been trying to find you since one o'clock, ma'am,' he said. 'Bad business.'

'When did the fire start?' Violet asked.

'Must've been around noontime, ma'am. Seems the little girl spotted the smoke when she went upstairs to do her lessons in the dispensary.'

'Yes,' Violet said. 'I let her go in there to do her homework: she has a key of her own. It's quieter for her there than at home.'

'Well,' the policeman went on, 'the little girl alerted the neighbours, and the Fire Brigade got there about twenty past. Neighbours said she went repeatedly up and down the stairs, in spite of the flames and smoke, saving all she could, this heap of stuff you see here. Reg'lar little heroine, ma'am.'

'Trust Queenie to come up trumps!' Violet remarked with a sort of desperate elation. 'I must go and see her to – '

The constable lowered his eyes and fell silent for a while, and my companion stiffened visibly. I instinctively slipped my arm round her shoulders.

'I'm very sorry, ma'am,' the policeman said at last. 'It was the smoke, you see, the last time she went up. Firemen had a job reaching her, and by then it was too late . . .'

'Poor Queenie!' was all I could say, but Violet was beyond words. She seemed to shrink inside my embrace. My heart went out to her and at last she rallied.

'Have her parents been informed?' she asked the constable in a hoarse whisper.

'Oh, yes, ma'am, around one o'clock. She's in the mortuary at the London Hospital. There'll be further enquiries later on. I take it you'll be requiring someone to take this stuff away?'

Violet nodded again, and the policeman touched the brim of his helmet, then went off to make arrangements. By then a small crowd had gathered in the court, and an elderly woman stepped up and laid her hand gently on Violet's arm.

'She tried to save all she could, doctor, before the smoke, the smoke . . .'

My foot blundered against a bundle of papers, which were riffling in the breeze. I picked the bundle up. It was a charred penny exercise book which bore the inscription: QUEENIE BRYANT – ARITHMATIC. I have it to this day.

Violet thanked the little knot of people for their condolences and insisted, against my strong urging that she accompany me forthwith to Coptic Street for a sedative and an early bed, that we go straight away in our waiting cab to offer what comfort, material and moral, we could to Queenie's people. This mournful duty having been accomplished, I at last escorted Violet into the cab, en route to the Junior Minerva.

She was silent for a long while amid the soporific rumbling of the cab-wheels and I took her hand in mine.

'My poor Violet!' I said. 'It is tragic! Poor Queenie, and all your work gone like that.'

With a little squeeze of response, she disengaged her hand from mine. Her back resumed some of its old straightness and her voice came calm and clear.

'On the contrary, James! Today my work has just begun! There are other rooms in the court, and the dispensary will re-open in a set of them tomorrow. She shall not have died in vain.'

'You may rely on me, heart and soul!' I said.

Silence fell again, then I voiced a thought I was sure my companion was sharing at that moment.

'If I thought Agar had had a hand in this . . .'

Violet's eyes met mine, and in them I read relentless nemesis!

Just then the cab pulled up before the door of the Junior Minerva, and we got out, this time to go inside the club. I repeated my suggestion that she take something to make her sleep and turn in immediately, but she insisted that her mind was running too fast, and that she would merely go and freshen up, to rejoin me in ten minutes in the common room. We had much to arrange for the opening of emergency premises for the dispensary on the morrow.

I installed myself in a chair, and reached into my jacket pocket for my tobacco tin and rolling-papers, but pulled up before the ferocious glance of a beetle-browed young woman who was reading a hefty tome in a neighbouring armchair. I recalled the disappearance of my grand silver cigarette case – it seemed a thousand years before – in my incarnation as a society physician. Whatever had become of it?

The image of a scorched penny exercise book, however, soon drove thoughts of tobacco from my mind. Queenie . . . I remembered the little white apron, brushed so often over the skinny knees; the eager, artless questions as we shared the mixing bench. She had dared to dream of a future. And Agar – that sniggering dandy with the rotten teeth – what part had he played in her death?

The arrival of Violet, crisp and fragrant in a fresh blouse, dispelled my gloomy ponderings for the moment. Her expression was set and grim.

'First, James,' she said briskly, 'the dispensary. Every minute its re-opening is delayed will spell an added victory for our adversaries. I have an idea: perhaps it is at our lowest moments that we should be boldest! I propose, here and now, the founding of a new institution, dedicated to the raising of the physical and psychological health of the people which, in perpetuation of Queenie's memory, shall be named the Bryant Foundation!'

I sat forward in my chair.

'Bravo' I exclaimed. 'I second your proposal with all my heart!'

'Subscriptions will be solicited with the utmost vigour as from tomorrow – '

'There I must disagree.'

I took out my cheque book and fountain pen, and wrote out a cheque to the Bryant Foundation for one hundred pounds.

'I counter-propose that subscriptions be taken as from now!' I said, handing my colleague the cheque.

She looked at it in silence for quite ten seconds.

'It is wonderful of you, James, but I cannot possibly – '

'You cannot! But it is to the Foundation that I have written out the cheque. Or perhaps you imagine you can keep me off the board?'

She took the cheque and folded it carefully, then looked at me solemnly.

'My Mr Greatheart! It shall be in my safekeeping for now. We shall talk more of this later.'

'As to tomorrow,' I said. 'What exactly have you in mind?'

'I am sure Finn the landlord will have no objection to our using another set of rooms he has vacant on the other side of the court. We must arrange for credit from the wholesale pharmacists, and Finn no doubt will be able to rent us some sticks of furniture. We shall have to start at the crack of dawn.'

'In that case,' I said finally, 'I absolutely insist that you take a strong sedative here and now, and be off to bed. I shall be round here as early tomorrow morning as the boots may decently admit me.'

25

The next morning sped by in a welter of carters, furniture vans, chars, helpful neighbours, packing cases and carboys, straw, redirected patients and prowling firemen and policemen. As usual, Violet was magnificent, drowning her grief at the loss of her young assistant in work, and all of her patients were given their consultations, even if not a few had to wait longer than usual in the improvised waiting room, whose carbolic-reeking floor was scarcely dry by the time the first of them had arrived.

So that week fled by, the fitting-out and shaking-down of the new People's Dispensary step-by-step with our coping with a full complement of patients, occupying virtually all our waking hours. That Monday, Ferraby was good enough to send me news that Lance had taken a turn for the worse over the weekend and had been despatched, in the care of a brace of qualified nurses, a week in advance of his father and Lavinia to Montpellier, to be operated on at once by Descadilhas. It looked as if Lavinia's supposedly celebratory trip to the French sanatorium would be a rather mournful one.

I had popped in at the British India offices on the Wednesday morning to be told that the latest mail-boat had had to put in at Brest for repairs, owing to started plates as a result of stormy weather in the Bay of Biscay. It was expected to be fit to sail again soon with its cargo of news from India.

That afternoon we received a visit at the new dispensary from a Sergeant Prudhoe of the local divisional C.I.D. He was a well set-up, youngish man in a brown billycock.

'Afternoon, ma'am, sir.' The sergeant addressed us in an unobtrusive northern accent, declining my colleague's offer of a seat. 'Just to let you know that the Fire Brigade have sent us their report on the fire on Sunday.'

'And their findings, sergeant?' Violet said.

'Accident, ma'am. No real evidence to suggest otherwise.'

My colleague compressed her lips and her brow was creased by a frown.

'And your findings, sergeant,' she pressed. 'Are they in agreement with that?'

'Mmm, in general, ma'am – '

'Then pray be particular, sergeant!'

'Well, ma'am, there was no evidence that the dispensary door had been forced, though the lock's a pretty old-fashioned one – easily teased open with a bit of wire – and there were no unaccounted-for objects, paraffin cans, burnt wadding, or the like, in the rooms affected or among the salvaged objects outside.'

'Where did the fire start?' I asked. 'Were you able to establish that?'

'Fire Brigade said the surgery, sir, just under the trapdoor to the loft.'

I felt we were treading on dangerous ground here!

'The loft, sergeant?' I asked nervously, recalling my escapade with Rosie Bartlett scarcely a week previously.

'Yes, sir. There were two clear sets of recent men's footprints in the dust up there – it's a common loft, you know, like a huge sail-loft – one a narrow size eight . . .'

Just then the sergeant looked down at my feet, which I shuffled uneasily.

'About on the lines of yours, sir, and the other a square-toed six or six-and-a-half. The footprints went back and forth, as if someone had been pacing up and down the loft, or looking for something there.'

Or for somebody, I thought, like Rosie Bartlett.

'That's not all, either,' the sergeant went on, 'for there were discarded burnt vestas at intervals along the floor of the loft, as if someone had been lighting his way along. Along with that, we found that the front door of the empty oil shop at the Winthrop Street side of the building had been forced recently. The lock had been wrenched right off. Looked like a jemmy-job. Mind you, an empty building's always a standing temptation to housebreakers and larrikins of all sorts. I've had a word with Finn about that. Rum thing was, though, that the lock had been wrenched off from the inside, as if somebody'd been trying to get out, not in, but the bar had been carefully replaced from the inside. Still, that makes no odds as far as the fire went. My considered opinion is that some moocher or other got into the dispensary and climbed up into the loft to see what he could prig, striking vestas along the way to see what he was doing. One of the burnt vestas must've found its way down the hatch into the consulting room and smouldered away among some combustible material, lint or dust behind a cupboard, or what have you. It only needs a bit of a draught – under the door, perhaps, from somebody closing a door rooms away – and Bob's your uncle! No one suspicious was seen loitering round the court near the time of the fire, or no one anybody's prepared to report. You know what it's like round here. That's about it. Oh, and I was to tell you, ma'am: inquest's to be held on Queenie Bryant tomorrow. Well, if that's all, ma'am, sir, I'll be off. Day to you both.'

With those words, Prudhoe touched the brim of his billycock to both of us in turn and left.

'They were looking for Rosie!' Violet said grimly.

'I'm inclined to agree,' I said. 'I recall Agar's remark when he came to the dispensary about the hidden nooks and crannies that were to be found in old houses. I incline, too, to the sergeant's view of the cause of the fire as accident. If Agar is on the brink of some spectacular coup, it would surely be rank stupidity on his part to stir up the local police with such an act!'

'Judging by friend Prudhoe's verdict,' my companion said sardonically, 'Agar has avoided even that.'

'All the same,' I said, 'I think that, on the evidence, the intruder on Sunday simply threw away an imperfectly spent vesta which eventually caused the fire.'

'Be the evidence what it may, James, I for one shall forever lay poor Queenie's death at Agar's door.'

'By the bye,' I said, changing the subject, 'have you any news of Rosie?'

Violet shook her head.

'Not yet,' she said, 'but we must assume that no news is good news. In the meantime, we must be content that she is at least out of harm's way. If only we could find corroboration for her testimony, we might be able to bring Agar down.'

Things took their course and Queenie's death was recorded at the Coroner's inquest next day as having been owing to misadventure. Her funeral was later fixed for the following Monday, the twenty-first of July, the eve of Lavinia's twenty-first birthday.

The ceremony itself was simple and dignified, and I was particularly touched by the brave figure Violet made as she paid her salt tribute at the graveside. I knew then, that, come what might, I would make her my wife.

After the funeral came the renewed, relentless round of duties

126

in the improvised new dispensary, and I needed no rocking to sleep when I turned in on that Monday night. I little dreamt what a bombshell was about to burst among us.

26

It seemed as if I had only slept for a few minutes when I was rudely awoken by the sound of pummelling on my door and the landlady's agitated voice.

'Two policemen to see you, Dr Mortimer!'

I staggered out of bed and grabbed up my watch, which by the grey morning light told six twenty-five.

'Coming!' I shouted and, with a curse, pushed my feet into my slippers and pulled on my dressing-gown. I opened the door and followed my thoroughly flustered landlady downstairs to her front parlour, where two men in serge suits and bowlers were standing on either side of the fire-screen.

'Dr Mortimer?' asked the elder of the two men – a heavy, pasty-faced man with a walrus moustache – as he took off his bowler.

'Yes,' I said, and waved vaguely at a couple of chairs, which offer the elder man declined on behalf of both of them with a slight shake of his head. I slumped down into an antimacassared armchair and shivered slightly. I glanced over to my landlady in the doorway: she was actually trembling. The younger man was lean and of average height, and sported a moustache scarcely less luxuriant than that of his superior under his rather bulbous nose and closely set-together keen eyes. He glared at me steadily. He made no move to take off his hat, until a glance from the bulky man brought him to heel. This did not diminish the intensity of his stare by one jot or tittle.

'I am Inspector Moultry,' the heavy man said in a calm, matter-of-fact voice, 'and this is Sergeant Wensley. We are detective officers from Leman Street Police Station, and we have reason to believe that you may be able to help us in tracing the whereabouts of Miss Lavinia Nancarrow.'

I gripped the arms of the chair and jerked myself forward.

'Lavinia!' I exclaimed. 'But surely she must be at home! Today is her twenty-first birthday: she is leaving for the Continent with her guardian.'

The two men stared at me for quite ten seconds, while my landlady shivered in the doorway.

'When did you last see Miss Nancarrow, Dr Mortimer?' the inspector asked at last.

'Let me see,' I said. 'It must have been more than a fortnight ago, the Sunday before the Sunday before last – '

'The sixth!' Sergeant Wensley snapped, taking out a notebook.

'And you're sure that was the last time you've seen her since?' the inspector went on.

'I have just told you, inspector – '

'And on that occasion,' he went on imperturbably, 'did she give any indication of her further movements, apart from this, er, planned foreign trip?'

'No, that is all she told me. But surely her guardian will have been able to explain all this to you.'

The detectives fell to staring at me in silence again, and I became irritated.

'Anyhow,' I said, 'what are Miss Nancarrow's movements to you? At twenty-one she is at liberty to go where she pleases!'

'Well, not quite yet, Dr Mortimer,' the inspector replied. 'First she will have to explain to us what she knows about the murder of Mr John Ronald Agar!'

27

I was aghast at what the inspector had just told me, and for a moment I could only gape at him in disbelief, while the two detectives held me in their cool, insolent stares.

'But it is absurd!' I finally burst out. 'Lavinia could not possibly have had anything to do with Agar's death, if, as you say, he is dead!'

'He's dead right enough,' the sergeant added.

'You are on Christian-name terms with the young lady, then, Dr Mortimer?' Inspector Moultry went on.

'I know Miss Nancarrow well!' I said, bridling at his tone.

'Of course, Dr Mortimer,' Moultry said in a conciliatory murmur, 'she was your patient for a while, wasn't she?'

They had already been to see Ferraby, I thought. I wondered what else he had been blabbing to them!

'Nothing serious, was it?' the inspector said. 'Miss Nancarrow's illness?'

'I am not at liberty to discuss my patients' conditions, inspector – '

'Of course not, doctor! Rather a highly strung young lady, I understand, if that's not too unprofessional a remark!'

'She is sensitive, impressionable.'

'Yes,' Moultry went on, 'but otherwise strong and healthy?'

Strong enough – in a highly strung rage – to have murdered Agar, seemed to be their drift, but I was determined not to give them a foothold on that particular path.

'Fit enough, but not particularly strong, no,' I said, thinking of the swansneck-slimness of her trunk as I had supported her when I first examined her. But there was strength in those long, thin hands.

'Agar seems to be familiar to you, Dr Mortimer,' Moultry said.

I hesitated before I spoke. What implications would my answer have for Violet?

'Did you know Agar, doctor?' Wensley snapped.

'Yes,' I said at last.

'Did you know him well?' Moultry followed up.

'Mostly by report. I learnt that he had been La – my former patient's tutor for a brief period in India.'

'Did you meet him?' Wensley asked.

'Three or four times. I called on him at his studio in Fournier Street on two occasions, out of curiosity.'

I still had the fading bruises on my ribs to prove it.

'Just to see what he was like at home, as the saying goes, hey, doctor?' Moultry said pleasantly. 'Did you like him?'

Again I hesitated but I knew there could be only one answer.

'Agar was an entertaining man, inspector, and good company, but no, I did not like him very much.'

129

'Have you ever given Agar money, doctor?' Wensley broke in. I actually laughed.

'Certainly not!'

'Did you form any opinions as to Agar's associates on your visits to him in Spitalfields, Dr Mortimer?' the inspector asked.

'They were not the type of people I should expect to find associated with a gentleman and a scholar . . .'

'Quite!' the inspector went on. 'But Mr Agar was an artist, and it's in their line of business, so to speak, to associate with all sorts and conditions, isn't it? Did you, er, get acquainted with any of these, er, rough diamonds, doctor?'

'I did not seek to do so, inspector.'

'Can you give us any idea, then, of what relation Agar stood in with regard to Miss Nancarrow, Dr Mortimer?'

'All I know is that he was tutor to her and Lance Boynton-Leigh in Calcutta for a time, and that he was in the habit of calling on them in Ginger Lane from time to time. I know of nothing else between them.'

'I see,' the inspector said. 'And Mr Boynton-Leigh: what did you make of him, doctor? Quite a man, hey? I shouldn't like to cross him!'

'Mr Boynton-Leigh is a man of great integrity, inspector, and of remarkable moral scruple.'

'Did he ever talk to you about his relations with Agar, doctor?' Wensley put in.

'No, never.'

'Would you say Boynton-Leigh was capable of murder?' Moultry asked.

'Quite out of the question! Perhaps in an act of passion, but then he would give himself up immediately, if he didn't blow out his brains beforehand out of sheer conscience! Boynton-Leigh is above all a man of conscience, inspector. In fact, I have never met anyone else so conscientious. He would be incapable of planned, cold-blooded murder!'

Moultry exchanged a rueful glance with his subordinate, as if in confirmation of an impression.

'Could you tell us about your own whereabouts and activities from, say, yesterday teatime, doctor?' Moultry went on.

'I had no teatime, inspector! I worked through till nearly nine at the People's Dispensary in Whitechapel, then I saw my colleague on to her train – '

'Which colleague would this have been, doctor?' Moultry asked.

'Dr Violet Branscombe, inspector.'

'Oh, yes, the young lady with the bicycle! She's quite an old friend of ours, doctor! And after that?'

'When I'd left her around nine, I took a cab back here, had a bite of cold supper and turned in about eleven – '

'That's right!' my landlady piped up from the doorway. 'And my doors have been bolted ever since!'

'Righto, mum!' the inspector said. 'We won't keep you any longer. We can see ourselves out . . .'

My landlady made a muttering exit, and the inspector turned back to me.

'Dr Branscombe can verify what you've just told us, Dr Mortimer?'

'Yes,' I said, praying the while that they would not make difficulties for Violet.

Sergeant Wensley put away his notebook and pencil, and both detectives resumed their bowlers.

'That'll do for now, doctor,' Moultry said, with a smile and a nod. 'You'd better get dressed: it's none so warm this morning! May I say that it is in Miss Nancarrow's most vital interests that she should come forward as soon as possible, and if anything concerning the matters we've just discussed should come to your mind in the meantime, please don't hesitate to step round to Leman Street at any hour of the day or night: either me or Wensley here will be on duty.'

'But inspector!' I began to protest, 'Can't you tell me something more about – '

'I really should get dressed, if I were you, doctor. There's a most unseasonable chill in the air. Good morning to you!'

28

I washed and dressed in great agitation, gulped down the tea my landlady made for me, and dashed out and hailed a cab to take me to the Junior Minerva Club, where I found Violet eating breakfast in the dining room. Not that I, in my fever of speculation, could have faced breakfast at that moment at any price, though Violet took my news with remarkable sang-froid, and went on serenely buttering her toast while, from a facing chair, I recounted the details of my brush with the C.I.D. men.

'God bless the hand that struck the blow!' was her response to the news of Agar's demise, but it was uttered without the vehemence that I would have associated with surprise. 'A surer Hand than that of the Law has found him out!'

'You do not seem to be surprised at my news,' I could not help but remark.

'I should have been surprised had it happened later rather than sooner!' she replied, and attacked her toast with more vigour than ever.

'I don't give a fig now for Agar!' I said, lowering my voice, as I perceived that we had a small but growing audience among the other breakfasting members. 'It is Lavinia I am concerned with. What on earth can have become of her?'

'If the police do not choose to tell you more than they did this morning, there is nothing you can do about it: you must wait for the evening editions of the papers. They will be out early this afternoon. In the meantime, you have at least the satisfaction of knowing that she is not in the hands of Agar.'

'But his crew of pimps and bullies!' I objected. 'They will be – '

'Gone to earth, make no mistake about that! From now on you will not so much hear the name of Agar mentioned in the East End. His "lay" will have died with him.'

'And the studio in Spitalfields,' I went on. 'All those paintings . . .'

'Under police guard by now, and I'm sure they will hardly be disposed to offer us an invitation to view.'

Something occurred to me.

'Good God!' I hissed, arousing the attention of the toast-eaters at the next table, then, more quietly: 'Rosie!'

Violet said nothing, but the guarded look was still in her eyes.

'Don't you see?' I went on in a sort of urgent mutter. 'Now that Agar is dead, Rosie will be a prime suspect. She has made threats against his life in half the public houses of the East End, and now she has gone to ground. When the people she is with read of the case in the newspapers, you don't think they'll – '

There was disdain in my companion's answering glance.

'You may be quite sure, James, that they will act with the same discretion as they have shown up to now. Rosie will be perfectly safe.'

'But if only we could – '

'You must consider, too, James, that if we pursue these matters too officiously, the police may draw the conclusion that we are anxious not to unearth, but to conceal, any new evidence.'

'But that is absurd!' I objected. 'As far as we ourselves are concerned, we have cast-iron alibis for last night.'

Violet gave me another guarded look but did not take me up on the topic.

'Let us above all keep our heads, James: we shall wait for the evening papers, and then hold a council-of-war.'

I hold it to have been a dispensation, not of medicine, but of Providence, that no hapless patient was poisoned by the potions I made up that morning, such was my absorption in this latest twist in the mystery. At last I could bear it no longer, and as soon as the last patient's heels could be heard going down the stairs, I plonked the last wrapped medicine-bottle into the new helper's basket and dashed into the consulting room.

'There is something I can do!' I said as, with hasty thanks, I devoured my share of the coffee and spiced-beef sandwiches Violet had sent out for not ten minutes before. 'Inspector Moultry said that if anything came into my mind about the death of Agar, I was to look him up in Leman Street.'

'You have remembered something, then?'

'No, but what better to jog my memory than a visit to the scene of the crime?'

'Ginger Lane? But what can you do there? It will be crawling with policemen.'

'There may be some trace unremarked by the police, some feature which perhaps I have not sufficiently noticed on my previous visits, which may give some indication as to what has become of Lavinia.'

'At least it will give you something to do until the evening papers come out,' was my colleague's eminently sensible summing-up.

'And you?' I said. 'Have you anything in mind for this afternoon?'

'I have in mind a line of enquiry suggested to us by Mr Politis last Sunday, but which has been rather pushed into the background by subsequent events. I refer to the history of the family portrayed in the lost Zoffany, whose possession – or suppression – evidently meant so much to Agar – '

'Ah!' I exclaimed. 'The Fairmeads of Rainton Hall. Capital idea!'

'With particular reference to the Misses Leigh.'

'Yes, indeed! I shall be all ears at our next meeting!'

We agreed to meet again in the Junior Minerva for tea at five, and I left for Leman Street Police Station.

I simply gave my name there, and the barrier of the enquiries counter was swung up immediately to admit me to the inner corridors, where I found Moultry in the passage outside his office. He was evidently giving some last-minute instructions to a couple of plainclothes men. The men strode off, and he spotted me.

'Ah, Dr Mortimer! Speak of the devil!'

'You were expecting me, inspector?' I asked, puzzled.

'I was about to look you up, as a matter of fact.'

'Oh?'

'Yes. Wanted to know if you knew a woman called Rosie Bartlett.'

I was put immediately on the alert. Perhaps another detective was asking Violet the same question at this very moment, and if our stories did not tally . . . Nothing else for it, then: the truth.

'Yes, inspector, I do know Rosie Bartlett.'

'And may I ask how you came to know her?'

'She is an unfortunate woman – of the streets – one of the many who have sought succour at the Whitechapel People's Dispensary. I met her there.'

'Yes, I see: the connection's right enough, then.'

'The "connection" inspector? What "connection"?'

'Oh, just with an, er, account which has reached us – shall we say information received – that around midday on Tuesday the eighth of this month you were seen to enter a cab in Durward Street in company with this woman – your arm round her shoulder, in fact – the said cab having moved off into Old Montague Street. What about it, doctor?'

'It is preposterous, inspector!' I exclaimed, perfectly truthfully. 'I have travelled in no cab with Rosie Bartlett, anywhere, at any time. I will take my oath on that!'

Moultry looked crestfallen. If he had thought to start a hare there, I had spoiled his sport.

'I see, doctor,' he said. 'You're very definite on that. What were you doing, then, at that time, if I may ask?'

'I would be escorting Dr Branscombe by cab to her club in Bloomsbury,' I said, again perfectly truthfully but not, of course, adding that Violet had been dressed in Rosie's clothes, while the latter had been on her way, in Violet's clothes, to the refuge in Hackney.

'Mmm, pity,' Moultry mused out loud. 'That puts back Bartlett's last sighting by quite a bit. If there'd been anything in the story, you'd have been the last person to see her since before Agar's death.'

As I had surmised, with her public threats against the dead artist's life, poor Rosie was obviously a strong suspect in the case.

'I can only suggest, inspector, that in future you choose your informants more carefully.'

'Mmm, . . . quite, doctor!'

'And now, inspector,' I went on, 'have you any news of Miss Nancarrow?'

''Fraid not, doctor. Have you remembered anything?'

'No, inspector, but I have been going over in my mind all I

know about the case – the Ginger Lane establishment, Agar, everything – and it occurred to me that a visit to Number One, and in particular a thorough examination of Miss Nancarrow's bedroom, might jog my memory.'

'Well,' the inspector said, removing the lid from a flimsy cardboard box on the desk in front of him, 'here's something from Ginger Lane to get your teeth into for a start; or rather from the old churchyard that abuts on to the garden there.'

I leant across the desk and peered into the box. Resting on cotton wool were the large fragments of what had apparently been a powerful mirror.

'Brute of a thick mirror, that!' Moultry said. 'Must've been used for some very definite purpose, possibly scientific. What do you make of it?'

I remembered the powerful glint I had noticed at the far end of the churchyard on the sunny evening when I had made my first visit to the Boynton-Leigh house. This must clearly explain it.

'Looks like the sort of thing one might use to demonstrate the spectrum,' I suggested.

'Sort of thing a schoolmaster might use, you mean, or an artist?'

'Possibly: I'm afraid I'm not really up in such things, inspector.'

'Mmph. We shall have to make further enquiries about this object.'

'And my visit to Ginger Lane, inspector?'

'Yes, doctor, trot along there by all means! Sorry I can't go along there with you, but pressure of work, you know. Precious lot of villainy goes on between the Tower and Commercial Road! We can't be everywhere at once, though the public seems to expect it. Wensley'll be there, though: if you've any questions, he's the lad. Before you go, though – '

'Yes, inspector?'

'About Dr Branscombe . . .'

I suppose it had been foolish of me to hope that Violet might be kept out of this, especially after the investigation into the fire at our old dispensary.

'What about her, inspector?'

'You were present after the fire at her, um, practice, I understand.'

'Yes, I was.'

'Have you any particular view on that, doctor?'

'I tend towards the official view, inspector: that it was probably accidental.'

'Bad business about that poor lassie, Queenie Bryant, too.'

'A very bad business indeed, inspector!'

'I daresay Dr Branscombe was very much cut up about that. I certainly would have been in her shoes.'

'She is naturally upset about it, inspector.'

The inspector smiled a doughy sort of smile and folded his hands in front of him.

'She's quite an institution round here, you know,' he said, 'with her bicycle and all. Tell me, do you know her well?'

'She is a fine young lady!' I said with some heat. 'Straight as a die!'

'Oh, I don't doubt that, Dr Mortimer. There are schools of thought as to lady doctors, of course, but for my money she's doing a grand job here. But that's not the same thing. Do you actually know her?'

I was genuinely nonplussed for a moment.

'Now that you put it like that, inspector, I cannot really say I do. I know her background, her work, and I esteem her, and like her enormously, but . . .'

It was more than that now, and I think Moultry must have guessed as much. He smiled, and put his head slightly on one side.

'Yes, doctor, that's what I meant, that "but . . ." But no matter. Perhaps you can help me with some more recent information about your colleague.'

'What is that?'

'Where she spent Monday night?'

I sat bolt upright in my chair.

'What? Why, at her club, where she always spends the night. Look here, inspector, where is all this leading?'

The doughy smirk vanished, and the inspector's stare grew harder.

137

'Towards the detection and conviction of the murderer of John Agar!'

'But it is fantastic to suggest that Dr Branscombe could have had a hand in this! You cannot imagine what it would cost her practice in terms of retaining the confidence of the local people to have C.I.D. men continually tramping up and down her stairs at the dispensary. Especially after the fire, and all she has gone through.'

'Oh, but I can imagine it, doctor, and that's why I haven't been to, er, tramp up her stairs there about this particular matter yet.'

'You have already questioned her, then, inspector?'

'After we'd called on you earlier on this morning, we paid a discreet visit to Dr Branscombe's residential club in Bloomsbury. Absolutely no tramping or clumping, I assure you, doctor!'

So that was why she had seemed so unsurprised to hear my 'news' of Agar's death that morning.

'And she gave no satisfactory account of herself, inspector? I find that hard to – '

'She did not, Dr Mortimer. In fact, she refused to speak at all!'

I was frankly staggered. It seemed from this that Violet must be positively provoking the thing she must have dreaded most in the world. I felt that I must do something to limit the damage this apparent stance of hers might cause.

'I am to see Dr Branscombe this afternoon, inspector, and I shall speak to her most earnestly about what you have told me. Allow me to say that I am completely convinced that there will be a simple explanation to this, and I will do my best to persuade her to talk to you about the matter. In the meantime, inspector, you will stay your hand?'

'I can make no such promise, doctor, but I repeat that I will be very pleased to receive some sort of explanation from her just as soon as possible, very pleased. I hope I'm not a heavy-handed man, but this is a murder case, and time is of the essence!'

'Yes, yes, inspector. I take your point!'

I thanked him and got up to go, and he ushered me to the door with all of his initial easy-going cordiality, repeating his invitation to consult him on anything that might come to mind.

'Any time, Dr Mortimer, day or night!'

I regained the street, and had much to think about as I made my way up Commercial Street. Did I really know Violet Branscombe?

<h1 style="text-align:center">29</h1>

The constable on duty at the door of the house in Ginger Lane directed me straight to Sergeant Wensley, who was standing on the first step of the stairs talking to a man in a top hat who had an attaché case in his hand. The detective gave me a sharp glance from his perpetually narrowed eyes and a curt nod, and I waited a moment or two till the conversation was over and the top-hatted man had bustled fussily out through the front door.

'What can I do for you, then, doctor?' Wensley said without enthusiasm as he stepped down on to the chequered floor of the hallway.

'I thought a visit to the house here would jog my memory as to the events surrounding – '

'I don't remember our having told you anything about Agar having been murdered here, doctor.'

'I was going to say,' I went on, 'as to the events surrounding Miss Nancarrow's disappearance, which you did tell me about. And wasn't Agar murdered here, then?'

Wensley merely grunted and intensified his stare.

'D'you want to see over the whole house?' he asked.

'Only the rooms I'm familiar with, sergeant: Mr Boynton-Leigh's study and Miss Nancarrow's bedroom.'

Until that moment, I had been too put out by Inspector Moultry's disconcerting line of questioning at Leman Street Police Station to even think of the Boynton-Leigh ménage, now evidently minus Lavinia as well as Lance.

'Are Mr Boynton-Leigh and his attendants here now, sergeant?' I asked.

Wensley paused on the stairs and turned round.

'Evening papers not out yet, then, doctor?'

'No. At least, I haven't seen any on the way here.'

'Hmph. I'll give you five minutes' head start on 'em, then. Mr Archibald Boynton-Leigh's in police custody, on suspicion – '

'Good Lord!' I exclaimed. 'You really think Boynton-Leigh has – '

'I said on suspicion, doctor! And it gets more and more suspicious the longer he keeps mum!'

'You mean he won't say anything about Lavinia's disappearance, or about Agar's death?'

'We'll start with Miss Nancarrow's room, doctor. You lead the way, please.'

By going without hesitation to Lavinia's bedroom, I seemed to have passed some sort of hurdle in Wensley's apparently fathomless fund of suspicion. I paused at the threshold.

'And Mrs Penruddock? Ord?' I asked.

'Skedaddled!' was the laconic reply. 'And if Ord's who we think he is, he's got plenty of other reasons besides this affair for making himself scarce! An old pal of ours, is Mr Ord!'

Hope rose in my heart. If the departure of Demmy from Ginger Lane at the same time as that of her 'baby' had been more than coincidental, I could scarcely doubt that at least Lavinia would not lack faithful attendance wherever she might be now.

We passed through the door into the silent bedroom where an air of oppressive stillness reigned. I looked around quickly, but could discern no fundamental difference in the appearance of the room from when I had last been in it. It was then that my gaze fell upon the splendid bronze candlesticks which continued to keep guard against the wall under the windows on either side of the bed. Something was not quite right about them. I stepped towards them, under Wensley's keen gaze. That was it! The stout red candles were a good handsbreadth shorter in their sconces, yet the visible inch or so of each squared-off wooden wick was quite uncharred! I reached out my hand.

'Just a minute, doctor!' Wensley snapped. 'You're not to touch anything!'

I pondered what I had just seen and wondered if I could have been mistaken, but no: the proportions of candles to holders were noticeably different. Odd. I walked slowly round the room, looking here and there, but I noticed nothing else. The age- and grime-obscured paintings were in their usual positions on the walls. I nodded to the sergeant, and we stepped on to the landing, where he again gave me precedence until we were in the master's study. Here no effort of Wensley's could possibly hide from me the implications of the chalked, slim masculine outline on the rug which the forensic investigators evidently had not thought worth their while to take away, and which covered the floor in front of the mandarin's desk-table. Nor could the complete absence of any visible traces of blood within the area of the carpet described by the chalk conceal another, equally inevitable implication.

'I see you have quite a puzzle on your hands, sergeant,' I remarked. 'Whatever happened to Agar, it's Lombard Street to a China orange he shed no blood on that rug!'

'Hmph!' Wensley snorted. 'Rum business all round. If we brought this forward in evidence, any Grand Jury would laugh the case out of court!'

Things were taking shape in my mind. Agar's body had borne no traces of blood when it had met the rug, so, barring poison, strangulation and sandbagging, it had been brought there after his death, long after death, if the blood – assuming there had been any – had had time to reach an innocuous dryness. But where, in that case, had the body been brought from? I inspected the rest of the study, but could find nothing which jarred with my former impressions of it except, yes, the library steps seemed distinctly more ricketty than when I had first set eyes on them, with, I fancied, a notable list to port. I turned to face Wensley again.

'That it, doctor?'

I nodded, and this time the sergeant escorted me out on to the landing.

'Well, doctor?' he said. 'Has your memory been jogged?'

'I'm afraid not, sergeant. At least, not yet,' I said, as he led me downstairs to the front door.

'Tell me, doctor,' Wensley said as we stood in the doorway. 'What d'you smoke?'

'Smoke, sergeant? Cigarettes, usually. Why?'

'What brand, doctor?'

'No brand: I roll my own with mild Virginia.'

Wensley drew an envelope out of his pocket, opened the unsealed flap, and took out a small white cardboard tube, at the end of which was the fag-end of a cigarette. He held the object up to me.

'Know anybody who smokes these?' he asked.

'Foreigners mostly, I should think. They look like a Russian make. Where did you find it?'

Wensley studied me for a moment, then evidently decided to throw me a bone.

'It was found in the gutter just outside Dr Branscombe's old dispensary,' he said. 'And you don't know who might have chucked it there?'

'No, sergeant,' I replied. 'I don't know who threw it there. I hope you find him, though.'

Wensley nodded and left me alone on the doorstep, and I recalled when I had last seen someone throw away such a cigarette butt. It had been on the stairs up to Agar's studio in Fournier Street, and the smoker had worn a cap with a stiff, shiny visor. He had had pale eyes like a wolf's.

30

The first thing I did on regaining Cobb Street was to buy an evening paper, and I unfolded it as I made my way to a cabstand. What I saw on the front page made me halt and draw in my breath sharply. Under the headline BLACK BEAUTY MURDER was a crude police-court type of sketch, or rather caricature, of Lavinia. There was something about the mouth and eyes that suggested tigerish ferocity and nameless passions, and there was a rider: WHO HAS SEEN HER? The text read as follows:

At about six o'clock yesterday morning, the body of Mr John Agar, an artist who resided in Fournier Street, Spitalfields, was found at the Aldgate mansion of Mr Archibald Boynton-Leigh, a retired Calcutta merchant of reclusive habits. Mr

142

Agar, the police report, apparently died of a stab-wound from a short, sharp instrument . . .

I immediately thought of Rosie Bartlett's scissors . . . The report went on:

Between midnight and one o'clock on the same morning Mr Boynton-Leigh had already made a sensational appearance, with his coachman, at Leman Street Police Station, where he had reported the disappearance of his ward, Miss Lavinia Nancarrow, along with her former nurse and companion, Mrs Demelza Penruddock, on the eve of Miss Nancarrow's twenty-first birthday.

Mr Boynton-Leigh's son Lance, we understand, has recently undergone a serious operation to the brain in France, and is in a critical condition in hospital there. The former Calcutta merchant reported the presence of Mr Agar's body to the police at about five o'clock this morning, and as he is at present assisting them with their enquiries behind closed doors, we have been unable as yet to secure an interview with him.

The deceased, Mr Agar, aged thirty-four, was a cultivated bachelor, a graduate of the Slade School of Art. Mr Agar had turned his hand to many employments while striving to make his name as an artist, and had travelled in many lands. Among those of his Spitalfields neighbours who have any knowledge of English we have encountered a marked unwillingness to express any view on the case.

As of this going to press, the police have refused to be drawn as to any definite link between the disappearance of Miss Nancarrow and the apparent discovery of Mr Agar's body at her home only hours later. Inspector Hector Moultry, of 'H' Division (Leman Street) is handling the case, and states that he is for the moment treating the two events as separate occurrences, and urgently appeals to the public for any information they may be able to furnish concerning the death of the unfortunate Mr Agar, or the whereabouts of Miss Nancarrow, who is remarkable for a streak of pure silver hair along the whole length of her hair-parting . . .

There followed by the way of padding a quantity of superfluous commentary on the strange, reclusive habits of the denizens of Number One, Ginger Lane, as well as much on the supposed dangers inherent in the alarming growth of 'alien' immigration into the East End, a topic which was resumed in the editorial column a few pages on. I turned over the rag impatiently for the 'stop press' column on the back page, where I found, under the heading BLACK BEAUTY MURDER CASE confirmation of the disappearance of the grim coachman, Ord.

As my cab trundled along the dusty streets I sank back in my seat and tried to take in the experiences of the afternoon. It was clear, then, as far as the moulders of popular opinion were concerned, that Lavinia was now the Black Beauty Murderess. On the face of it, of course, there was every reason to see her in that light. She vanishes inexplicably, then a dead man is found in the house where she lives. Therefore . . . But if a man is killed by a jab from a short, sharp instrument, why is there no blood on the rug on which his body is found? And Lord! What on earth did Violet mean by refusing to give the police an alibi for the night of the murder? Then that disconcerting question Moultry had put to me concerning her: did I know her? Not her qualities – strong, proud, stubborn, great-hearted – but her life. What had her life been before I had first laid eyes on her bicycle wheels? On that count, no, inspector, I did not know Violet Branscombe! Nor for that matter – even less so – did I know Lavinia, apart from her qualities: beauty (what beauty!); eager vitality; hunger for experience. By their deeds I should know them.

As to Violet, she was full of her afternoon's activities over tea at the Junior Minerva, her researches into the Boynton family having borne fruit. There was however only one subject I wished to discuss with her in the light of my chat with Inspector Moultry, and indeed, her eager tone and attitude were exactly those of someone who seeks to fend off a painful topic with bright conversation on another tack. I listened with all the attention I could muster, while preparing in my mind my line of approach in the matter of her seemingly defective alibi.

'First of all,' she began, as she poured out my tea, 'I consulted the *Gazetteer*, and found a Boynton in Yorkshire, not far from Bridlington. Now there is a Boynton Hall there, but it has long been the seat of the Stricklands, quite outside the scope of our enquiries, as is Boynton Hall in Barmston, also near Bridlington. My next stop was the College of Heralds, where I learnt that the Boyntons are armigerous. From Adam de Boynton, a Hull fish-monger who, having made his fortune in that town, in 1377 married into an estate in North Grimston, not far from Malton, in the Yorkshire Wolds. Well, the family had its ups and downs in the succeeding centuries, and by the 1750s was in dire straits, until its fortunes were recouped by Richard Cary Boynton, who went out as a trader to Calcutta in 1760 – '

'Calcutta!' I exclaimed, replacing my cup in its saucer with a clatter, and forgetting for the moment the grave matter of Violet's alibi.

'Yes!' she went on. 'Archibald Boynton-Leigh's branch of the family! I was on their trail!'

'And the, er, manor?' I asked. 'Are there still Boyntons there?'

'I have wired to Beck Hall today.'

'You know the name of the manor-house, then.'

'Presently. There is better to come.'

'Go on!'

'I had an hour or so in hand before tea, so it crossed my mind to call on Mr Politis in Bloomsbury – '

'Zoffany!' I said, and with a little smile of triumph, Violet rubbed her hands on her napkin, then took a stout brown-paper envelope, backed with cardboard, from her reticule.

'Mr Politis is such a dear!' she said, as she carefully drew out a photograph from the envelope and held it out to me. 'From his catalogue: he insisted I borrow it.' It was my turn to rub my hands on my napkin, then I took the photograph, which was of an obviously eighteenth-century portrait of a blunt-featured girl of about twenty with cold arrogance in her eyes. The likeness conveyed nothing at all to me. At the foot of the photograph there was the caption: PORTRAIT OF MISS BOYNTON OF BECK HALL, 1779.

'Miss Boynton,' I said, 'not Miss Leigh. Still, it is a definite discovery: you are to be congratuated!'

'Thank you, kind sir! The painting, which incidentally was by way of being a potboiler of Zoffany's, and not in particular demand from collectors – '

'With the possible exception of a certain fanatical German-American gentleman, and his late agent – '

'Indeed. Well, the picture is still in the family, in the form of Miss Theodora Boynton, of Beck Hall, North Grimston, near Malton in Yorkshire.'

'We must follow this up!' I said eagerly. 'Heaven knows what it might lead to, especially if Agar has already been up there! How did you couch the wire?'

'That we would be most obliged to be allowed to visit Beck Hall to view the painting.'

'Good,' I said, putting down my now-empty cup. 'Now, Violet, a most serious fact has been brought to my attention by Inspector Moultry – '

'They have been questioning you about Rosie? I simply told them the truth about my – our – movements on the eighth. I trust, James, that you too – '

'Yes, yes, I told them the same. It is not that. No, I refer to the matter – which I own I find astonishing – of your apparently refusing to give Moultry any confirmation of your whereabouts on Monday night.'

The shoulders of my flaxen-haired comrade-in-arms straightened in the best parade-ground manner, and her lips set into a most uncompromising line.

'Then the inspector has not respected my confidence! Really, James, I must insist – '

'No, Violet, it will not do! I assume the right of a – a loyal comrade to demand that you give the police an account of your movements on Monday night. You owe it to – '

'It is out of my hands for the moment, James, but you have my assurance that the situation is a temporary one, and that I shall put things right in good time.'

'But no truces can be called for individuals in a murder enquiry, Violet. Can you not simply give Moultry such times and places as will satisfy him that you were not in the vicinity of Ginger Lane late last night, without naming anyone in particular? It would after all be up to him to disprove your alibi.'

'An alibi without corroboration would be more incriminating than complete silence, James, and once embarked upon that course I should sooner or later be entrapped into lying. That I will not do, for the sake of the public trust I hold. And besides, a citizen has the right to refuse to speak to the police: I repeat that my silence will only be temporary.'

'But this is murder! The police will not bother their heads over constitutional niceties or legal fictions! And think of your reputation – that of the dispensary – if you are arrested!'

A calm half-smile settled round Violet's lips.

'You have put your finger on it, James. I am certain that if I established an alibi by revealing the person involved, my work in the East End would be finished, and my name there would henceforth be mud!'

'It is Rosie Bartlett, then, that you are protecting!'

My companion made no answer to this, but instead took my hand in hers across the table, and fixed her eyes on mine.

'James,' she said, in a low, urgent tone, 'if I never ask anything of you again, will you grant me one thing?'

'What is it? Name it.'

'That you allow me, without further question, to deal with this matter in my own time, as I fully intend to do. The fact is, I have given my word. Surely you would not wish me to go back on it, and – besides the grievous consequences I have mentioned – lose my self-respect?'

I saw it was no use, and that I must for the foreseeable future work in the dark, as far as the motives of my closest associate were concerned. But I was inclined to ascribe her attitude not so much to self-respect as to a mulish pride.

'In that case,' I said wearily, 'I must respect your wishes. You are the best judge of your own conduct. I shall not mention it further.'

I felt her hand squeeze mine, a grip which was relaxed, and the hand withdrawn, as soon as the avid glances of the tea-takers at the surrounding tables were turned on us.

'You will understand, James!' Violet murmured fervently. 'It is for the best! And now your news . . .'

I gave it in detail, in spite of the uneasiness I felt at the peril in which she was so wilfully placing herself. Violet's eyes narrowed.

'They have no real evidence!' she murmured. 'The lack of blood on the rug clearly indicates that the body was laid there long after Agar's death.'

'I suspect that Agar died earlier on that night,' I replied, 'possibly while Boynton-Leigh and Ord were galloping around looking for Lavinia. Or else why would Ord have driven his master straight into the lion's mouth – Leman Street Police Station – knowing that Agar's body was lying in the house they had just left, and that he himself, especially with his apparently shady past, would be a prime suspect as soon as the police got wind of the murder? God help whoever the police can trace who might have been seen near the house at that time! They will worry him like terriers.'

'If they have no real evidence,' Violet went on, 'surely the police cannot hold Mr Boynton-Leigh for much longer? Didn't Sergeant Wensley say something about a Grand Jury? I believe the police have to present a convincing case to them before anyone can be brought to trial. Unless – '

'Yes?'

'Unless he has already confessed in order to save Lavinia. If Boynton-Leigh is nearly so devoted to her as you say he is, he will surely be prepared to do even that in order to protect her from suspicion.'

'Mmm,' I murmured in turn. 'That would be perfectly in character for him. And if he confesses and stays silent, refusing legal assistance, they can charge him and hold him without evidence. Hang him, even, if it comes to that!'

'Can one be hanged on a confession alone?'

'I believe there have been precedents and, really, once the police have brought someone before the courts, whatever happens to the accused afterwards is no longer their responsibility. Like Pilate, they can wash their hands of him. I scarcely think an officer like, say, Wensley, would have many qualms in a situation like that!'

Violet gave a shudder.

'I know him by repute,' she said. 'He is by all accounts a devouringly ambitious and relentless officer! Do you know what they call him in Whitechapel?'

'No, what?'

'Weasel Wensley! He is a sergeant already, and he cannot be out of his twenties!'

We were not to know then that Frederick Wensley would go on to be one of the founders of the Flying Squad, and retire, forty years later, as – to quote a press encomium – 'The most famous detective in England'.

'Violet,' I said in a low voice, 'we must be constantly on our guard, and upon that score, it shall now be my turn to demand a promise from you.'

'What is it, James?'

'From now on, apart from the matter we have just discussed, there will be no secrets between us.'

'I willingly promise you that, James.'

Evening surgery was over by a quarter-to-seven and, after I had dropped my colleague off at her club again and taken supper there with her, I made my way back to my rooms for an early night, for I felt absolutely done-in after the day's turmoil. My mind, however, was racing to such an extent that I only passed what the French call a 'white night' of little and fitful sleep. On the Wednesday morning, then, I was sitting half-awake over my breakfast when my landlady gave me a message, brought by an Express Messenger from Violet in Bloomsbury. The text consisted of only three words, but they caused me to halt my spoon short of the top of my boiled egg: LAVINIA NANCARROW FOUND.

31

I was all agog on meeting Violet in the common room of the Junior Minerva, but a bucket of cold water was promptly thrown over my expectations when, without a word, she simply handed me a photograph. It was of a stained, crumbling headstone, with – only just legible despite the excellent quality of the photograph itself – the following inscription:

SACRED TO THE MEMORY

OF

LAVINIA NANCARROW

OB. 11TH JUNE 1797

AGED 4 MONTHS

D. OF CAPTAIN MATTHEW NANCARROW

BENGAL ARTILLERY

AND OF

HIS SPOUSE LOETITIA

SUFFER LITTLE CHILDREN TO COME UNTO ME

'Your informant's report has arrived at last from India, then,' I said somewhat wearily, as I sank back, disappointed, in my cane chair.

'Oh!' Violet exclaimed hoarsely, as she read the disappointment in my eyes. 'I am sorry, James, but I have been so excited by my news from India that I fear I have broken the news about Miss Nancarrow rather melodramatically. You must have thought – '

'No matter,' I said, 'and Lord knows we have been waiting eagerly enough for this stuff to arrive! But where on earth – '

'The stone was in South Parks Road Cemetery in Calcutta.'

'Yes, but however did your informant get the idea of looking there?'

'I think I have already told you that Mr Kearney was formerly with the Pinkerton's Bureau in New York, and has now set up on his own account in Calcutta. He writes that in this country, when someone needs spare identities for some reason – usually for election purposes – the most popular place they look for them is in the nearest cemetery. There is more than one European cemetery in Calcutta, of course, but he is evidently terribly thorough. I have a whole parcel of reports from him.'

To illustrate her point, Violet waved a stout packet, wrapped in waterproof paper, over the little cane table on which it had been lying.

'And Boynton-Leigh?' I asked.

Her face flushed with enthusiasm – how charmingly ingenuous she was on these occasions – Violet drew from the open packet a thick wad of folded foolscap, densely covered with purple typewritten text: Yankee efficiency at its peak.

'All here!' she said breathlessly. 'But we will not have time to do it all justice this morning . . .'

I looked at my watch: ten-to-eight already. We would have to be making for the dispensary.

'The photograph would indicate, then,' I said as we went to the door, 'that Lavinia's name was simply chosen at random from some long-forgotten family line in the Calcutta cemetery. So much for Boynton-Leigh's story of her being the orphan of a dear friend. What an old humbug!'

'Not entirely,' Violet demurred, as we stood on the doorstep while the porter hailed a cab. 'There could be poetic truth in it. perhaps the dear friend was his lost young self.'

'Suggesting that Lavinia was fathered by him in his unhappy, unregenerate youth, so that, after he had seen the light later on, the wayward young fellow he had been was dead to him.'

'Something of the sort,' my colleague agreed, as we got into the cab, 'and the only link with the old life – Lavinia – would have to be kept quite separate.'

'In Simla,' I said, 'so that he could carry on in Calcutta in a state of staid self-righteousness: church sidesman, and all! I repeat, what an old humbug! Anyway, at least he had the decency to give her a good start in life, with a nurse who clearly dotes on her, and a good education. And then to bring her into his home when Mrs Boynton-Leigh was out of the way at last.'

'All goes well,' Violet mused. out loud, as the cabwheels rumbled hollowly over the wooden sets of that stretch of road that fronted Blackfriars Station, whence we would go on by train to Whitechapel. 'All goes well until Agar is appointed tutor to Lance and Lavinia, then the "brainstorm", as Percy Tooke put it, and Boynton-Leigh ups sticks and brings his little brood to Aldgate, with virtual purdah for Lavinia. What did happen in Calcutta? It will be a treat to delve into Kearney's report!'

We got out of the cab, paid the cabbie, and dived into the smoke and clatter of the station, our speculations stilled till we should have more leisure to indulge in them.

The morning went pretty busily at the dispensary, and at

about a quarter-past-twelve, just as the last patient had left and I was dismissing the bottle-laden delivery boy, the clump of masculine boots on the stairs heralded an unexpected visitor. I left the door of the pharmacy slightly ajar, so that I could hear what might pass in the adjoining consulting room, and laid hold of my loaded stick. I listened and waited.

I heard Sergeant Wensley announce himself, then refuse Violet's offer of a chair. My heart sank. Since the gamekeeper, Inspector Moultry, had failed to get what he wanted out of her, he had sent his retriever!

'I won't beat about the bush, doctor,' Wensley said. 'I now require you to give me an account of your movements from the late evening – say nine o'clock – of Monday, the twenty-first of July, to the morning of Tuesday, the twenty-second of July.'

'I have already told Inspector Moultry, sergeant,' Violet explained, 'that I spent that time in professional consultation, and that I was nowhere near the house where Mr Agar met his death.'

'We now have reason to believe that after you left your residential club in Bloomsbury at approximately ten-past ten on Monday night, you took a cab, which put you down at about eleven o'clock at the corner of Greatorex Street and Whitechapel Road, within half-an-hour's easy walking distance from One, Ginger Lane.'

'Did I not leave a message with the club porter, to explain to any emergency-callers that I might be absent for upwards of an hour?'

'We also have reason to believe that you went caped and veiled!'

'It was late at night, sergeant, in the East End!'

'You were then lost to view till yesterday – Tuesday – morning. You will admit that you had ample time – even on foot – to visit Ginger Lane, with time in hand there, before returning to the area of the Whitechapel Road, or wherever you went to after that.'

'And if I'd walked in the opposite direction, sergeant, I would have had ample time to take a spot of midnight supper with the Khedive of Egypt on his steam-yacht at Wapping Old Stairs!'

I groaned inwardly: there would now be consequences.

'Very well, doctor,' Wensley said with a sort of quiet menace. 'I see that we will have to carry on this conversation at another place.'

'Am I then under arrest? I believe some sort of warrant is customary.'

'Not for the moment, but I must ask you in the meantime not to leave the country or in any way remove yourself from Her Majesty's jurisdiction. Morning, ma'am!'

The boots clumped again on the stairs and died away. I rushed into the consulting room.

'Now you have really done it, Violet!' I protested. 'You will now be treated as a hostile witness, and taken down under warrant to make a statement at Leman Street Police Station. This time they will make you talk.'

'My conscience is clear, James. They cannot make me talk when there is nothing to talk about. Really, another offence should be added to the Statute Book: the police's wasting the ratepayers' money!'

'But what do you propose to do?'

'Join you at Cohen's for a capital luncheon. Then we shall retreat to the Club to do justice to Mr Kearney's voluminous report from India.'

32

The report turned out to be really admirable, though my interest in it was tempered by my uneasiness at what had happened at the dispensary just before we had gone out to luncheon. I was expecting to hear the relentless clump of Wensley's boots on the faded carpets of the club common room at any moment. Violet, however, was as imperturbable as some Bloomsbury Boadicea, and pored over the papers with undiminished relish.

'Mmm . . .' she murmured, as she adjusted her pince-nez and brought a typewritten sheet up to her eyes. 'Kearney could find no record of any birth of a child of the name of Lavinia Nancarrow, a year on either side of her supposed birth-date of July the twenty-second, 1869.'

'Do you think there is any significance in that?' I asked. 'Any financial interest served by obfuscation of the date of her twenty-first birthday?'

'As far as we know, Lavinia Nancarrow has no financial resources whatsoever besides what Boynton-Leigh may be prepared to allow her. What in fact do we know? Ah!'

Violet tapped the sheet with her forefinger.

'This at least seems substantial: Mrs Penruddock – the nurse Demmy – leased a bungalow in Simla on the tenth of October, 1869 – '

'Lavinia would have been nearly three months old.'

'Assuming she was born on the date suggested in 1869,' Violet said in qualification. 'This is interesting: "Lavinia Nancarrow was enrolled at Madame Ropars' School for Infants, September 1875." She is taking on reality! But instead of going on to the Bishop Cotton's School, the recognised place of education in Simla for the children of respectable folk who could not afford to have them educated in England, she goes on to Madame Ropars' Junior, then Senior establishments till she's nearly sixteen.'

'Obscurity,' I suggested. 'Boynton-Leigh could certainly have afforded to send her to the Bishop Cotton place.'

'To further set her apart, we learn that most of her lessons at Madame Ropars' establishment were conducted in French. But here: this brings us up-to-date. Mrs Boynton-Leigh dies in Calcutta on the twenty-first of September, 1885, and Demmy gives up the lease of the Simla bungalow on the eighth of November that year.'

'That corresponds exactly with Lance's account of Lavinia's having appeared in Calcutta six weeks after his mother's death,' I said.

Violet laughed her throaty laugh.

'According to the caretaker of the Boynton-Leigh house in Calcutta,' she went on, 'when questioned by Kearney, Boynton-Leigh showed "much bobbery . . ." '

'I beg your pardon?'

'"Bobbery": anger. He showed much bobbery, then, around the New Year of 1889, this being followed, in time if not in consequence, by his purchase, on January the twentieth, of one-way steamship tickets to England by British India boat for himself, Lance, Lavinia and Demmy.'

'So,' I summed up, 'they all end up in Ginger Lane, Lance being packed off to Dartmouth shortly thereafter, and Lavinia into purdah. And Agar?'

'Rather little. Agar seems to have fallen between two stools in India: he was neither a tourist nor a salaried servant of the Raj in any capacity, and he certainly wasn't engaged in trade, at least not locally. India is above all a country where everyone has a place, and if by some chance one does not fall into this pattern, it is very easy to leave no mark at all on the country, as far as officialdom is concerned. Unless one commits some glaring crime, and the police are involved, it is relatively easy to pass through the country unnoticed.'

'You are not telling me that Agar managed to perform this Indian Rope Trick!'

'No, there is one exception to the rule: the club. For many Europeans there the club is their identity: one could say that they exist by virtue of their being mirrored by its conventions. It is the one and only way of knowing how they are getting on as members of European society there. In Agar's case, membership of a top-hole club would have been invaluable in his quest for Zoffany paintings, always provided, of course, that he had no recourse to anything remotely resembling vulgar touting for trade. That would have earned him immediate blackballing.'

'Some form of temporary membership, you mean?' I asked.

'Yes, and in this case the Bengal Club, the top of the heap! That is, for the higher reaches of business, the old merchant class. The Indian Civil Service – the "Heaven Born" – have other outlets, and the military their messes.'

'And who better to put Agar up for temporary membership than Boynton-Leigh, most "burra" of all the burra sahibs!'

'You have it!' Violet confirmed. 'Kearney has been able to trace his election to October 1888. He must have timed his arrival in Calcutta to just before the advent of the Cold Weather, when the influential members of the European community would be returning from the hill-stations.'

'And his departure?'

'From India? We don't know exactly. But from the Club: now that is interesting . . .'

Violet drew the paper even closer to the lenses of her pince-nez, and I squirmed until my cane chair squeaked.

'What is interesting?' I said. 'I am on tenterhooks!'

My confederate's eyebrows rose, then she laid down the sheaf of papers and looked straight into my eyes.

'Hijras!' she said mysteriously.

'What on earth are they?'

'Hijras,' Violet repeated. 'Indian eunuchs. A sort of caste of low female impersonators. They are hired to bestow good luck at Hindoo weddings and births, and to entertain raffish bloods at "smokers" and so forth. They sing, dance, play musical instruments and do . . . other things. Except for the brief appearances at weddings and births I have mentioned, they are kept at arm's length by all decent people. To be known as a consort of hijras in India is to be a social leper.'

'And I take it Agar's addiction to such, er, entertainments reached the ears of the Club secretary?'

'Yes,' Violet said. 'It seems Kearney has an inside correspondent in the Club, who told him that the Secretary learnt through the servants' grapevine – everywhere and inescapable in India! – that Agar was in the habit of smuggling hijras into his quarters late at night, but one at a time, and there was no music or dancing.'

'When would this have been?'

'Round about the Christmas of 1888, a few weeks before the Boynton-Leigh household left so abruptly for England.'

'This casts a light on Agar's, er, preferences . . .'

'Quite,' Violet agreed, 'and it could scarcely have gone unnoticed by Boynton-Leigh, his sponsor at the Club. He must have dismissed Agar as the young people's tutor in pretty short order. And of course Agar couldn't possibly have stayed on in Calcutta.'

'But that in itself would not have forced Boynton-Leigh to

leave the country too,' I said. 'Even in the unlikely event of his having done so because of Agar's conduct, there is the fact that he seems to have taken up with him again as soon as he had followed the Boynton-Leigh ménage back to England. We have still to establish the exact nature of the hold Agar must have had over them. We see the jerkings of the puppets, and the sardonic leer of the puppetmaster above the screen: if only we could see the strings!'

'One thing seems clear,' Violet said, 'and that is that Lavinia Nancarrow – or whoever she really is – is not the orphan-of-a-friend of Boynton-Leigh's.'

'I am convinced that she is his natural daughter,' I said, 'which calls up another spectre – '

'Ah!' Violet whispered. 'You mean some unnatural passion?'

'It would explain her earlier unease at remaining under his roof, in spite of her late protestation of her belief in his good intentions towards her – and God knows what coercion may have been responsible for that!'

My companion's expression clouded and grew grim.

'The drugs, James,' she said. 'The drugs! Do you think he could have used them on her to force her to . . .'

'Murky waters!' I said.

'But that is not the last skeleton in the Boynton-Leigh cupboard,' my colleague went on. 'It seems his father, Richard Tenniel Boynton, was a decided old rip.'

'It is hard to see Boynton-Leigh as anyone's son.'

'According to Kearney, he was one of the old brigade of Peninsular adventurers: he had fought in the Mahratta and Sikh Wars, served several native rulers as a mercenary, and made and run through several fortunes before he was forty. He was one of the last Calcutta nabobs to keep a beebee-khana, too.'

'What, pray, is a "beebee-khana"?'

'It means a "ladies' house": a harem of native women. Quite the thing in the earlier years of the century, but the custom began to be frowned upon once British wives started to be shipped in in growing numbers. When Richard Boynton married Rachel Leigh – she was a Bristol tobacco-heiress – he was well over forty and set in his ways, but his new wife's large fortune was by way of being his last hope, so out went the harem!'

'And I'll warrant Boynton-Leigh has a number of unacknowledged half-brothers and sisters dotted about the Subcontinent. But these speculations are worse then useless without solid evidence, for they only cloud our judgments. We must have more evidence. If only we could find some new line.'

'But perhaps we have one,' Violet said brightly, as she searched among the papers on the table, until, with a smile of triumph, she thrust a sheet of pale blue notepaper into my hand. I read out what was written there.

Dear Dr Branscombe,

It is kind of you to remember our poor pictures. There are so few left now to come and enjoy them with me. Do please come down and stay at Beck Hall any time you wish, and I include your Dr Mortimer in this invitation. We are quiet here, and there are none of your London airs about us, but the country round about is not without its charm. Loftus, the innkeeper of the Gloucester Arms, will drive you up to the Hall.

I met your dear father at Tunbridge Wells with Mama in '59, not long after the Mutiny. What a fine man he was! I look forward to seeing you here. God bless you, my dear! Very truly yours, Theodora Boynton.

'I almost forget to tell you about it,' Violet explained, 'amid the excitement caused by the arrival of Kearney's material from India.'

'Excellent!' I replied. 'Let us take up the invitation this very weekend: strike while the iron is hot.'

Violet looked away from me and her voice seemed without conviction.

'Yes, do let us, James . . .'

'We need every scrap of information we can glean about the days and ways of Jack Agar,' I said, 'and I can hardly credit that he would have let a Zoffany escape him, however disconsidered this particular example might have been among the connoisseurs, and however deep it might be buried in the wilds of Yorkshire!'

158

I paused in some trepidation before I made my next statement, for I did not wish to seem as if I were trying to go back on a pledge. 'Now, Violet, I cannot forbear from mentioning the matter on which I gave my promise this afternoon. I mean the matter of Wensley's visit.'

The back of my comrade-in-arms stiffened in her cane chair as if she were bracing herself for an Afghan charge.

'Oh, make no mistake,' I said. 'I have given my promise, and I shall not attempt to broach the reasons behind the matter under discussion, but for God's sake, Violet! I can smell the danger you are in! I beg you, if you have any consideration for me, any thought for your – our – work, will you tell me when you intend to give the police an account of your movements on Monday night?'

Violet looked at me gently for a while, then spoke in a husky whisper.

'I shall act as soon as the time is ripe, James, that is a promise!'

33

At noon the next day we sat down in the dispensary consulting room to a sandwich luncheon. Our mood was sombre, set by Wensley's warning on the previous day: we knew that the axe was about to fall. For a while we ate in silence.

'James,' Violet finally said, 'if I am detained . . .'

'Yes, Violet? If you are detained . . .'

'Will you please inform Eleanor Ramsbotham at the New Woman's Hospital in Seymour Place. She will appoint a helper for you here.'

'Very well, Violet, my dear, but for the last time, won't you – '

She shook her head and smiled calmly, then stretched out her hand across the table and, grasping mine, gave it a squeeze.

'All will be clear soon, dearest James. You will know it has been for the best.'

I reflected ruefully that though I might be her 'dearest James',

I was evidently deemed not to be worthy of her deepest confidence. Even then I had still fully to learn that, once pledged, Violet Branscombe's word was set in granite.

'And you will go up to Beck Hall?' she asked quietly.

'Yes, I will, Violet. I shall see what is to be done there in our case.'

Just then there was a gentle tap on the inner door, not at all the sort of knock we had been bracing ourselves for.

'Come in!' Violet called out in firm tones.

Percy Tooke, out of breath, and with his eyes glittering, stepped in soundlessly.

'Tooke!' I exclaimed. 'I had expected to hear from you long ere this!'

'No time for that!' the surveyor gasped. 'Wensley! Followed him from Leman Street. He's detailed two plainclothes men round Old Montague Street. It'll be so they can watch the entrances on Durward Street and Winthrop Street: the oil shop!'

'He must be about to make an arrest,' I said. 'What about the opening of the court on to the Whitechapel Road?'

'He's waiting round the corner out of sight with a police van. I've a coach waiting at the Durward Street entrance. If we hurry we may get away before the plainclothes men are in place.'

We tore on our outside clothes and followed Tooke to the door out into the court, but to our dismay, Violet suddenly parted company from us and, lifting her skirts, dashed straight to the Whitechapel Road entrance, and disappeared round the corner! We hurried in pursuit, only to see her being helped up into the police van by Sergeant Wensley. The sergeant got in and the van moved off briskly.

'By Gad, Mortimer!' Tooke yelped. 'They've got her!'

'But not for long, Tooke, if I can help it! This coach you say you've got: have you hired it for the day?'

'Yes, it's at your disposal.'

'I'm obliged. Well, d'you know any decent solicitors?'

'Mmm, there's old Gillis. Works from a room above my office in Crutched Friars. Seems a shrewd old stick. We've a game of chess together on occasion. Has a biggish criminal practice, if the company he keeps is anything to go by . . .'

Tooke led me to his vehicle, and I got into it, while he

mounted up and took the reins. Soon we were galloping citywards.

Old Gillis could not see his way at that moment to dashing out with us, but he let us borrow his young partner, Mr Zeinvel who, from his lacquer-like hair to his patent leather boots, was the very picture of legal smartness. Tooke asked if he might put me and Zeinvel down a block away from Leman Street Police Station, which suggestion I fell in with without question, having become accustomed to his penchant for secrecy. Even with my mind in turmoil over what had befallen Violet, I could not help but be struck by the fact that, since he had appeared, he had not once mentioned Lavinia.

Sergeant Bovill, a youngish fair man whom I did not know, was sent to receive us when I made my business known at the desk. We were ushered into a private room, bare except for an institutional table and four chairs, at which we were bidden to sit. Bovill said his piece.

'I have to tell you that Dr Branscombe positively refuses to speak to either of you, gentlemen.'

'Has the lady been charged yet?' Zeinvel piped up in his squeaky but confident cockney voice.

'Not as yet. She's helping us with our enquiries.'

'Then you must know that by law,' Zeinvel went on, 'she's not obliged to say anything.'

'Well,' Bovill said, unperturbed, 'there's obstruction of the police in the execution of their duties, and in connection with a very grave crime! We could charge her with that, if you insist.'

I seized Zeinvel's arm.

'Dr Branscombe must not be charged with any crime!' I hissed. 'It would destroy all she has worked for!'

The young lawyer paused then addressed Bovill again.

'And in your opinion, sergeant, what form has this obstruction taken?'

'I express no opinion, but the fact is she has consistently refused to speak.'

'If she refuses to speak at all,' Zeinvel countered, 'how do you know she doesn't want to see us?'

'We put it to her,' Bovill said wearily, 'and she shook her head. And we've also advised her as to her rights.'

'And have you any reason to believe,' Zeinvel went on relentlessly, 'that in refusing to speak, she is attempting to prevent the lawful arrest or detection of someone else?'

Bovill's heavy lids seemed almost to engulf his eyes for an instant, and he got up slowly.

'If you'll wait a tick, gentlemen, I'll speak to the inspector again.'

Bovill left the room, and Zeinvel turned to me.

'The lady's people ought to be informed, doctor,' he remarked. 'If you can give me some details.'

'She lives in a residential club in Bloomsbury, Mr Zeinvel,' I explained. 'Her parents are dead. There are some aunts in the West Country, I believe, but I shall act on her behalf in any matter that may arise.'

'Very good, Dr Mortimer.'

'Now, Mr Zeinvel, please tell me exactly where Dr Branscombe stands, and how we are to get her out of here.'

'Well, briefly, the citizen has a duty to assist the police, especially in a crime as serious as murder, and the police have a perfect right to ask questions, even though the citizen is under no legal obligation to answer them.'

'Without wishing to appear churlish, Mr Zeinvel,' I said with disgust, 'that is as clear as mud! If I take it to mean what you seem to suggest it means, then my colleague has a perfect right in law to remain silent if she chooses.'

'Ah!' Zeinvel said with a bright little smile. 'These matters are always difficult for the layman to understand. Seen in isolation – and isolation from actual cases and circumstances forms the basis of a legal fiction – Dr Branscombe would indeed enjoy the right to stay silent, but as it stands the police may in this context construe her silence as an attempt at preventing their arrest or detention of another person. That in turn would constitute obstruction of the police in the execution of their duty, which is an offence.'

'But according to the papers, they've already detained and charged Boynton-Leigh!' I said. 'So how on earth can she be attempting to prevent them from doing that? On that score, she doesn't qualify for being in this hole.'

'I gather they haven't actually charged him with murder yet, doctor, and there's still Miss Nancarrow. We still don't know what they propose to do with regard to her, when and if they do find her, and I'm sure they're not going to tell us! No, doctor, pending further evidence – '

'Which Dr Branscombe is withholding from them,' I mused aloud gloomily.

'Excellent!' the dapper solicitor exclaimed. 'We'll make a lawyer of you yet, Dr Mortimer!'

'But then you're saying there's nothing we can do!' I protested. 'My colleague must be left to stew here, with all the time the threat of a criminal prosecution being dangled over her head, which would mean the destruction of all she has worked and striven for!'

'Now, Dr Mortimer! *Nil desperandum*! You must leave this in my hands: I've pulled far harder cases than this through. Tell me, can you think of any reason why Dr Branscombe should adopt this extraordinary attitude? I need hardly add that anything you say to me will be in strictest confidence. Is she perhaps, um, intimately involved with anyone in the case?'

'All I can say, Mr Zeinvel, is that she is a woman of extraordinary scruple, and once she has pledged her word for any reason wild horses could not force her to go back on it. She is as proud as the devil!'

'Mmm, I see. Well, I'm afraid neither pride nor scruple have any standing in a court of law, and when someone is eventually charged with the murder, and it all comes into court, she will be obliged to speak, or go down for contempt.'

The idea of Violet, her career in ruins, 'going down' for any reason whatsoever, made my heart sink into my boots, but Inspector Moultry's arrival with Sergeant Bovill put a stop to my gloomy ponderings. The inspector hailed me in friendly enough fashion, but studiously ignored Zeinvel who, I guessed, had before now laid the lash of his legal acumen across more than one back in the establishment.

'Step this way, doctor,' Moultry said. 'Though much good it may do you. It looks as if the same cat has run away with the tongues of both Mr Boynton-Leigh and your lady colleague! Perhaps we've coined a new disease, hey, doctor: forensic mutism!'

163

It was only then that he deigned to look down at the young lawyer.

'You'd know something about that, Zeinvel!'

'I must ask to be spared these sarcasms, inspector!' the solicitor replied, his face as straight as a Cherokee's.

Moultry led us briskly to the interview room, where Violet sat facing Sergeant Wensley across a table. The inspector nodded at Wensley, who moved his chair along and made room for me. I gripped the edge of the table and leant forward.

'Violet,' I murmured gently. 'What can I do?'

She looked straight ahead of her and made no reply, so I lowered myself into an empty chair, in order to be eye-to-eye with her. She looked straight through me.

34

I sat for twenty minutes with Zeinvel on a bench in the public corridor of the police station, and told him everything I could recall about the case, then we left the building together. He looked thoughtful for a moment, then said he had certain enquiries of his own to make farther east, and would not be joining me in Tooke's hired coach.

'Very well, then, Mr Zeinvel,' I said, as we prepared to go our separate ways, 'you have my address and my proposed whereabouts in Yorkshire over the weekend. You have helped me a great deal this afternoon, and I feel I am leaving Dr Branscombe in safe hands.'

The young lawyer waved his hand in deprecation.

'However,' I went on, 'there is one thing I must impress on you above all, and that is that you are to adopt no course of action that will possibly result in my colleague standing in the dock on a criminal charge. At all costs, please avoid that!'

'I understand perfectly, Dr Mortimer: rest assured I will do all I can to get her released without directly challenging or provoking the police. And before I go I'd like to warn you not to seem to be trying to influence any known suspect or potential witness in the case. The consequences of that could be very grave. Well, I hope to have something to report to you very soon. Good luck, Dr Mortimer!'

We went our various ways, Zeinvel to his investigations, and I to rejoin Tooke in the coach.

'I expected to see you with Dr Branscombe on your arm!' Tooke said ruefully from the driver's seat above me as I got into the coach again. 'Where to next?'

'The New Women's Hospital, Seymour Place,' I said, and Tooke urged the horse on to the start of our journey.

At the New Women's Hospital, I was directed to a kind of cubicle in the ward where, in white coat and with her hair thrown up in a bun, Dr Ramsbotham was officiating. She turned out to be a strapping, dark-haired girl with a sort of still authority about her. She rose briefly and gave me a cool, dry handshake, before waving me into the chair in front of her writing table. Her sherry-coloured eyes registered no emotion as I explained the purpose of my visit.

'I shall send Jane Bonsor – she graduated from the Sorbonne with Violet and myself – to look after the Whitechapel Dispensary until this absurd business is over,' Dr Ramsbotham said crisply. 'Will you be able to show her the ropes this evening?'

'Yes, indeed. I thank you on behalf of both Violet and myself.'

'We are on active service, Dr Mortimer, and each must play her part. No need to ask you, either, how Violet is facing up to prison: she is true steel. You have had the opportunity to get to know her pretty well, I understand?'

'The privilege, Dr Ramsbotham. It has been an honour to work with her.'

The stern-faced young woman nodded.

'You do her no more than justice,' she remarked without emphasis. 'I trust she is having all the legal and other assistance she needs.'

'I am attending to all that,' I said.

Another grave nod, and then Dr Ramsbotham wrote out a note for me with the address of a private hotel in Holloway before finally nodding me out with an injunction to keep her informed as to Violet's case and a coolly civil 'Good evening.'

By now it was tea-time, and I decided that, after he had driven me to Holloway, Tooke should be given his freedom for the day.

'I am sorry that I have not been able to give you any news about Lavinia,' I said as I got out of the coach at the entrance to Dr Bonsor's private hotel. I must confess I broached the topic with some awkwardness, since Tooke had not alluded to it all day.

'Oh,' the surveyor said in a philosophical undertone, 'I saw you had enough on your plate for that. Suffer in silence, and all that. I feel in my bones that she has Demmy with her, though, and that thought gives me some comfort. And they're still no forrader in finding out who did that blackguard Agar?'

'That's how the matter stands at present, I'm afraid.'

It crossed my mind at the mention of Agar that Tooke himself had had a very respectable motive for wanting the artist – his 'hated rival, don't you know' in his own words – out of the way. A man furthermore who by his own admission is 'out of his mind' with love for a woman will scarcely stop at half-measures, especially if he feels that his lady-love is under some threat from that rival. And, again, the way Tooke had dealt with the garrotters who had attacked me in Plumber's Row had left me in no doubt as to his capacity for physical violence. I decided to come directly to the point.

'I say, Tooke,' I said, just as he was about to gee up the horse, 'where were you at the time when Agar died?'

The prominent grey eyes levelled with mine from atop the coach, then for a moment or two I thought that this time the surveyor had really taken leave of his senses, for he burst into peal upon peal of helpless laughter. Presently he found his voice again.

'Where was I, Mortimer?' he wheezed. 'Where was I? Why, I've the ripest alibi imaginable: I was on the other side of London, drinking bedtime cocoa with a vicar!'

35

Dr Bonsor was a fair, pretty girl of about twenty-four or five, clearly the baby of the trio who had taken their degrees at the Sorbonne. She received me in the parlour, and after she had read Dr Ramsbotham's note, described her recent voluntary work in a sort of Church mission in Hoxton, which had just closed owing to the drying-up of the bequest that had sustained it. She would be very pleased to take up the temporary post in Whitechapel. Tea was brought in by a general maid, and we discussed Jane Bonsor's new duties, after which I escorted her by cab and train to the distant dispensary, where her experience in Hoxton helped her through her duties very satisfactorily. I explained to the regular patients that Dr Branscombe had been temporarily detained elsewhere.

By seven-thirty, I had handed out my last wrapped-up medicine-bottle, and I stepped into the consulting room to congratulate my new young colleague on her sterling effort, and to hand her into the safekeeping of her young man attendant, who had been coughing diplomatically in the waiting room, and who I found, when I invited him in, to have rugger-blue written all over him. Evidently she would not lack an able-bodied escort home on the evenings when I should be absent from the dispensary! It was scarcely five minutes after Dr Bonsor and her swain had left, and I was tidying up in the pharmacy before leaving, when there was a rap on the inner door. I stepped out into the consulting room and asked through the frosted glass of the door panel who it was.

'Zeinvel, doctor! May I speak to you?'

I opened the door and ushered the breathless young man into the patient's chair.

'I may be on to an alibi for Dr Branscombe!' he exclaimed.

'That was certainly quick work!' I cried, excited. 'Please explain.'

'You remember what you told me, doctor, about Sergeant

Wensley's interrogation – or rather, attempted interrogation – of Dr Branscombe, when he went through her movements on Monday night? The bit about her having been seen outside the Greatorex Street entrance to the Whitechapel Road Synagogue?'

I nodded impatiently.

'Cabmen's testimony!' I snapped. 'You can tell by the gaps!'

'I've just been talking to the hot-potato man who lives just across the street from the entrance to the synagogue,' Zeinvel went on, 'and he told me that around eleven on Monday night, he'd just finished hawking his potatoes round the pubs, and was putting his barrow and stove away for the night, when he chanced to look across the road and see a woman in a cloak coming out of the synagogue entrance. She turned on to the Whitechapel Road and he thought no more of the matter.'

'Well, I'm damned!' I said. 'It must have been her! I cannot believe that coincidence could stretch as far as two evasive caped ladies out at that hour on the Whitechapel Road. Did you enquire at the synagogue itself?'

'Yes, but apparently it was deserted and locked up at that time. If she met anyone in the porch before the hot-potato man spotted her, we've yet to find out who it was. I have to report as well, Dr Mortimer, that the registrar of the London Hospital has no record of anyone of the name of Rosie Bartlett among their patients on Monday night or immediately before or since.'

'In any case,' I commented, 'she would not have been admitted under that name.'

I was somewhat disappointed by this latter piece of news, but at least we had something to go on as to Violet's activities on the night of Agar's death.

'It's the time element I'm worried about, doctor,' Zeinvel went on.

'The time element?'

'I mean,' Zeinvel explained, 'if Mr Boynton-Leigh should decide to break his silence and give some sort of reasonable account of his actions on Monday night, they'll have to let him go on the pitiful evidence they seem to have against him at the moment, especially if he brings in a decent solicitor. Then with Miss Nancarrow and Rosie Bartlett still missing, that'll leave them without a main suspect.'

I rubbed my hands through my hair and groaned.

'Yes, I see, I see! Violet would then be their prime suspect! It's like sitting on a powder-keg. If only we had more time.'

At last we agreed that Zeinvel should continue to work fast and furiously at the case while I made my dash to Yorkshire in search of fresh evidence. We could only hope and pray that in the meantime, Violet would not be charged with murder by default. The lawyer wished me luck and left.

That evening I dined off devilled kidneys swimming in mustard in a chophouse in the Strand, and afterwards lingered thoughtfully over my tankard of porter. I reflected gloomily on the tenuousness of my prospects of finding some sort of clue in Yorkshire. After all, my conclusion that Agar must have been in Beck Hall in search of Zoffanys some time in the past was no more than speculation. However, I had given my word to Violet that I would go, and in any case, I could not possibly leave that particular stone unturned with things at their present pass: we were hardly spoilt for evidence to play with at the moment. My deepest misgivings concerned the tortures of suspense I must suffer on account of my tow-haired comrade, whom I now realised that I loved. What if the nabob should decide that Lavinia was by now out of the reach of the law, and that he might safely make a statement, and so go free? And if Lance was found to be unmistakably on the mend after his operation, would Boynton-Leigh feel the urge to be at his son's side, and so pronounce the Open Sesame to Moultry and Wensley? And if, and if, and if . . .

I drained off my porter and slammed down the pot on the oaken table. There was only one alleviation for suspense, and that was action! I paid the waiter and strode out of the chophouse to my nearby rooms, where I consulted the Bradshaw for night-train depatures for York. I learnt that one would be leaving St Pancras in an hour. I told my landlady of my intentions, left an encouraging note for Jane Bonsor, then flung some things into a Gladstone bag. On an afterthought – I am one who marvels at those who can sleep on train-journeys – I stuffed into my coat pocket my copy of the masterwork of that wayward and nefarious Knight, Sir Thomas Malory.

169

36

I managed to catch the nine-fifteen northbound train at St Pancras and, settling myself comfortably in a corner seat of a first-class compartment which I had all to myself, I opened the *Most Piteous Tale of the Morte Arthur Saunz Guerdon*. I was already familiar with the account in the scholarly Introduction of how Malory had whiled away the time between battles in the Wars of the Roses with such pastimes as rape and highway robbery, and indeed had been no stranger to the prisons of whatever Majesty had been on the throne at the time. Sir Thomas, it seemed, had been 'mad, bad and dangerous to know.' The style, too, was the man himself: virile, insensitive and matter-of-fact, which traits showed clearly through the rough, fifteenth-century English.

I read slowly, but with some interest as the train clattered, screeched and whistled through the summer night. The book was a sort of adaptation, according to Malory, of a 'Freynshe' book he had taken as his authority, but the courtly nuances of the original had all but vanished amid Malory's harsh, bustling style and treatment. As for the matter in hand, for all the hearty plainness of the narrative, I could see nothing in it that might have caused Boynton-Leigh to keep it out of Lavinia's hands. Kings, knights and ladies would now and then trespass outside the lawful bounds of marriage, but this was dealt with in a brisk, blunt way, quite free of deliberate bawdy. The thought occurred to me that the obviously Roman Catholic tincture of the work might have offended the nabob, but could he be such a fanatic devotee of the Church of England? Again, if before her seclusion Lavinia had been weaned on the pious decorum of Lord Tennyson's version of the *Morte d'Arthur*, she would have found little to recommend this prosaic treatment of the legend. I sank into a routine of ploughing through a page or two, then dozing, or rather musing, for a few minutes before tackling the next page. By the time we were screeching into Peterborough, I had reached

Book Four, the Day of Destiny. Mordred, King Arthur's treacherous nephew, has taken advantage of the King's absence on the Continent to seize most of the country. He determines to take Queen Guinevere for his own, and she takes refuge in the Tower of London, to which Mordred lays strong siege. The Archbishop of Canterbury intervenes, berating Mordred for his conduct, then utters the following words, which aroused me from all my drowsiness.

'For ys nat kynge Arthur youre uncle, and no farther but youre modirs brothir, and uppon her he hymselffe begate you, uppon his owne syster?'

To the best of my knowledge, this did not appear in the Tennyson version. Incest! I laid the book face-down on the upholstered seat and stared at the black window, which reflected my own puzzlement. Could this, then, be the reason why Boynton-Leigh had rejected the book? I could imagine how this sin – by no means rare in High Victorian England – might wreak havoc in the mind of a morbidly self-demanding man, a man who seemed in his conduct to elevate guilt to the level of a religion. But on whose account? Not surely, that of Lavinia and Lance: I could hardly entertain that. But then there was that shadowy business of the letters which had apparently played a part in the nabob's 'brainstorm' just before they had all fled from Calcutta. Why must Lance and Lavinia never correspond? I could make nothing of this.

By now it was past midnight, and my heart sank lower as the dead, small hours approached. The thought of Violet's present incarceration was gnawing at me like a dog on a bone. At last I dozed for a while, mesmerised by the clicking of the wheels of the train over the ties, then I recalled Violet's expressions of her cold detestation of Agar and his unspeakable treatment of some of her girls. She had referred to him as a sort of microbe, fit only to be wiped out as a clinical measure. Perhaps – and I thrust out the idea as soon as it had come unbidden into my mind – I was even at this moment hurtling north in the quixotic service of a cold-blooded murderess! Absurd! But why had she not confided in me, even if she had given her word to someone? The truth was, I was already thinking of Violet Branscombe as my wife-to-be, and was measuring her by the impossibly high standards of the prospective bridegroom. Nor would Moultry's teasing question quit my mind: did I really know her? One thing at least was clear to me: my feelings were thoroughly engaged, for this suspense on her behalf was torture.

I sank into a wretched half-doze near Grantham, and I cannot account for the couple of hours that passed before I became aware of the dimly lit platform of Doncaster Station gliding by. At last the train pulled into York at the withering hour of twenty-to-four on Friday morning, the twenty-fifth of July. I stuffed the Malory back into my pocket, grabbed my bag, and stepped shakily out on to the platform in the pre-dawn chill. I made straight for the refreshment room, where I sought to bring myself back to life with hot, black coffee, before it was time to catch my connection to Malton and the Wolds at twenty-past four.

I arrived eventually at Malton, feeling more dead than alive, at five o'clock. I then reasoned that if I weathered out the wait till the ten-to-eight train to North Grimston came in, I should be in the latter place just after eight, at which hour retired maiden ladies in the wilds of Yorkshire would scarcely be disposed to receive unheralded gentleman callers. In short, I had allowed haste to get the better of judgment, and in correction of this, I stepped straight over to the Station Hotel, roused the duty-man, and had him prepare me a room, with strict orders not to call me before ten.

I woke up shortly before ten, refreshed by my sleep, and rang for breakfast, which arrived along with the daily paper. I was glad that I had left the paper till after I had done justice to the breakfast, for what I read in the first of the national columns would certainly have robbed me of all appetite for the meal: ALDGATE MURDER SUSPECT RELEASED.

37

I positively slung the breakfast tray on to the side table, and sat up in bed as I read the brief article:

In a surprising development yesterday evening, the Metropolitan Police released Mr Archibald Boynton-Leigh, the Calcutta merchant who had been held for questioning since Tuesday morning in connection with the violent death of Mr John Agar, an artist, at Mr Boynton-Leigh's house in Aldgate, East London, sometime around midnight on Monday night. The whereabouts of Miss Lavinia Nancarrow, Mr Boynton-Leigh's beautiful ward, remain shrouded in mystery, but Inspector Moultry, who is in charge of the case, holds out the prospect of an imminent arrest . . .

There followed the testimony of the usual 'eye-witnesses', who claimed to have spotted Lavinia in a couple of dozen places between Land's End and John O'Groats. I flung away the paper and leapt out of bed, first attacking my shaving kit and the basin of hot water on the dressing table under the window, then throwing on my clothes and rushing downstairs to the lobby, where I paid my reckoning and tossed my bag into the nearest waiting cab in the rank outside. I had not time to palter around with railway timetables, even less so in view of the fact that North Grimston was only four miles away. I directed the cabbie to put me down at the door of Beck Hall itself, and prayed that Miss Boynton would be at home in both senses of the word.

My head was in too much of a whirl to allow much appreciation of the unfolding Wolds as they sped by the cab window, but I have a vague memory of great swelling chalk hummocks, much like the high Sussex Downs, but with something broader and bleaker about them. There were many sheep and precious few trees.

I felt I did not need many guesses as to the object of Moultry's 'imminent arrest', and I began to curse myself for not having stayed in London and done my damnedest to help Violet there as events unfolded, instead of traipsing round the wilds of Yorkshire. But there might – just might – be something here. If only the fellow would drive faster! There was comfort in the fact that Zeinvel was handling the affair in London: he was a live wire, if ever there was one!

And where the dickens was Lavinia? She seemed to have vanished, along with the self-effacing Demmy, out of human ken. She had by now taken on for me the aspect of a creature of legend – of fiction, almost – like Poe's Lenore. I remembered the sweet burden of her slim torso, lithe as a snake's, when I had examined her on our first meeting.

Then there was Tooke, with his zany alleged alibi: that he had been drinking cocoa with some suburban clergyman at the time of Agar's death! And yet nothing could have been more real, more genuine, than his unforced laughter when I had taxed him with this. One could almost say that it was so mad, it must be true. Percival Tooke was without doubt the Joker in the pack of this case, and I should have to devote more time to scrutinising him when once immediate pressures had been lifted.

I was jerked back to earth as the cab swayed round a sudden bend in the road, and a wooden hollow revealed itself with, at its centre, a perfect little William-and-Mary mansion in mellow orange brick. The wheels of the cab crunched on gravel, and we were soon at the front door of Beck Hall. I jumped out and bade the cabbie wait till I had rung the front door bell. At length, a rosy-faced girl answered my ring and, taking my card and explanation, went to see if Miss Boynton was at home. I had a longish wait, then back she came: Miss Boynton would see me directly. My heart leapt, and I paid the cabbie and handed my bag to the maid, who put it on an ancient-looking chair in the hall, and led me to the breakfast room, where a tiny lady in a flouncing dress that might have been in vogue in the sixties rose from the table to greet me. I hurried over and took the mittened little hand briefly in mine, while the small-featured rosy face with its faded blue eyes was wreathed in a smile.

'Dr Mortimer!' she cooed in a fluting treble. 'Dr Branscombe wrote to me about you. You are most welcome, though I am disappointed to see that you seem not to have brought your colleague with you.'

'She is unfortunately, er, detained, ma'am,' I said. 'She has many commitments in London.'

'Ah!' the old lady said. 'London! I have not set foot there since before Mr Dickens passed away. But you shall give me all the latest news. Lowesby shall prepare a room for you.'

'Most kind of you, ma'am, but I fear I must be away again before the evening is out. Pressure of duty . . .'

'Such a disappointment, but you will surely take a bite of breakfast with me?'

I allowed myself to be pressed to a cup of coffee, and Miss Boynton, after the fashion of lonely old folk, regaled me with the account of her meeting in Tunbridge Wells in 1859 with Violet's late father, Colonel Hereward Branscombe, later so justly famous as the hero of Maiwand. I was able to assure my hostess that Violet was showing every sign of being a chip off the old block when, to my relief, the old lady suggested we go into the library, where the family paintings were to be seen. I got up and joined her at the door of the breakfast room, and she linked her arm in mine in an old-fashioned gesture and led me slowly into the library.

It was a remarkable collection by any standards, exclusively of family portraits, and by the time we had come to the Zoffany, I had received a comprehensive account of the fortune of the Boynton clan from about the time of the Battle of Edgehill. At last we stood under the cold stare of Miss Arabella Boynton, her look of disdain in 1779 frozen for ever by Johann Zoffany.

'Such hard eyes!' my dainty hostess remarked. 'But it was a hard age, and they had no doubts at all about anything. Do you know, Dr Mortimer, that ever since I was a little girl, whenever I have done something silly, I have never been able to face that stare. I wonder how her children put up with her, if she ever had any.'

'These paintings are clearly an important part of your life, Miss Boynton.'

'Yes, indeed: there could never be any question of my parting with them.'

I was on the alert.

'Someone has raised that question, perhaps?'

'A young man has been here twice, Dr Mortimer, to look at Miss Arabella there. Why, the last time can scarcely have been a month ago. There is something positively ill-bred about such persistence, though he was a thoroughly gentlemanly young man.'

'He actually tried to buy the picture on those two occasions, then, Miss Boynton?'

'Mmm, only on his first visit. Let me see, that must have been quite two years ago. On his more recent call he seemed more interested in the papers than in the painting.'

'The, er, papers, Miss Boynton?'

'Yes, Dr Mortimer, that is one of the most interesting features of the collection: we have kept practically all the original papers – bills, receipts, letters from artists, and so forth – pertaining to each individual portrait.'

'But that is most interesting!' I exclaimed. 'Do you think I might . . . Would it be possible for me to . . .'

The old lady laughed.

'Of course, Dr Mortimer! I shall take them out and show them to you, but I warn you, there are quite a few, and if you try to do them all justice, they might take out quite a tidy bite from your valuable time.'

Miss Boynton went over to the wall-sash, and soon the maid was sent in search of the library-desk keys, which my hostess used to unlock a lower drawer of the desk, from which she took a stout metal deed-box. She unlocked this in turn, and placed it on the desk, with a gesture of invitation in the direction of the chair.

'For your delectation, doctor. Please give a ring when you are finished.'

I stammered my thanks, and the old lady glided out of the room, while I jumped into the chair and, with trembling fingers, tackled the yellowing bundles, tied up in faded, silk ribbons. This complete historical record of the provenance of the paintings in the Boynton collection might have been of absorbing interest in itself, if I had not had but one aim in mind. I spent the better part of two hours in single-minded pursuit, of sifting and re-sifting, before I realised that, alone among those of all the pictures in the library, the papers pertaining to the portrait of Miss Arabella Boynton were missing.

38

Once I had made certain that the Arabella Boynton papers were missing, I carefully replaced the rest in the box, which I locked and put back in the drawer, which I also closed and locked. I sat back in the chair and looked around me, receiving a look of cold contempt from Miss Arabella. I considered the implications of what I had just discovered. Agar had taken the papers – of that I had little doubt – but for what reason? Of what use were documents of verification without the actual object they were supposed to verify? Or had Agar been such a confirmed pilferer, such a recidivistic Autolycus as to filch, magpie-like, any unconsidered trifle that took his fancy?

Just then the maid Lowesby came in: please, sir, it was time for luncheon, and would I join Miss Boynton in the dining room? I handed the girl the key to give to her mistress later, and followed her to the dining room, where a place had been laid for me.

'It is really most kind of you, Miss Boynton. I will not pretend that I have no appetite!'

'Brain-work is always the most demanding, doctor. I trust you found the papers interesting?'

'Immensely. They are a complete record of your family: why, there are Boyntons scattered all over the world!'

'Yes, it has been the old story: too many younger sons, and not enough acres! Luckily, the Empire has provided room for them all.'

'As far afield as India,' I remarked.

The little pink face took on a slightly sniffy look.

'Indeed, I understand we have a flourishing branch in Calcutta: trade, I believe.'

The disdain in Miss Boynton's voice was unmistakable, and it was clear that Archibald Boynton-Leigh and his menage would not be 'known' to my hostess in any sense of the word! I did not pursue the matter.

'I wonder if I might ask you, Miss Boynton,' I said, as the soup-plates were being cleared away.

'Yes, Dr Mortimer?'

'This, er, persistent young man who came to look at your pictures: have you heard any more from him?'

'No, he has not troubled me again. You are not by any chance acquainted with him?'

'No, not at all!' I hastened to say, being anxious not to be taken for an agent of Agar's. 'It was just that he sounded like a singular individual altogether.'

A shrewd look came over my hostess's face.

'I have run across one or two artists in my time, Dr Mortimer – at home and abroad – and they have had one thing in common.'

'Yes, Miss Boynton?' I asked, as I applied sauce to my fish.

'They do not pay their dues!'

I left it at that.

'I expect you often look at those most fascinating papers you have just let me see, Miss Boynton?'

'Why, there you have me, Dr Mortimer! I don't think I have actually read them since I was a girl! It is enough for me that they are there, and besides, my eyes are not what they used to be.'

'I see. I was looking at another Zoffany the other day.'

'A most prolific artist: always hard-up, I expect!'

'No doubt! The painting I refer to was a conversation piece, as they call them, a family group of the late seventeen-hundreds. There were a couple of girls in it – very striking – by the name of Leigh. You are not by any chance familiar with the name?'

'Leigh? Now let me see. Mmm, no. I cannot say that I know any Leighs: should I know them?'

'No, no matter, Miss Boynton, merely a shot in the dark.'

Soon the conversation trailed off into generalities, and I mined my memories of my brief tenure as a society locum to regale my hostess with the London tittle-tattle she was clearly dying to hear. This line-of-goods was so much in demand that it was nearly half-past two when I was finally able to rise from the table and offer my thanks. I promised to convey Violet a renewed invitation to come up and stay, then Miss Boynton insisted on showing me to the door herself, and into her trap, in which I was taken by her old coachman to North Grimston Station, where I found I had an hour in hand before the arrival of the three fifty-two to York. My mind was racing, ringing the logical changes which had been set in motion by my discovery of Agar's apparent theft of the Arabella Boynton papers, and I was loath simply to vegetate in the rather mournful little station. I decided to take a turn round the village and I left my bag with the porter.

A rather pleasant spot, I realised, in its wooded nick of the Wolds, and served by two rushing streams. The soughing wind in the canopies of august trees cooled my fevered brain somewhat. I made my way through the cluster of white houses to a long, low church, along whose graveyard path six lime trees stood sentinel. There was a clearly medieval tower, topped by a statue, and inside all was dim and ancient, all the angles of the building being aslope and aslant, with here and there carvings of men and beasts, actual and mythical, portrayed with the ferocity of expression found in carvings on the prows of Viking ships. This was the real Norman spirit, and if further proof were needed, there was the characteristic zigzag axework on columns and piers.

I walked slowly up the aisle, bathed in grey light, then stood before the altar. I offered up a prayer for Ruth, then for someone in prison.

A cough from behind me warned me that I was not alone, and a verger appeared with a pair of stout candles in his hand. He approached the ancient iron candleholders which flanked the altar, and began to remove the guttered-out stumps from the iron sconces. I noticed a high-stepped blackwood pulpit to the right of, and slightly behind, the altar, and reflected idly how easy it might be to stumble on those teetering steps.

My gaze swung round again to the verger, who had laid down the fresh candles on one of the pulpit-steps, and seemed to be having some difficulty removing the stumps from the sconces. He succeeded at last with the first candleholder, but my eyes had now become adjusted to the dimness, and I saw that in fact there were no sconces atop the ancient candlesticks. I went on staring with a sort of childlike wonderment, then I offered up a prayer of heartfelt thanks, and ran laughing like a madman out of the church.

39

I arrived in York with a good forty-five minutes in hand before the departure at half-past six of the King's Cross train. My first stop on alighting was the station telegraph office, where I wired Inspector Moultry, with the urgent request that he take no further action with regard to Violet until he or his representative should meet me off the train at King's Cross at ten-fifty. In case he should feel any hesitation about falling in with this, I added that I believed that I should be able immediately to take him to the murderer of Jack Agar!

My next stop was the nearest newspaper stall, where I bought copies of all the evening papers, and retired to a platform bench to scan them. I opened each with trembling hands and a muttered prayer, but to my relief found no further mention of the Aldgate Case. There was still time, then, to forestall any move against Violet and to test my brainwave as to the manner of Agar's death. How I wished the man to hell!

In the remaining twenty minutes before the arrival of my train, I snatched a sandwich – or something resembling one – and a cup of coffee in the refreshment room. The journey down was smooth and expeditious and, comfortably ensconced in my first-class smoker, I got to work on the, if not three-pipe, then ounce-of-rolling-baccy-problem of Violet's unaccounted-for activities between eleven and midnight on Monday night. She is seen, then, to emerge from the porch of the locked-up and deserted synagogue at the corner of Greatorex Street and the Whitechapel Road at around eleven, then, in Sergeant Wensley's words, is 'lost to view' till Tuesday morning. This of course would have occasioned neither surprise nor suspicion at her club, for a doctor may be called out at any time and for any length of time. I mulled over what little I knew about this, then sank into a half-doze just after Newark. I came out of my doze as we were nearing Grantham, and the solution plopped gently into my mind like a ripe fruit. On my first hearing through Zeinvel of the hot-potato man's testimony, I had omitted to make the distinction between a cape and a cloak.

The rest of the journey proceeded smoothly, until at last, my pulses racing, I found myself striding towards the barrier at King's Cross. I saw both Moultry and Wensley waiting stolidly behind the ticket collector, to whom I handed my ticket.

'You have not charged Dr Branscombe?' I asked Moultry.

'Let's talk about that when you've told us your story, Dr Mortimer,' was the inspector's cagey reply, while Wensley fixed me with his notorious weasel glance and said nothing.

'Have you a cab waiting?' I asked as we walked towards the Euston Road entrance.

'We've a police van at your service!' Moultry replied, while his colleague muttered something about his hoping it would be worth it.

I preceded the detectives into the big, horse-drawn van, then Moultry asked me from the pavement where we were going.

'Number One, Ginger Lane, Aldgate,' I said.

'You won't be able to show us any murderer there,' Wensley remarked. 'Place is empty, locked-up!'

'But it was in the paper,' I said. 'Boynton-Leigh has been released.'

'So he has,' Moultry replied. 'But he's putting up at the Strand Palace at the moment.'

'Then he has broken his silence?' I asked.

'He got news that his son was out of danger after his operation in France,' Moultry said, 'then apparently decided that, well, he might get over there to see him a lot quicker if he came clean about what happened in Ginger Lane on Monday night.'

In other words, I thought, a little judicious blackmail on the part of the C.I.D. All the same, I was delighted at the news that Lance had come through his ordeal.

'Then he has not left immediately for France?' I asked.

'Not just yet,' Moultry explained. 'At the moment he's briefing what must be about the biggest army of private detectives ever assembled in London to find Miss Nancarrow before he leaves.'

181

'Pity he hadn't come clean in the first place,' Wensley grumbled. 'Then he'd have had the whole Force at his back.'

'Right, then, doctor,' Moultry said, as he leant against the superstructure of the van and lit up his pipe. 'About this murderer you were going to tell us about.'

'Please, inspector!' I begged. 'You have been good enough to come this far: let us go directly to Aldgate! I will explain everything on the way.'

Moultry studied me for a moment through the blue haze of his pipe-smoke, then straightened up and spoke.

'Righto, then,' he said wearily. 'I won't give anyone the chance to say I left any stone unturned. One, Ginger Lane, driver!'

The two detectives got in beside me and the heavy van rumbled off in the direction of the Pentonville Road.

'At least we won't need a search warrant, sir,' Wensley remarked in one of his rare attempts at humour. 'not with that trick door-knocker!'

'You mean there's no one there at all?' I exclaimed. 'No servants or caretaker?'

'The house is perfectly safe, Dr Mortimer,' Moultry said. 'Nobody can approach it without being observed.'

A sudden fear seized me.

'Has anything been moved – furniture, fittings, anything – since Mr Boynton-Leigh was released?'

'Not that we know of,' the inspector replied. 'As far as we know, Mr Boynton-Leigh just dashed over there from Leman Street, packed some clothing and personal things, and booked into the Strand Palace. We certainly do know that he hasn't been back to Ginger Lane since.'

I was much relieved by this information: my theory might now have a sporting chance of being demonstrated.

'You've both examined the house and contents thoroughly?' I asked.

'With a fine tooth-comb!' Wensley snapped with more than usual ferocity.

'Are the library steps still in Mr Boynton-Leigh's study?' I asked.

'Yes,' Moultry replied. 'Do they signify in some way, doctor?'

'They are crucial to my demonstration, inspector! But that can wait till we arrive at Ginger Lane. I should like to return to the topic of my colleague, Dr Branscombe – '

'That young lady is her own worst enemy, Doctor,' Moultry said. 'She has only to give us a simple statement as to exactly what she was doing in the East End on the night of the murder, and no one would be more pleased than me to – '

'If my line of thinking is borne out tonight, inspector,' I said, 'I fancy you will scarcely require even that.'

'Mmph!' Wensley snorted. 'Sounds like a pretty tall order, doctor!'

'Well, do let's have this theory of yours, Dr Mortimer,' Moultry prompted.

'First of all,' I said, 'I can reveal whose was the hand which was behind the death of Jack Agar.'

'Well?' Wensley asked. 'Whose?'

'That of a very old Chinaman: a Chinaman with rare skills in his hands!'

40

Wensley jumped out into the night before we turned off Cobb Street, no doubt to make contact with whoever was watching the house in Ginger Lane without being observed. We sat in the van outside the house till he quietly rejoined us.

'Anything to report?' Moultry asked.

'Nothing fresh, sir: usual gawpers this afternoon, and some young 'uns trying to climb over the graveyard wall, but no one's been near the house itself.'

'Well, come on, then,' the inspector said, stifling a yawn. 'We'd better go in and look for Dr Mortimer's Chinaman!'

Wensley got out in front of us and, after he had satisfied himself that no one was watching from any angle of the Lane, grasped the brass fingers of the knocker and gave it a simultaneous lift and half-twist. The door lay open to us, and we got out of the van and went into the hall.

'What next, then, doctor?' Moultry asked.

'I'd like the library steps in Boynton-Leigh's study brought into Miss Nancarrow's bedroom, inspector.'

The inspector nodded at Wensley, who clumped up the stairs ahead of us, and soon we could see the yellow glare of gaslight on the first-floor landing. There was a rattle of keys, then more clumping, and presently the sergeant passed along the landing, pushing the delicate steps along on their squeaking castors. The keys rattled again from the direction of Lavinia's room, then Wensley said: 'Everything ready, sir!'

We went upstairs into Lavinia's bedroom, where I went over to the window and managed, with some difficulty, to lug the waist-high bronze candelabrum about eighteen inches away to the right of its usual position midway between the bed and the windowsill.

'That candlestick was in its usual place when we found it,' Wensley protested. 'Just under the windowsill, where you've just taken it from!'

'Please bear with me, sergeant,' I said. 'I shall be explaining that in due course.'

I stepped over to the bed, stripped off the bedclothes and, tossing aside the pillows, pulled out the bolster, which I lifted up and weighed between my hands.

'Pretty well-packed,' I remarked. 'Nice and solid!' I passed the bolster to a mystified Wensley.

'Now, gentlemen,' I began, 'this bolster represents a man – say an art-dealer – who has just popped in here, up to no good. He hasn't come without an appointment, mind you, but that is known to only one of the normal occupants of the house. To our visitor's consternation, the person who has fixed the appointment with him is nowhere to be found, so quietly, stealthily – he is an old hand at this game – he tries the doors to all the rooms. Nobody. The house appears to have been abandoned.'

'He must know the trick with the fancy knocker, then,' Wensley put in, 'else how'd he have got in?'

'Yes, sergeant,' I said, 'he knows the fancy-knocker trick, as he's a sly and observant customer and, anyway, the person who made the rendezvous with him told him about it, as he's not the sort of chap you'd want even your servants to know is calling on you. Anyway, our visitor looks in all the rooms, and is especially interested in Miss Nancarrow's bedroom, or more particularly – for reasons which I shall explain in due course – in the grimy old paintings which you see up on the wall here. Now the pictures are dark and dirty enough in themselves, but being hung so high up on the wall, one needs steps to appreciate the detail, even in full gaslight.'

I took those very steps and placed them so that they faced the wall about a foot away from its surface.

'Would you please bring me a tray from the kitchen, sergeant?' I requested. 'Any old tray will do.'

Wensley left the room to return shortly with a common tin tray, which I placed, like a breastplate, between my chest and the bolster. I manoeuvred the steps along the wall from painting to painting, squinting as I went, until they stood under the last painting but one.

'All goes well,' I said, as I climbed the steps, clasping my cumbrous padding to me. 'Our art dealer is not a heavy man, and he is nimble on his feet, but he tends to lose himself in his art. At this penultimate painting he places the edges of the castors rather too close-into the gap between a couple of exposed floorboards. He is absorbed by a detail in the picture – again, I will explain this later – something almost completely obscured by dirt and old varnish. He finds he must lean just a little to the left, and – '

'Look out, doctor!' both detectives cried at once, as the steps, their left-hand side castors jammed against the floorboard-crack, canted over, teetered, then toppled over with a splintering crash. I let go of the steadying-post of the falling steps and tried, catlike, to jump to the ground instead of crashing willy-nilly on to my side only, in turning, to fall face-forward on to the candelabrum which was now well clear of the wall. The short-ened red candle went clattering across the floor, and there was a metallic clunking noise as something connected through the bolster with my tea-tray breastplate. I leapt aside and the tray clattered to the floor. There was a visible dent near its polished centre, but it was not the tray upon which the eyes of the two detectives were rivetted, but the bolster – my art dealer – which was hooped at a sinister angle over the antique candelabrum, now propped up steeply against the wall. At the apex of the bend in the bolster protruded the sharp, bronze point of the spike upon which the stout candle is customarily impaled in ancient holders of that type, as I had seen earlier on that day in the example in the church in North Grimston.

Wensley stepped over and gingerly tested the point of the spike with his finger, making a clucking sound with his tongue as he did so.

I turned to Moultry, who was shaking his head slowly from side to side.

'Inspector,' I said, 'allow me to present to you the killer of Jack Agar!'

41

Moultry shot me a canny glance.

'This is all very fine, doctor,' he said, 'but you've still to explain how the candlestick came to be so far out and away from its usual place under the window and against the wall.'

'For the moment, though, inspector, do you admit that my demonstration explains how Agar came to be found here, when all of those who had a motive for killing him were apparently known to be elsewhere?'

'I admit nothing, doctor, and I must say that's a pretty big "apparently": one or two people have still to establish their whereabouts and movements on the night of the murder. I shall be wanting more in that line; and at the very least I want more evidence before I can act on this theory of yours. Anyway, what put you on to the candlestick in the first place?'

'When I was here with Sergeant Wensley the other day, I noticed that the candles were a good third of their length shorter than when I had last laid eyes on them. Now, since the wicks are unburnt, how does one account for the wear? I was on the point of going over and pulling one out – or rather off – when the sergeant very properly prevented me from doing so. Then something I saw during my trip to Yorkshire suggested the true state of affairs. I saw that if a candle in an ordinary sconce took a knock, it would pop cleanly out, but in the case of a candle stuck on to a central spike, the whole of the base of the candle would be torn and spoilt as it was wrenched away. It would need a fairly hefty blow to do this, too, such as an eleven- or twelve-stone man's weight falling against it. Anyone who wanted to tidy up the damage would have to cut off the base of the spoilt candle neatly up to the sound part – and of course do the same for its undamaged companion for the sake of symmetry – before impaling them on the spikes again.'

'Why not stick on new candles?' Wensley put in.

'Lack of time,' I explained, 'and in any case, supposing you haven't fresh supplies handy, where do you buy a box of outsize red Chinee ceremonial candles after midnight in Aldgate?'

To this, Wensley had no immediate reply but a grunt.

'Funny how these Chinese things are all different from ours,' he muttered after a little pause.

'What about the blood, then, doctor?' Moultry asked. 'I don't see any trace of it on the floorboards, unless there's still some of it in the cracks.'

'Most of the bleeding was internal, if you'll recall, sir,' Wensley said, 'in the what-d'you-call-it sac.'

'The pericardium, sergeant,' I explained.

'That's right!' Moultry said with a chuckle. 'Maclure the police surgeon said that when they opened him up, the thing was so full of congealed blood it was like a black pudding!'

'Agar must have remained slumped over the tilted candelabrum for hours,' I said. 'The spike would have acted as a sort of bung, so I don't suppose cleaning up would have been any major undertaking.'

'Well,' the inspector said with a sigh as he contemplated the fatal corner, 'we'll be having to have those boards up before we're much older. Who moved the candlestick out from the wall, then, doctor, and why?'

'Why would you move anything cumbersome away from a window, inspector?'

'If I wanted to climb out, I suppose.'

'Or let somebody in!' Wensley countered. 'The question is, who was inside, and who were they getting ready to let in, or out?'

There was a longish pause, then Moultry gave me a long, hard look.

'Supposing, Dr Mortimer, just supposing, there's something in this theory of yours, why would Agar be so intent on climbing up the walls of Miss Nancarrow's bedroom? What was so interesting to him in the pictures?'

'If you'll bear with me, inspector, as I proceed with my demonstration, that will become clear by-and-by. The solution to this case is a mosaic made up of a great many pieces. But you are fond of material evidence. Very well, I shall give you some on account, so to speak! I peer into my crystal ball, and presently the mists clear, to reveal you and the sergeant here, on the scene of the so-called crime, removing the contents of Agar's pockets. Among those contents figure a wad of cotton wool and a small bottle containing an 80/20 solution of methylated spirits and ethanol: am I right?'

Moultry's eyes narrowed.

'Common enough artists' materials, doctor.'

'But you did find them on his body?'

'All right, then, doctor, what was he carrying them for, according to your theory?'

'He had a specific use in mind: the removal, not the laying-on, of paint and varnish!'

'You're saying he was up the steps to remove something from one of the paintings? What?'

'Again, I shall return to that.'

'Well, doctor,' Moultry said. 'I'll promise you this: if there turns out to be blood on that candle-spike, we'll have the floorboards up, then we'll see. Now what about this statement from Dr Branscombe? We shall still be wanting one, you know, theories notwithstanding.'

I took the next step in the knowledge that, though Violet might be bound by a pledge of secrecy, I was not, and that my principal duty lay with getting my colleague freed from police custody. My more immediate purpose was to lay the case open to such an extent that Moultry would scarcely need a statement from her any longer.

'At about eleven on Monday night,' I began, 'Dr Branscombe alighted in Greatorex Street from the cab mentioned by your informant. She was wearing a caped coat when she'd gone out that night – ' Wensley nodded in confirmation ' – and when I heard of the testimony of a local hot-potato man to the effect that at that time he had seen a woman coming out of the porch on the Greatorex Street side of the Whitechapel Road Synagogue in a "cloak", I took his description to be merely a slipshod way of describing a cape, the little shoulder-mantle of a lady's coat. I now realise he meant neither more nor less than a cloak – a nurse's cloak, to be specific – which she flung over her other clothes in the synagogue porch. She then crossed the White-chapel Road and entered the London Hospital – I've no doubt she had a nurse's headdress concealed upon her also – where Rosie Bartlett must have been lying.'

'But we weren't looking for either of them, then!' Moultry objected. 'It was probably at least an hour before Agar died, and he was seen to leave the Warsaw Café, alive and well, at nearly eleven-thirty.'

'Yes,' Wensley said. 'There was no need for her to go about secretly.'

'As you know,' I explained, 'Agar had a score to settle with Rosie, so she had to keep her movements secret. Do you concede that Rosie might have been – was – in the hospital at the time, inspector?'

Another longish, hard look from Moultry. I was encouraged, though, by the strong engagement in his expression. I felt I was at last getting through to him.

'Please just go on and have your theory out, doctor,' was the inspector's cagey reply. Evidently I was to get no prompting from him.

'Dr Branscombe goes into the hospital as a nurse,' I went on, 'and escorts Rosie – who must have recovered to an extent that would allow her movement – away to some place of greater safety.'

'From Agar, you mean?' Moultry said.

'From Agar, inspector,' I said positively.

'Are you sure she – or they – weren't running away for something else, doctor?' Wensley said with an unpleasant little smile.

'But you will admit, gentlemen,' I said, a little desperately, 'that my theory holds water, that is, in default of actual information?'

There followed the longest pause of the interview and Moultry actually exchanged significant glances with his subordinate. 'We checked on admissions and discharges at the hospital, of course,' the inspector said at last, 'and there was only one that might've fitted the bill. A Mrs Shaw, or so she called herself, a private patient, surprisingly enough.'

'Oh?' I queried. 'Why surprisingly?'

'They described her as a "poor, rough woman". She'd been in for nearly a fortnight with severe, feverish bronchitis – touch-and-go, they said – but she discharged herself at around eleven-fifteen on the Monday night. She was still pretty shaky, Sister said, but insisted on leaving.'

'Alone?' I asked.

'Apparently. Just got dressed, collected her things and went.'

'Had she had visitors?'

'Just a veiled woman – three or four times – and Mr Venables, the clergyman-like gentleman who'd first brought her in.'

I thought of the Women's Refuge in Hackney: no doubt this clerical-looking Samaritan had been some sort of helper there. Moultry soon confirmed this.

'What was given as her address when she was brought in?' I asked.

'The gentleman – Mr Venables – just said that she was an unfortunate woman who he was looking after.'

'They usually end up in the workhouse hospital,' Wensley put in.

'Well,' Moultry went on, 'Mr Venables gave them his own address – place in Hackney, very respectable – for reference, and that's where the hospital bill was sent.'

'You have questioned this Mr Venables?' I asked.

'Naturally,' Moultry said, 'and he told us the last he'd seen of Mrs Shaw was when he visited her after teatime on Monday. Said he'd no notion of her present whereabouts. Discreet-seeming, circumspect sort of cove.'

I had no doubt at all of that! So Rosie had taken seriously ill at the refuge in Hackney, and had had to be sent to the London Hospital. This Venables had presumably made arrangements for

190

getting her out of harm's – Agar's – way after she had become more-or-less fit to travel, and had probably given her her last-minute instructions during his teatime visit on Monday. Violet, whom Rosie trusts implicitly, is deputed to escort her to safety and awaits, in nurse's cloak and rig, at the Hospital entrance at the appointed hour, no doubt with a confidential means of transport at hand. She meets Rosie, they get into the conveyance, and Violet – again in Wensley's words – is 'lost to view' till she turns up on Tuesday morning at the Junior Minerva. I outlined my suspicions, minus any details of the Hackney people, to the two detectives.

'Where did they go afterwards, then, doctor?' Moultry asked. 'We must've questioned every cabman in the Division, as well as every railway ticket-clerk, ambulance driver, boatyard gaffer and ship's master!'

'Hired coach strikes me as the best possibility,' I suggested. 'In or out of the Division!'

'Lor', doctor!' the inspector exclaimed. 'No one in their right mind's going to book a coach in advance, with a ready-made witness up on the driver's seat, to go to do a murder, or get away from one, come to that! Not even through a third party. Your own common sense'll tell you that records and bills are kept of these things.'

'Precisely, inspector!' I said. 'Neither Dr Branscombe nor Rosie Bartlett had any thought of murder in their minds on the night of the twenty-first of this month! And dangerous as Agar and his East End myrmidons were, they were not the police. What power had they to quiz all the coach-hire firms in London?'

'You mean we haven't been trying our best to make up an alibi for Bartlett and Dr Branscombe?' Wensley sneered.

'I merely suggest, sergeant, that your priorities may have led you away from the truth of the matter.'

'So you're saying,' the inspector remarked, 'we should act on this notion you've got as to Dr Branscombe being elsewhere at the time of Agar's murder on a mission of mercy, ferrying this Bartlett woman in an above-board way away to safety some-where. Why, doctor, we don't even have any proof that "Mrs Shaw" was Rosie Bartlett.'

'Then I'll try to give you some, inspector: did you get a full physical description of Mrs Shaw from the hospital staff?'

Moultry nodded.

'And did they tell you she had old transverse bruises all over her face?'

The inspector turned wearily to Wensley.

'Coach-yards, sergeant,' he said. 'This time within a five-mile radius of here south of the river and west of the Tower. Get help from the Divisions concerned. That's after you've had a chat with this hot-potato wallah opposite the Whitechapel Road Synagogue. Take the candlestick along with you to Leman Street, too, and I'll want some men round here to take up the floor-boards. Oh, and Wensley . . .'

'Sir?'

'If you don't get a move on, I'll be there before you!'

I felt elation rise within me as the sergeant set to work quickly but carefully, and untangled the bolster from the candelabrum, which he wrapped tenderly in a pillowcase, then strode briskly out of the room.

'What can I do in the meantime, inspector?' I asked eagerly.

'Go home and get some sleep, doctor: you look dead on your feet. I think you've done quite enough for one day!'

Moultry was perfectly right, for my frantic mental efforts over the last forty-eight hours, combined with insufficient sleep, had left me tottering. Soon I would be unable to think straight, and would be of no use to anybody, so I reluctantly took the inspector's advice, and trans-shipped from the police van to a cab on the way to Leman Street and, once having gained my rooms, flopped into bed and slept till after nine on Saturday morning.

I took a hurried breakfast, and dashed down to the dispensary, where Jane Bonsor was already coolly in charge, and so passed the morning in my normal duties. At midday I wolfed down a sandwich, then made straight for Leman Street Police Station, where I was allowed to pass through to Moultry's office.

'Any results, inspector?' I asked.

'Looks like Rosie Bartlett's in the clear,' Moultry replied.

'What!' I exclaimed. 'But that is splendid! And Dr Branscombe?'

'Wensley's luck was in at Shipley's Yard, near Waterloo Station,' the inspector answered somewhat indirectly. 'A coach and driver had been ordered there on Monday morning by a Mr Smith, to go to the London Hospital for eleven-fifteen that night. Driver said he'd picked up a short lady wearing pince-nez, with white eyelashes and a very straight back, dressed as a nurse.'

'Dr Branscombe to a "t"!' I remarked.

Moultry smiled his doughy smile.

'This lady,' he went on, 'was accompanied by a shabbily dressed woman who didn't say anything, and who had marks on her face. The driver positively identified her as Rosie Bartlett from her police photograph.'

I reflected that the pair had evidently had the sense at the hospital entrance not to draw attention to themselves by wearing veils.

'And what according to the coachman was the women's destination, inspector?'

'Victoria Station, where they arrived around midnight. The two women left the coach, then the lady came back alone about twenty minutes later.'

Rosie had been put onto the boat-train, I would be bound!

'And what happened to Dr Branscombe then?' I led the inspector.

'The lady,' Moultry – not to be led – replied, 'asked to be put down at the corner of Bloomsbury Way and Oxford Street. They arrived there just before one in the morning.'

'So there was no possibility of either woman having killed Agar between eleven on Monday night and well after one on Tuesday morning!' I exclaimed.

'Begins to look like it, doctor. What wouldn't I give for a little chat with Miss Nancarrow at this moment!'

The finger of suspicion had evidently swung back on to Lavinia, but that would have to wait. First, my tow-haired comrade!

'About Dr Branscombe's detention, then, inspector: I really think now that on the evidence – '

I was somewhat disconcerted when Moultry quite cut across my bows by seemingly ignoring my question.

'By the bye, Dr Mortimer,' he said serenely. 'You've still a lot to tell us about the background to Agar's death, according to your, er, theory. We're still waiting for the results of the forensic tests on the candlestick and floorboards from Ginger Lane, and I suggest we have another little talk when they're in. We'll keep you informed.'

'But inspector,' I began to protest. 'Violet – '

'Good day for now, then, Dr Mortimer, and thanks for all your help!'

I stood, fuming inwardly, for a moment or two: it was intolerable! I remembered Zeinvel. Yes, he would know how to settle Moultry's hash! I'd go immediately to Crutched Friars.

'Very well, inspector,' was my parting shot. 'You shall be hearing from me sooner than you think!'

I turned on my heel and made for the corridor, but Moultry's voice arrested me at the door.

'Oh, and Dr Mortimer,' the inspector said, as if on an afterthought, 'you might just care to pop into the interview room at the bottom of the corridor on your way out. Someone there to see you.'

I strode down the corridor in the grip of a great surmise and opened the door of the interview room. Standing alone in the middle of the room was Violet, smiling radiantly. I rushed in and, folding her in my arms, poured out my heart to her.

At length she broke away and, linking her arm in mine, led me out into Leman Street.

'Come, James,' she said quietly. 'We have much to do.'

42

We retired to a little Italian place for luncheon, and I apprised Violet of all that had befallen me since we had last met, then she explained to me the reasons for her silence.

'After Rosie fell ill at Hackney, my acquaintance there – '

'Mr Venables?' I queried.

'Just so. Hilary Venables decided that there was nothing for it but hospital, if she was to live, and so she was moved to the

London. We were on tenterhooks lest Agar should get wind of her whereabouts. I visited her as often as I could without arousing suspicion, and on each occasion she made me swear solemnly that I would tell no one where she was. The poor thing was frantic with terror! Well, Agar's tentacles began to wave ever closer, until finally we decided that Rosie must be got out of the country, at least for the time being, until we could present a cast-iron case against Agar. Hilary had had previous experience of, er, getting people away, and he made all the arrangements.'

'Rosie was put on the boat-train at Victoria, then?'

'Yes, friends from the Sorbonne were awaiting her at Boulogne, but when the news broke of Agar's actual death next morning, it was decided that she must be got out of Europe altogether to avoid the French extradition laws. I received a visitor not two hours ago, who informed me in previously agreed language that Rosie was now safe under the care of the Sisters of Mercy at Marrakesh! Moreover, I was given to understand by the same conventions that she had released me from my vow of silence, and so I was able to give Inspector Moultry his statement!'

She must have read the disappointment in my eyes, for she seized my hand and wrung it warmly.

'But that by no means dims my gratitude for the efforts you have made towards my deliverance, dearest James! I scarcely think the police would have released me so promptly, statement or no, without the spur which your discoveries have applied to them.'

I smiled and squeezed her hand in return.

'What exactly did Moultry say to you?' I asked.

'That in view of my statement, and the new evidence that had come to light, he did not think it appropriate to detain me further, but that I was to hold myself in readiness to help him in his further enquiries, and that any further attempts on my part to withhold evidence would meet with the gravest consequences.'

'Then we are not out of the wood, yet!' I remarked. 'We must thoroughly lay this case to rest before we can have any rest. But tell me, how was it that you were "lost to view", as Wensley put it, on Tuesday morning, when the hired Shipley's coachman put you down in Bloomsbury Way? Surely the boots at your club must have admitted you: why then did he not tell Wensley that? Devotion to you, no doubt.'

'Billy devoted to me, forsooth! Why, he is a regular limb of Satan! No, it was Wensley's fault. The man is a brute. When later on he asked Billy if he had let me in in the early hours of Tuesday morning, Billy asked him why he wanted to know, and he promptly boxed the boy's ears for cheek. That put his back up, and he simply repeated to Wensley that he "hadn't seen nobody" all that morning. I was woken up by Moultry and Wensley at seven on the Tuesday morning, and the rest you know.'

'And you were prepared,' I remarked, 'to sit in prison with the prospect of disgrace and ruin – at the very least – hanging over your head, till word should reach you from North Africa that you might speak.'

'I keep my word, James!'

'Violet, you are as magnificent as you are impossible, and I serve notice on you that I shall not rest until I have made you my wife!'

All the reply I got to this was a blush and a repetition of her injunction that we had much to do. We heard no more from Leman Street, as, back at the dispensary, the afternoon advanced into teatime, which in turn merged into evening surgery, and Jane Bonsor was given a cordial farewell. I ate a most contented supper with Violet at her club where, as far as anyone knew, she had been spending a few days in the country, then, my nerves easy, I slept deeply and long that night, and was joined at breakfast in my rooms on the Sunday morning by Percy Tooke.

'Sorry to burst in on you like this, Mortimer, but have you got any news?'

I sat him down and rang my landlady for a spare cup-and-saucer and more rounds of toast.

'Yes, Tooke,' I said. 'Dr Branscombe is in the clear.'

'You mean – '

'Out, free! Better get some toast inside you. No need to ask if you've had any breakfast!'

I poured the surveyor a cup of coffee while he nibbled in his bunny-like way at the toast, liberally plastering each round with butter and marmalade, as I told of my experiences in Yorkshire and during the previous day.

'By Jove, Mortimer!' the little man spluttered, as he goggled at me in awe across the crumb-strewn table. 'Not a bad show!'

I refilled my own cup and stretched out my legs. I shied at the compliment and tried to fend it off with mild levity.

'Don't mention it, Tooke, all done by mirrors.'

The little man coughed violently and his face turned scarlet. I attributed his reaction to his undoubted bolting of his toast and sat up in my chair.

'Do go easy on that toast, old man,' I said. 'Dry tack: apt to stick in the throat.'

The lovelorn surveyor gulped down a draught of coffee and seemed to regain his aplomb.

'All the same,' he said, returning to his subject, 'tribute where it's due, and all that. And, Lavinia?'

'I'm truly sorry, Tooke, but we're no forrader there: you'd do well to go and look up Moultry in Leman Street. And you'd get my news a lot quicker if I had your private address.'

Tooke put down his cup with a clatter and jumped to his feet.

'Damn' decent of you, Mortimer, feeding me up like this. I'm happy to hear about Dr Branscombe, too: nice to see justice done for a change. Deuced happy about that. I'm sure you're doing your best about Lavinia, too. Must be off, now, though, following up some leads of my own. Remember, Crutched Friars will always find me.'

Before I could draw breath, Tooke had scampered out of the room. I pondered his visit as I finished my coffee. I went back over that coughing fit of Tooke's: had it just been the dryness of the toast, or something in my innocent jest: all done by mirrors? I got up and strolled over to the window, and gazed out at the Cambridge blue summer sky, and at the white clouds that were scudding across it. Bright, glittering things, mirrors, I mused idly. What could rival the sheen of a polished mirror, brighter than burnished silver? Brighter, even, than the silver of my fine new silver cigarette case, the loss of which still rankled with me. I went back to my room, sank into the armchair, and began to look through the morning papers. An hour must have passed in this desultory Sunday fashion, then an advertisement caught my eye. An advertisement for a patent boot polish: YOU WILL NEED NO MIRROR WHEN YOU USE HONEYSUCKLE WAX!

I flung down the paper and sat bolt upright in my chair. No! I could not believe it! Had I been used all along? There was only one way to find out: I must change into my oldest togs and set off for Whitechapel. There was not a moment to lose.

43

I took the stairs up to the new dispensary three at a time, bursting in abruptly on Violet who, with the new lad, was busy behind a heap of discarded packing cases and cartons.

'Better late than never, James!' my colleague remarked. 'I suggest you start with the – '

'Violet, I think I have it!' I gasped.

'Have what, James? You look quite overwrought. I hope you slept properly last night.'

'It's Lavinia!' I exclaimed. 'I think I know how we might find her. I'm sure Tooke has her, and he is here.'

'Good heavens! Where? Outside on the landing?'

'No. No time to explain now. Will you please send for Charlie Noble!'

Charlie was one of the less reputable of our allies among the street urchins, but satisfy him on two points – that you were not a policeman and that you were a friend of Dr Branscombe – and he was yours. A judicious tanner or a twist of 'baccy did not do any harm to your cause, either. My colleague sent the lad out to look for Charlie.

'What is this all about, James?' Violet asked.

'No time, Violet. You must do something for me: it will take five minutes.'

'Yes, what is it then?'

A padding on the stairs announced the arrival of a barefoot, bandy-legged mannikin in cut-off men's trousers and the ruins of a fisherman's guernsey, about four sizes too large for him.

The tiniest and greasiest of cricket-caps topped the close-cropped bullet head, and little, pale-blue eyes regarded me out of a wizened, blackhead-pimpled face. Charlie was rolling the disgusting bowl – and an inch or so of stem – of a broken clay pipe in and out of his mouth with his tongue. He looked at me in silence for a while, then turned to Violet, who nodded approvingly.

'Charlie,' I said, 'I want you to do something for me.'

'Yerss?'

'Go out by the court entrance and buy a pair of herrings from the woman with the barrel up the road.'

'Yer mean 'er as stands next to the ragman?'

Since for many in the East End the Sabbath had ended at dusk on Saturday, the Sunday streets were still a-bustle with traders.

'Yes, that's the one,' I confirmed.

'An' then?'

'I want you to study the face of every man you see within sight of the court entrance, without being noticed, mind you.'

The look of contempt I earned from Charlie was quite enough to reassure me of the unlikelihood of anyone being studied by him and knowing it.

'And come straight back here and describe them all.' I had finished my request.

Charlie rolled the pipe-bowl perilously in his maw, snatched the sixpence I held out to him, then scampered downstairs.

'Why do you think Mr Tooke is watching this place?' Violet asked, while the new lad was engaged in the pharmacy. I told her of his breakfast-time call. She returned to the attack.

'Why should the information you gave him make him wish to come here? Surely his first port-of-call would be the police to find out if they could shed any new light on the case.'

'If my surmise is right,' I said, 'he would first come here to satisfy himself that you are really at liberty again. How long have you been here?'

'Since about eight-thirty.'

'Mmm. He left me at about half-past nine, and I lounged about with the morning papers for nearly an hour after that.'

'He could have been here,' Violet said, 'taken a good look at me, and gone, with half-an-hour in hand.'

199

'No, wait!' I exclaimed. 'He would first have changed out of his decent clothes to come and loaf around here with ragmen and fishwives. He'd have had first to go back to wherever he lives to get a change of clothes.'

'Or to Crutched Friars,' my colleague suggested. 'Perhaps he keeps them there. But I still don't see why – if he does have Lavinia under his hand – he should worry so much, as you have told him the police are considering the possibility that Agar may have died by accident.'

'Their "considering the possibility" hardly puts Lavinia in the clear: it is not at all the same thing! On the contrary, she will now be the focus of their interest. No, Tooke will want to get her as far out of British jurisdiction as possible, and from the wrath – and long purse – of Baba! That's what I – Ah! Here's Charlie back.'

The urchin slapped an odoriferous newspaper bundle on to the table, along with four pennies change, which latter I handed back to him. He then started on a monotonous litany of description, in the course of which I stopped him at 'littlegingertash'.

'What was that again, Charlie?' I interrupted him.

'Little geezer in a cheesecutter and pea-jacket, buck-toofed like a rabbit, wiv a little ginger tash.'

'That'll be him!' I said. 'Where was he standing?'

'On va corner of va court, readin' va Pink 'Un!'

I added another threepence to Charlie's bounty and, dismissing him with thanks, turned to Violet.

'I must get out of here by the back stairs,' I said. 'Give me five minutes' grace, then I want you to come either to the window that overlooks the court, or down to the front entrance. On any pretext you like, so long as Tooke can see you.'

'And then what?' Violet asked.

'Just come back in here and carry on with what you are doing. Don't, whatever you do, look as if you are watching the court opening. I just want Tooke to see that you're at large. I'll come back later – soon, I hope – and explain in detail. Give me five minutes.'

I scampered out by the back stairs and emerged into Durward Street, then turned sharp left into New Road and arrived at

Whitechapel Road again. Two or three minutes must have passed since I had left the dispensary. I counted on Tooke's attention being concentrated on the comings and goings in the court, so that his back would be turned to me. I darted across the road, then slipped into the deep doorway of an oil shop, from which I could scan the other side of the road. Yes, it was he all right, in a short seaman's jacket and cheesecutter cap. He was leaning against a hitching post, and had a copy of the racing paper Charlie had mentioned open in front of him. He looked for all the world like any absorbed Sunday loafer, and his left profile was turned to the opening of the court. I waited amid the cries of the soused-herring woman and the hoarse bellowing of the ragman. My pulses raced as occasional traffic hold-ups temporarily obscured my view of the other side of the road, but then, briefly, the brim of Tooke's cheesecutter tilted upwards. He had seen Violet! He then unfolded his legs in leisurely fashion, straightened himself up and off the hitching post, folded the Pink 'Un, which he slipped into his pocket, and turned to face in my direction. Instinctively, I shrank deeper into the doorway, but Tooke's view could not have reached into the distant dimness of my refuge, and he simply turned on his heel and began to stroll down in the direction of Aldgate East.

Between Whitechapel High Street and Aldgate East Station he stopped twice to peer into plate-glass windows, and on each occasion I instantly turned my back to light a cigarette under my lapel. At last; at the end of the High Street, he crossed over into the opening of Mansell Street, the direct route to the workings of the new Tower Bridge, then still under construction. I guessed he would take a brief look round him before actually turning down Mansell Street, so before his foot had actually mounted the kerb, I slipped into the doorway of a public house, where I counted slowly to five before cautiously re-emerging with pounding heart. Instead of trying to sleuth him down Mansell Street – Tooke was too experienced a shikaree for me – I crossed in front of the portico of Aldgate Station and set off on what I hoped was a parallel course down the Minories, where even on a Sunday the steady dull rumble of traffic marked out the route to and from the docks. At last the two roads converged at the foot of Tower Hill, then, with St Katharine's Dock on the left, I espied the narrow back of my alert prey. He was walking briskly ahead towards the bridge-workings.

It was now after eleven, but the sun was still somewhat in the eastern quarter, so if my theory was to be put to the test, I had to get myself into position pretty quickly. I must get below, opposite the bridge-workings. I retraced my steps and scurried down towards the river, sweating in the July heat, deciding finally to stop just downstream of Alderman's Stairs. I pulled the peak of my battered cricket cap over my eyes and sat, idler-fashion, on the edge of the quay, kicking my heels against the stone-revetted quayside. At intervals in both directions there were others, similarly disengaged. My gaze swept over the smoky glory of the forest of masts and funnels which clad the riverbank in those days, and up to Wolfe-Barry's stone-clad towers of steel which in three or fours years' time were to take shape as Tower Bridge. Nothing happened for quite a while, and I sat breathing in the sun-molten tar- and smokestack-reek, listening to seagulls creaking and brawling overhead. I contemplated a cluster of Thames barges, which lay moored, four-deep, just upstream of me. What a sturdy elegance the breed had, when beating along in full red sail, with their prosaic cargoes of bricks or field drains! Then the flashes started from the site of the bridge-workings opposite.

The Morse Code had been one of my boyhood crazes and I was able to read the message with ease: BRANSCOMBE FREE. PREPARE LEAVE ONE HOUR. And that was it. There were no more flashes, and about a minute later, a stubby, aproned female form emerged on to the deck of one of the barges, and hung what looked like a pillowcase to a line of otherwise blue dungaree washing. On a Sunday ... I squinted upstream at the squat figure, who had turned to face downstream as she backed down the hatch again. My heart leapt. Demmy! I had them! Calm, calm ... I remained where I was and drew out my tobacco tin and cigarette papers, with which I rolled a cigarette, lit it and smoked it through, while my insides churned with impatience.

After about five minutes I got up and strolled along the quayside till I was alongside the nearest barge. I hopped across the covered, tarpaulined hatches of the first two, and landed on the foredeck of the *Saltwell*, the only one with washing hanging out. I made my way round to the accommodation and tapped on the porthole of the hatch. Demmy's frightened goggle-eyes stared into mine.

'Oh, Lor'!' I heard her squawk. 'What'll become of us now!'

44

It was Lavinia who let me into the cabin. She had on a plain, grey cotton dress, covered with a housewifely apron, just the sort of thing a bargee's missus might wear, and her hair was scraped back into an unbecoming bun. The silver streak had evidently fallen victim to the dye-bottle. She looked somehow sallow and without mystery in the light of common day. Her eyes avoided mine, while Demmy cowered behind her.

'I am so sorry, James,' Lavinia said at last, 'but it was the only way. I'm so glad Dr Branscombe's been set free. We should never have left her to be tried for murder, though, please believe that! Percy has been following the case most carefully, mainly through you.'

'I am not your judge, Lavinia,' I said, as for the first time I came to a full understanding of how I had stood vis-à-vis Tooke. 'But tell me, had Tooke ever approached Ferraby – as he later approached me – concerning your plight in Ginger Lane?'

'Once, at Dr Ferraby's consulting room in Eaton Place; or rather, he tried to. Dr Ferraby didn't even invite him to sit down or trouble to ask him who Percy was enquiring about, but merely told him he didn't discuss patients with outsiders and ordered him out. That was one of the things that finally made us decide on elopement as the only way out. Percy had rather hoped to make an ally of Dr Ferraby, to influence him to prevail upon Baba to change his attitude towards us, a forlorn hope, as you yourself came to see.'

'I see,' I said. 'So when Tooke saw that Ferraby had been replaced by a much younger locum, he decided to try me as a prospective listening post, and when, moreover, in the course of his staged initial encounter with me – a less daunting venue than Eaton Place – he spotted that I had a fine, highly reflective cigarette-case . . .'

Lavinia's eyes were downcast again.

'Percy taught me the Morse Code in Simla – we have loved each other since we first met there – and I needed something with a good shine to it to answer the messages he was flashing to me over the churchyard wall in Ginger Lane.'

'So – ' I finished her confession for her ' – he flashed the information about my case to you, so that when I first examined you, you put on a fit of the vapours in order to distract me, while you slipped your hand into my pocket and filched my cigarette case!'

'Oh, that was beastly of me, I know, James, but there was really no other way! Baba had confiscated my last little mirror, and the time of our escape was approaching, so that I desperately needed some way of answering Percy's signals. Oh, I know we – I – have used you all along, but really – '

I held up a deprecatory hand.

'It is no matter, Lavinia. Tell me, why did your guardian confiscate your mirror? Did he suspect something was going on between you and Agar?'

'No, it was just that Ord spotted me using the mirror one afternoon, and reported it to Baba, who suspected I was using it to attract the attention of passers-by. Luckily Percy caught sight of Ord before responding with his mirror which, in his haste to get away, he let slip into the churchyard.'

That explained the fragment of optical glass the police had found in the churchyard, I thought.

'Baba's suspicion increased even more after that,' Lavinia went on, slipping her arm round the shoulder of her old nurse, 'and I've only Demmy's ceaseless vigilance on my behalf to thank for the fact that we were able to exchange any further messages at all!'

How valuable indeed I had been as an unwitting listening post! I reflected bitterly.

'Tell me, Lavinia,' I went on, 'where did you spend Monday night?'

'In an hotel, with Demmy, as Mrs and Miss Wright.'

The old nurse huddled closer to her former charge.

'Then you should be in the clear: your handwriting in the hotel register alone should be your order of release. All the more reason for coming forward.'

The great eyes shone with some of their former splendour.

'But, James, please, you won't tell the police. Percy says we must wait till things are absolutely certain, and – '

'No, I shall not give you away, Lavinia: or should I say Mrs Tooke.'

'Percy and I were married on Tuesday morning, before the news of Mr Agar's death came out. Percy arranged it all with a clergyman friend of his in Woolwich. They were chums at Wellington. He's been a real sport throughout: he hasn't said a word to a living soul.'

I recalled Tooke's laughingly announced alibi, which I had not been able to take completely seriously at the time, to the effect that he had been taking bedtime cocoa with a vicar at the time of Agar's death.

'And I take it Tooke went on to stay with this clerical chum of his in Woolwich after you and Demmy had signed in to the hotel?'

'Yes, James, he went straight on there, and stayed until we turned up to join him in Woolwich for the wedding at ten on Tuesday morning.'

I could now see plainly why, at our last meeting, Lavinia had seemed to go along willingly with her guardian's plan to have her placed in a French sanatorium. She had not wanted the elopement arrangements to be upset at the eleventh hour!

'What do you mean to do, James?' Lavinia said.

'First, I shall go and have luncheon, then I shall go to Leman Street Police Station and tell them all I know. I shall also suggest that they bring your guardian to hear what I have to say. He has been perfectly frantic on your behalf since you disappeared, Lavinia.'

'I shall never speak to Baba again, ever! He will use his money to separate Percy and me, I know he will! He will say I am insane, that we are not really married, bring in horrid, foolish doctors like Ferraby, lawyers – '

'I think you will find he has changed once he hears what I have to say, Lavinia.'

'No, never, James, I shall never – '

'I leave it to you, Lavinia. According to the message I have just intercepted, Tooke will be back here in forty minutes or so. I shall be going to Leman Street in a couple of hours. You will both have an hour to talk things over. In parting, I should add that your guardian has something very important to tell you, something it were better you should know before you decide to cut him entirely out of your life.'

I turned to leave.

'James!' Lavinia said behind me.

'Yes?' I said, turning back.

She thrust a square, flat packet into my hand.

'I meant to send this on to you afterwards,' she said, stepping back.

I left the cabin and the barge, regaining the quayside, where I tore open the packet. In it was my fine, new silver cigarette case, and a note which read:

'Dear James, Please do not think too badly of me. Truly yours, Mrs Lavinia Tooke.'

The screeching seagulls overhead seemed to be laughing at me.

45

I thought much on the wiles of women as I walked up towards the City in search of a disengaged cab. I set Lavinia's combination of slyness and feyness – or so I saw it – against Violet's solid worth, and wondered what sort of helpmeet Tooke would find in his darling. And how consistently I had underrated Tooke, though the way he had dealt with the garrotters in Plumbers' Row had given a jolt to my view of him hitherto. I should have relied less on appearances, more on evidence, and the evidence had been formidable! Here was a man who had faced sunstroke, thirst, the Pathan's musket-ball. He had played the Great Game for the highest stakes in the freezing passes of the High Himalaya, and finally had thrown up his commission and his career, crossed continents, cheerfully faced penury in England, all to be near the woman he loved. What woman could fail to respond to such dash, such juice! This would be a lesson to me for the future.

I finally managed to rouse a snoozing cabman in Fenchurch Street, who drove me to the dispensary, whence I escorted Violet to Cohen's for cold borscht soup, over which I told her of my discovery of Lavinia. Practical as ever, she got a lad to run up to the Strand Palace with a note for Boynton-Leigh while we finished our lunch, then, at around two o'clock, we set off for Leman Street Police Station, where we found Moultry and Wensley. We retired to a sort of boardroom, the inspector presiding at the head of a leather-topped table, with Wensley, company secretary-like with notebook at the ready, at his right hand. The sun filtered into the silent, stale-aired room through high-up, dingy windowpanes. Violet and I sat together on one side of the table. We told Moultry of our invitation to Boynton-Leigh to the conference and he nodded his agreement, and sent Wensley to instruct the desk-sergeant to send along the nabob as soon as he arrived.

'Lead off, please, doctor,' Moultry said in his brisk, civil way. 'Mr Boynton-Leigh knows the way here by now!'

'I should first of all like to ask you, inspector,' I began, as Wensley arrived back again, his note-book at the ready, 'whether the tests on the spike of the candelabrum which I suggest killed Agar have borne any fruit yet?'

'They have, doctor,' Moultry said. 'Traces of blood have been detected at the base of the spike – '

'They will try to wash it off with hot water,' Wensley added with a contemptuous snort, 'when it only makes it stick!'

'As I was saying, doctor,' Moultry went on, 'there were traces on the spike, and any amount of it on the edges of the floor-boards near where you put the candlestick in your demonstration of your theory on Friday night. It looks like a true bill, and if we can just clear up where Miss Nancarrow stands in all this – if we ever find her, that is – it's beginning to look more and more like misadventure.'

'I prefer to call it nemesis!' Violet said grimly.

'Be that as it may,' I went on, 'Agar came by his death as a consequence of the relation in which he stood to the members of the Boynton-Leigh household. Indeed, the relations between the various members of that establishment were all curious: Boynton-Leigh's attitude to his ward, Lavinia Nancarrow, at once doting and harsh; his savage contempt – now so mercifully softened by his only son's illness – for Lance; Miss Nancarrow's irruption, at the age of sixteen – virtually a woman – into Lance's life, and his subsequent confusion as to how he should relate to her. After Lavinia and her faithful nurse, Penruddock, are conjured up – I can think of no better way of expressing it – from Simla to Calcutta, after the death of Mrs Boynton-Leigh, the newly reconstituted household settles down to some sort of modus vivendi. Then in steps Agar, like some pantomime demon, in search of Zoffany paintings. He meets Boynton-Leigh in St John's Church in Calcutta, where the nabob is a sidesman, and where there are Zoffanys. Agar charms, he makes his mark, he is brought into the household as drawing tutor to the young people, then, only weeks later, something goes wrong: so wrong that Boynton-Leigh uproots them all and takes them off to England.'

'Agar was up to something,' Moultry remarked. 'Blackmail most likely. Something seems to come over white people in the tropics, and I daresay Mr Boynton-Leigh had his little secrets.'

'But why leave Calcutta?' I objected. 'Where was the point? If Agar was blackmailing him there, he could blackmail him equally easily in England, or in Timbuctoo, for that matter! No, it must have been something which made going on living in India impossible for Boynton-Leigh, and which made him, once in England, want to shut up Lavinia in a sort of periodically doped stupor. She was cosseted by him, and at the same time distrusted and reviled, as if she were some kind of reprobate who could not help herself. And yet again, Agar, a manifest and unapologetic scoundrel, seems to be the only visitor – apart from tradesmen, Ferraby, and myself – who is ever admitted to the house!'

'He'd have gone there to collect his blackmail payments,'

Moultry suggested. 'An instalment's due on Monday night, so he comes round at midnight knowing the servants'll be out of the way. He knows how to use the trick-knocker, and Boynton-Leigh, by long-standing agreement, will have drawn the bolt Ord always shoots before turning in at night. On Monday night, Agar finds that all the birds have flown, has a look in Miss Lavinia's room, sees something that interests him in one of the paintings on the wall, and ends up spiked like an invoice in a counting office after he falls off the steps while leaning to look closer at the picture!'

'The blackmail theory is a strong one,' I said, 'and the fact that Agar apparently chose to make his midnight call on the very eve of the departure of the members of the household for the Continent strongly confirms it.'

'Boynton-Leigh would be desperate to get the thing over with before their departure,' Violet suggested.

'Yes,' Wensley put in, 'good moment to put the screw on him!'

'The daytime servants lived out,' Violet added, 'and Ord, whose job we assume it was to bolt the door on the inside last thing at night, had driven his master out in the coach in search of Miss Nancarrow and Penruddock.'

'Let us go back to motive,' I said, 'and again to personalities. We have a fair notion of how Boynton-Leigh stood in relation to his ward, but how did she and Lance really get on? Yet again, there is their expressed attitude to their former art tutor, Agar. Mention of him drew only cold indifference from Lavinia, but Lance seemed to hero-worship him with a positively schoolgirl-ish intensity!'

Moultry coughed at this juncture.

'A year or two in Australia would cure him of that sort of thing!' the inspector muttered darkly.

'Then,' I went on, 'I considered Lavinia's pleas to me never to suggest to her guardian that she and Lance be allowed to correspond. This led me to suspect that a letter had been behind what Lance described as his father's "brainstorm" in Calcutta, which in turn led them into sequestered exile in Aldgate. What was the nature of that letter?'

'Some sort of love-letter?' Moultry suggested. 'From the lad to

Miss Lavinia? That'll be most likely what got his father's goat in India. Not much of a dark and dirty secret, though, I should've thought. Couldn't squeeze much blackmail out of that!'

'It goes deeper than that,' I said, 'much deeper. I learnt that Lavinia had an interest in the Arthurian Legend, and to help her pass the time during her convalescence from influenza, I gave her a copy of Sir Thomas Malory's version of the *Morte d'Arthur*; or rather handed it over to Boynton-Leigh for his approval, before he gave it to Lavinia. He threw the book back in my teeth, as if it had been a basketful of cobras I had offered her! This made me curious, and later I read it through. I found that the only feature that really distinguished it from Lord Tennyson's immensely popular and highly respectable version – which in normal times, Boynton-Leigh said to me, he would have been perfectly happy for his ward to have had – was the theme of King Arthur's unwitting incest with his own sister.'

'You mean,' Violet said, all attention, 'Lance and Miss Nancarrow are – '

'Half-brother and half-sister!' Moultry said.

'That would surely have been manageable,' I went on, 'even in Calcutta. The truth could have been tactfully broken to Lance and Lavinia, and they could have been quietly packed off separately to school in England like any normal sahib's children. Agar could have been squared somehow – God knows Boynton-Leigh's rich enough – but there would have been scarcely any need for him to have left India.'

'So you think Miss Nancarrow is Boynton-Leigh's natural daughter, then?' Wensley said.

'I believe so,' I said. 'But I don't think the matter ends there. Agar's intention was deeper and darker than that. He was a man with a sardonic mind, and a deep contempt for his fellows: it was his instinct to play out the farce for all it was worth. I have tried to put myself in his shoes. He was an artist, an acknowledged expert on Zoffany, with an agency granted by the American millionaire Frohwein to buy paintings by that artist for his principal. In the course of his researches, Agar came across a Zoffany previously thought lost, in the hands of a Highgate recluse. This group-portrait included two young girls, whose subsequent fate seems now to be lost in the past. The girls – the

Misses Leigh – were of striking, gypsy-like beauty, each with a streak of pure silver hair running through their otherwise black tresses. Well, this was one Zoffany Mr Frohwein was not going to be able to add to his collection, for the recluse absolutely refused to part with the picture, and Agar had to turn to other matters.

'Later on, the ups and downs – mainly downs – of Agar's life brought him to Calcutta, where he fell in with Boynton-Leigh and his establishment. He was introduced to Lavinia, and it must have seemed to him as if more than a century had been abolished, and he was pressing the warm, pulsating hand of one of the Misses Leigh in the painting in Highgate, so strong was the resemblance! The artist was fascinated, and got to work ferretting into Boynton-Leigh's antecedents. Among other things, he found out that the nabob was the son of a noted – not to say notorious – Peninsular adventurer, Richard Boynton. This worthy, one of the last of the burra sahibs to keep a harem of native women, had been obliged to pension off his houris in order to recoup his shaky fortunes by marrying a wealthy heiress, a Miss Rachel Leigh of Bristol, a young lady of strong Evangelical principles. This set off a train of thought in Agar's tortuous mind – '

'Deep waters, doctor!' Moultry muttered with narrowed eyes.

'Agar finally hatched out a plan,' I went on. 'He sought out those of the late Richard Boynton's "beebees" who were still alive and traceable, and found one who was still sufficiently bitter about her treatment at the hands of her late protector, and sufficiently impoverished to be willing to join in Agar's plot. He further learnt of a youthful indiscretion of Boynton-Leigh's, the inevitable fruit of an oppressively religious upbringing on a naturally virile young man: a clandestine liaison with a lowly native girl, of the sort who do not have pedigrees. There was a child, whom the young Boynton-Leigh put out to nurse in Calcutta – '

'Lavinia!' Violet murmured.

'Yes,' I confirmed, 'Lavinia! Soon afterwards he provided her with a new identity borrowed from a forgotten gravestone in Calcutta cemetery, and sent her, in the care of a trusted protégée of his – Mrs Penruddock – up into the crisp and healthy air of

Simla, where his daughter was brought up in modest gentility. By now Boynton-Leigh himself was married, but stole up to Simla whenever he could to spend time with Lavinia, who only knew him as "Baba". He watched her grow into a lovely girl, and came to feel a chaste adoration for her. Eventually his wife died, and he brought Lavinia down like a prize from the hills to join his household in Calcutta. Now of course Agar knew nothing of the details I have just conjectured – '

'Conjectured is the word, doctor!' Wensley remarked sceptically, but I pressed on.

'Agar was convinced only that Lavinia was Boynton-Leigh's daughter, and that was enough for his purposes. He waited for the right moment, then approached the nabob with a grave matter, something which might only be told in absolute confidence. He then told Boynton-Leigh that an old native woman had approached him recently with a tale of a secret, something which she felt that, nearing the end of her life, she must tell. But it was only for the ears of Boynton-Leigh. Nonsense, of course, Agar assured the nabob, and if it had been him she had been trying to work on, he would soon have sent her packing, but somehow he had thought he had better tell him about it before sending the woman away with a flea in her ear.'

'I take it this old biddy's the discarded native mistress of Boynton-Leigh's father,' Moultry queried, 'put up to it by Agar?'

'Yes,' I replied. 'Boynton-Leigh immediately came to the conclusion that his sin had somehow found him out, and he was of course agog to hear what the old woman had to say to him. Agar arranged a so-called secret meeting for him with the old "beebee", and she duly parrotted the tale Agar had coached her to tell. To the effect that, after she had been discarded by Richard Boynton, she had borne a daughter, whom she had not been able to keep on the occasional pittances her erstwhile protector had allowed her. She had at last been forced to farm out the little girl to poor relations, whose own fortunes had fallen lower and lower until when the child had reached nubile age – very early in those latitudes – the poor relations had in desperation offered her to a wealthy, repressed young European.'

Wensley clucked his tongue against his upper palate.

'They were making Boynton-Leigh think he'd unknowingly

fathered Miss Lavinia on his own half-sister. That your drift, doctor?'

I nodded.

'No wonder he didn't like Malory's book!' Violet remarked.

'A wicked business!' Moultry remarked. 'If it really happened.'

Just then we heard the handle of the open door rattle behind us, and we swung round to behold a dark-clad figure, who was clutching on the handle as if to support himself.

'Why, Mr Boynton-Leigh!' Moultry exclaimed.

'It happened,' the nabob groaned, 'very much as Dr Mortimer has just described it! I am naked!' And with those words, he slumped down on to the floor.

46

Moultry and I rushed over to the door to help Boynton-Leigh to his feet, then to a chair at the table.

'If you don't feel up to it, sir,' Moultry began, 'we can always – '

The nabob waved his arm impatiently.

'No, inspector,' he insisted, 'I am quite restored. I shall see this through right to the end! Dr Mortimer's supposition is true in most details, and Agar played his card ruthlessly to the end. I suspect he found out the whereabouts of my late father's, er . . . concubine through an old mali – native gardener – whom I had sacked for theft and for bullying the other servants not long after Agar came to teach Lance and Lavinia. We never saw the mali again. I could not possibly go on in India, of course, with the sword of public obloquy and ruin hanging over my head. How many other discontented cast-off servants of my father's might not be considering breaking their silence. The name of Boynton associated with incest! I suffered the agonies of the damned. But there was worse to come: the sins of the fathers were to be visited on the sons, even unto the third generation!'

'The letter!' I said. 'You were at cross-purposes all along, Mr Boynton-Leigh: Lance did not write it to Lavinia, but to Agar!'

'To Agar, doctor?' the nabob whispered. 'You are suggesting that my son's feelings towards him were – '

'I fear so, sir, and Agar planted it on Lavinia in Calcutta, which I surmise was the cause of your great sundering quarrel with Lance and Lavinia. It was a trick to strengthen Agar's hold over you: making you believe that your supposed incest with your alleged half-sister all those years ago was being repeated by your own children! I daresay Agar saw it as a capital joke!'

Boynton-Leigh cradled his head in his hands and stared at the table-top as he replied.

'I should have seen what Agar was doing to my boy when first I engaged him as the children's tutor, that Agar's degeneracy was finding an answering chord in Lance. But I did not allow myself to see it, or believe it. One of the native sweepers found the letter in Lavinia's room and, being of course unable to read it – for which thank God! – innocently brought the letter to me. Oh, my son! My son!'

Boynton-Leigh clutched his head in his hands and swayed for a moment, then, regaining his composure, went on.

'At the time, I was convinced that the filthy letter had been from Lance to Lavinia – it was couched in terms that left room for that interpretation – and the children's obstinate silence only confirmed my suspicions. I decided then on the course that led us to Aldgate.'

'Where Agar eventually visited you with a fresh ploy,' I said. 'The picture!'

'Yes, the picture. He claimed to have succeeded in reserving a painting – at considerable expense, of course – of one of my father's remote ancestresses, a Miss Boynton, along with the very papers exchanged between buyer and artist all those generations ago. Agar hummed and hawed about bringing me the painting and papers, the price going up with each delay, but at one of our midnight meetings just a week before I planned to travel to the Continent with Lance and Lavinia, I found myself in possession of both! The portrait was the image of Lavinia, and the papers irreproachable in their authenticity. I was then prey to divided emotions, for on the one hand, these supposed proofs further persuaded me that the resemblance had come down through my father's line, and that Lavinia's mother had been my own half-sister, and on the other hand, I had to counterbalance my immense relief at having secured the only surviving proof of my family's shame.'

'I can lay your mind at rest, sir,' I said, 'as to one thing: the painting you bought so dearly is not a portrait of Miss Boynton, or of any ancestress of your father's. The true portrait of Miss Arabella Boynton still hangs in Beck Hall in Yorkshire, and that portrait bears not the slightest resemblance to Lavinia. The picture Agar foisted on you was a fake, concocted from a portrait of a Miss Leigh, an eighteenth-century forebear of your mother's!'

Boynton-Leigh gave a start, and sat bolt upright.

'But the papers, Dr Mortimer! Surely they are absolutely genuine? I have had them verified by one of the most learned – '

'Genuine, but stolen, sir!' I replied. 'Those papers pertain to the real portrait of Miss Boynton, the one that is still in Yorkshire. The papers were filched by Agar from your trusting kinswoman at Beck Hall, and used by him to lend a spurious authenticity to the fake which he palmed off on you. You have been pitilessly abused, sir!'

The nabob flung himself back in his chair as if stunned, then a light seemed to dawn in his eyes.

'You have relieved me of a heavy burden, Dr Mortimer, and I shall be forever in your debt!'

'Please do not speak of it, sir! Pray go on with your narrative.'

'On Monday night, then,' Boynton-Leigh went on, 'I had arranged for Agar to call on me – at his urgent request – at midnight, according to our old arrangements, though to this day I have no notion as to what his purpose was.'

'More blackmail, most likely!' Moultry muttered.

'Well,' the nabob said, 'death cut the scoundrel off before he could try any more of his machinations on me!'

'Please describe exactly what happened on Monday night, sir,' Moultry said. 'You may remember something further to what you've already told me in your statement.'

'Yes,' Boynton-Leigh resumed, 'the servants – except for Ord – left shortly after dinner at eight, and the evening passed quietly till eleven, when we all retired for the night or, rather, all of us except myself. I went downstairs at about ten-past eleven and drew the front-door bolt to allow Agar to enter later on, then went upstairs to say goodnight to Lavinia and Penruddock, as was my usual habit. To my surprise, I receive no response from either! I tried their doors to find them unlocked, and their rooms empty. The sash of Lavinia's bedroom window had been forced from the outside, and the padlock which secured the grill of iron bars on the inside wrenched off. The window was wide open!'

'And the candlesticks, sir?' Wensley queried. 'I don't recall your having mentioned their position in your original statement to us.'

'Did I not, sergeant? Well, the candelabrum was naturally drawn out from under the window to allow easy entry and egress for the fugitives.'

'You're sure of that, Mr Boynton-Leigh?' Moultry asked.

'Positive, inspector.'

Both Moultry and Wensley fixed their eyes on me for a moment, then the nabob went on with his account of Monday night.

'I immediately alerted Ord,' he said, 'and we searched the house from cellar to attics, but found no trace of the missing women. I then had Ord get out the coach, and we went out into the night in search of Lavinia and Pendruddock – '

'And incidentally established excellent alibis – ' Wensley said.

'We had no thought of that, sergeant!' Boynton-Leigh protested. 'My first thought was that it was some trick of Agar's. But anyway, we returned at about five in the morning to find Agar's cold corpse bent over one of the bronze candelabra in Lavinia's room. I was at my wits end, feeling sure that the presence of Agar's body would inevitably be linked in the minds of the police with Lavinia's disappearance. With Ord's help, I removed the body to my study, then we set to cleaning up what little blood there was in Lavinia's room with hot water, after which we tried to return the room to its original state. I refastened the catch on the window-sash, then replaced the broken padlock of the grill with one Ord found in the stable. Ord then suggested we go through Agar's clothes for anything incriminating – '

'He would have!' Wensley muttered. 'If he's who we think he is.'

'Ord became increasingly agitated as the morning wore on, sergeant,' the nabob explained, 'until he left the scene abruptly when I later told him of my intention of confessing to Agar's murder in order to shield Lavinia from possible evil consequences. He naturally had no desire to be arrested as an accomplice to murder! I have not seen hair or hide of him since.'

'And your findings,' Moultry asked, 'when you searched the body?'

'Just what I told you in my statement, inspector: a handkerchief, cheroots and vestas in a little silver case, a pencil-case, some loose change, a little bottle of spirit and a wad of cotton wool – '

'Ah!' Moultry broke in, turning to me. 'You had something to say about the artist's materials, Dr Mortimer: what about the spirit and cotton wool, then?'

'First, inspector,' I said, 'may I ask Mr Boynton-Leigh a question?'

'Doctor?' the nabob quizzed.

'Did Agar on his, er, confidential visits to your house in Ginger Lane ever ask you about the family paintings on display there?'

'Mmm, as I recall, he did make allusion to them. Said something about his noticing that there were some he'd not seen in our house in Calcutta.'

'And did you tell him that some had been found stored in the attic in Ginger Lane? Pictures he could not have seen in Calcutta?'

'Yes, I may have done, though you will understand that on these occasions, once our, er, business was done, I had no other thought than to see the back of the fellow.'

'And Agar had never to your knowledge been in Lavinia's room?'

Boynton-Leigh's face reddened and he sat up rigidly in his chair.

'I should think not, Dr Mortimer! I saw to it that the door to her room was locked from the outside whenever the scoundrel called!'

'So, then,' I summed up, 'Agar knew there were possibly family portraits in Lavinia's room, a room he had never been in. His fake painting plot depended for its success on there being no other portraits extant of Leigh women – Mr Boynton-Leigh's mother's line – showing the tell-tale streak of white hair so striking in Lavinia – '

'With you, doctor!' Wensley growled, his eyes narrowing to sparkling flints. 'He had to see whether there was anyone with the streak in the pictures in Miss Lavinia's room, and since Mr Boynton-Leigh here hadn't mentioned it – '

'No, sergeant, I have never noticed anything of the kind!' the nabob remarked.

'And,' Wensley went on, 'since his lay had worked all right so far, he'd reckoned the pictures must be so covered in muck, the streak mustn't show – '

'And that's where the cotton wool and meths came in!' the inspector chimed in. 'I see what you were driving at now, Dr Mortimer. Good thinking, that! Agar carried the stuff with him – the only artist's materials found on his body – whenever he visited the house in Ginger Lane, on the offchance he might be able to nip into Miss Lavinia's bedroom and take a dekko at the paintings, with the cotton wool and meths handy to clean away any grime and old varnish. If Agar hadn't come a cropper, Mr Boynton-Leigh, I daresay you might be a picture or two short now! Instead, he – quite literally – overreached himself!'

'Nemesis!' Violet muttered again. 'God is not mocked!'

Moultry turned to Boynton-Leigh.

'All the same, sir, it was a mad, reckless thing you did, confessing like that, then keeping silent all that time! Far from diverting our attention away from Miss Lavinia, it only made us more eager to find her, not to mention the waste of our time.'

'It is easy to see that now, inspector,' the nabob replied, 'but it is impossible for you, sitting comfortably in judgment here, even to begin to understand what was passing through my mind on that appalling morning! But Dr Mortimer, I am sure we have all been astonished by the accuracy of your deductions today. Cannot you, for pity's sake, apply your acumen to give me some hope as to where my daughter is at this moment?'

I looked at my watch – my bargain of the morning had been fulfilled – and nodded.

'Sir,' I said, 'I found her this morning on the barge *Saltwell*, moored off Alderman's Stairs. She eloped with Percival Tooke on Monday night, and Mrs Penruddock was with them. They have watertight alibis for that night. Lavinia is well, and I have urged them both to come here now and give an account of themselves – '

Boynton-Leigh leapt to his feet and, leaning forward, gaped into my face like an idiot, while both the detectives rose in their chairs and shot me reproving glances.

'Tooke, doctor!' the nabob gasped. 'Tooke has my daughter? Why, he cannot look after himself, let alone a wife! And on a barge!'

'I must say, doctor,' the inspector said indignantly, 'you've taken your time in telling us! They might both be over the hills and far away by now!'

It struck me that, in spite of the bombshell I had just dropped, neither of the detectives had made any immediate move to go off in pursuit of Lavinia and Tooke, and just then I was given an indication why not, for, as if acting on a prompt, Wensley unfolded a large foolscap sheet with a ragged edge, as if it had been torn out of a ledger. He handed over the sheet to his superior, who nodded at him, then turned to the merchant.

'Do you happen to have anything on you in your, er, daughter's handwriting, sir?' Moultry asked the still-astonished Boynton-Leigh, who looked puzzled for an instant, then like an automaton drew out his pocket-book, from which he took out a photograph and handed it to the inspector.

'Taken on her eighteenth birthday,' the nabob said.

The two detectives conferred for a moment, comparing page with photograph, then Moultry nodded at Wensley, who addressed Boynton-Leigh.

'You can swear to this dedication being in your daughter's handwriting, sir?'

'Of course I can, man! Do you think I do not know my own child's hand!'

'I have here the page of the register of the great Eastern Hotel,' Moultry said, 'for Monday night, the twenty-first of July, with the signature of a Miss Jane Wright, described by the hotel staff as a slim, young lady in a veil, who took a double room with her mother, a stout, elderly lady in old-fashioned widow's weeds. The pair left the hotel at nine on Tuesday morning. We are agreed that the handwriting of "Miss Wright's" signature in the register seems identical to that of your daughter's writing on the photograph. This would stand up in any court of law as a first-rate alibi. May we keep this photograph by us for the moment, sir?'

Boynton-Leigh nodded and grunted his assent.

'Well, sergeant,' Moultry said, turning to his assistant, 'I think a little stroll down by the riverside might be in order, so if you'll – '

Just then a uniformed constable appeared in the doorway and announced two visitors, to do with the Aldgate Case. Moultry nodded brusquely at the constable, and all eyes were on the door, when in stepped Lavinia, on Tooke's arm, with Demmy bringing up the rear.

Boynton-Leigh let out a sort of animal bellow and sent the chairs scattering as he dashed across the room to his daughter. He flung himself down on his knees in front of her and buried his face in the hem of her dress. Violet and I averted our gaze.

'I'm so glad they saw sense at last, James!' my companion murmured.

'Yes,' was all I could say.

'Speak of the devil!' Wensley exclaimed.

'You shall have your statements, inspector,' I remarked to Moultry. 'The River Police will not nab all the glory after all!'

Violet and I at last were able to leave them all to it and, as we passed through the double doors, I suffered Tooke to shake my hand briefly.

'All's fair and all that, old chap,' he stuttered.

'I wish you both happiness,' I said coldly, and Violet, taking my arm, gave him a stiff nod and began to steer me into the corridor, but not before Boynton-Leigh had rushed up and wrung my hand. He said a number of complimentary things which need not be repeated here, then addressed Violet.

'May I say, ma'am, though we have had our differences in the past, he will be a happy warrior indeed who faces life's battles with you at his side! But you and Dr Mortimer shall be hearing from me anon. I am going back to my daughter. For the time being, my undying thanks!'

'Strange man!' Violet remarked as we left the building. 'There is a devil in him!'

We took a cab and I escorted her back to the Junior Minerva, where we were to take tea. She hesitated at the foot of the steps.

'James . . .' she said.

'Yes, Violet?'

Clearly something was in the air.

'Regarding the er, matter you raised in the Italian restaurant yesterday lunchtime.'

My heart began to pound.

'Yes!' I replied in the merest whisper.

She seemed to be having difficulty closing her parasol, while I hopped on hot coals.

'I have been thinking, James.'

'Yes, my dear?'

'I believe they do such things quite decently at Marylebone Registry Office. You may make arrangements . . .'

I was, as they say, walking on air!

Envoi

Even the mills of the Law did not have to grind particularly fine before the demise of Jack Agar was entered as a case of Death by Misadventure, and those who had been caught up in its meshes were free once again to pursue their several avocations.

The Percival Tookes took ship for Rangoon, where the artful surveyor had found a billet extending the Burmah railways. It hardly needs saying that Demmy accompanied them, so at any rate, the first generation of little Tookes would not lack for a devoted nurse! Lavinia must have been happy to find herself under eastern skies again. About two years after the events I have described, and after the birth of Lavinia's first child, James, there took place in Simla a no doubt rather awkward reunion between the Tookes and their firstborn and Archibald Boynton-Leigh and Lance, who were by then re-established in Calcutta after a world cruise undertaken to complete Lance's recuperation. Percival Tooke must evidently have mastered his aversion to the climate of Bengal, for shortly afterwards, he was taken on as a junior partner in his father-in-law's firm in Calcutta, though he and Lavinia kept their own domestic establishment in that city.

I think it may be surmised that it must have been with considerable relief that Lavinia – again from the independence of her own establishment – was able to share the burden of her father's adoration with little James who, as I write this, is head of the firm of Boynton and Tooke. Perhaps we may hope, too, in view of his sore trial, that the nabob at last found a measure of happiness in the discovery that those who wish to go on being loved by those they care for must first learn to let them go.

Certainly he seems very promptly to have learnt this lesson in respect to his son, who must soon have wilted in what must, for him, have been the humid tedium of his father's Calcutta counting house, for the next thing we know of Lance is as proprietor of a select, very successful small hotel in the hill-station of Naini Tal: 'Naughty Naini'. The former Dartmouth misfit quickly came into his own as quite the best-dressed man in Naini, a perennially eligible bachelor and the acknowledged leader of the Gay Set there, much in demand for amateur theatricals. I later learnt through travellers' tales that his portrayal of Nell Gwyn was the talk of the station.

Rosie Bartlett returned to England from her Moroccan adventure after she heard she was in the clear. She joined Hilary Venables as a helper in his women's refuge in Hackney and, so far as I was able to hear thereafter, found no further use for her scissors outside housewifery!

Violet and I were married in the August of that year, and Boynton-Leigh sent us as a wedding present the fine 'lost' Zoffany which Agar had used as model for the fake portrait of the nabob's alleged Boynton ancestress, and which the merchant had purchased by auction from the Crown, which held Agar's estate. We gave first refusal of the painting to Mr Politis, the Bloomsbury collector who, afire with the desire to foil his German-American rival Frohwein, had engaged us as his informal agents and, with the proceeds, we were able to go ahead with the establishment of the first Bryant Foundation socio-medical institute.

Not long after this, the house in Ginger Lane – in more recent years demolished to make way for one of Mr Oswald Stoll's talkie-palaces – was put up for sale, and we received an unexpected souvenir of this in the shape of a crate, without any explanatory note whatsoever. Inside were two fine bronze Chinese candelabra of a remote dynasty, which Violet immediately consigned to the attic of our home where, in all the houses we have occupied since then, they have remained.